Fall from Grace

by Sarah Costello

The contents of this work, including, but not limited to, the accuracy of events, people, and places depicted; opinions expressed; permission to use previously published materials included; and any advice given or actions advocated are solely the responsibility of the author, who assumes all liability for said work and indemnifies the publisher against any claims stemming from publication of the work.

All Rights Reserved
Copyright © 2016 by Sarah Costello

No part of this book may be reproduced or transmitted, downloaded, distributed, reverse engineered, or stored in or introduced into any information storage and retrieval system, in any form or by any means, including photocopying and recording, whether electronic or mechanical, now known or hereinafter invented without permission in writing from the publisher.

Dorrance Publishing Co
585 Alpha Drive Suite 103
Pittsburgh, PA 15238
Visit our website at *www.dorrancebookstore.com*

ISBN: 978-1-4809-2710-0
eISBN 978-1-4809-2848-0

Prologue

Samantha sat on the bed staring at her suitcase as she contemplated going back. Her doctor had urged her not to travel but time was running out and she needed to go home. Home. That was something she hadn't called Bradyville in a long time. The small town of her past was in reality nothing more than a distant memory but hopefully also a chance at happiness. The only person back home that she had connections to likely hadn't given her the slightest thought in the twelve years that she had been gone. If she stayed in New York there was still hope. Hope that one day things would work out the way she knew they were meant to. If she went home now, she might find out that it wasn't real. She may find herself right in the middle of a world that never existed and place that no longer wanted her. Samantha knew it was her own fault that her life ended up the way it had. Despite her successes in life she knew that she had given up a great deal to be where she was. Of course there were moments when it all seemed worth the pain and sins of her past. There had been many times in her life when she could say that she was right in staying away. Was it worth it though? Were those few fleeting moments worth the turmoil she had caused? In the back of her mind she tried to convince herself that if she just remained right where she was there was always the possibility that life could go back to the way it was in that small town. Was she actually ready to face the reality of that part of her life truly being over? This was the more likely scenario. She would be a fool to think that she could somehow seamlessly fall back into a community that she had spent so much time running from.

Samantha could hear the ticking of the clock on her bedroom wall as she contemplated one of the biggest decisions she would ever make. By choosing to go home she would undoubtedly be opening old wounds for the one person who she loved more than anything in this world. It was insane to think that her arrival could be met with anything other than hatred and resistance. But there was always hope. Hope for a boy and girl who once were madly in love. Although that boy and girl no longer existed, the man and woman who replaced them needed long overdue closure.

There was rarely a day that went by that Samantha didn't think of him. Back then he was tall, tan and full of life. His smile could melt her heart; his embraces had made her feel safe and his eyes held the promise of a future together. There was a point in her life where she couldn't have imagined being with anyone else and she knew that he had felt the same. Neither one of them could have known what the future held for them back then. They were young and in love. If you would have asked him he would have told you he'd die for her and she would have willingly done the same for him. Through all of the sadness and tragedies in her youth, he had always been there for her. The five years they were together and the feelings they shared were both honest and rare. They were envied by some and adored by most and her feelings for him could never be compromised. At least she thought.

Back then, neither one of them could have anticipated the events that would tear them apart forever. It was time to face him.

Part 1

August 2000

Chapter 1

Lucas sat there holding her, hoping that the night would go on forever. His arms surrounded her waist, his hands tightly clasped in front of her body. The wind whispered over the water as they sat by the edge of the creek. Neither said a word as they listened to the sounds of the night. The scenery that surrounded them felt romantic and incredibly sad at the same time.

"What are you thinking about?" he nuzzled his face into her hair, waiting for a response. He was a little afraid of what she was going to say. Lucas knew where the conversation was eventually going to lead. He dreaded putting such a damper on what had been such an incredible evening.

Without hesitation she responded.

"I was thinking about you." She said it with such ease that Lucas thought there might be a punch line to follow but she said nothing else.

He could feel her shiver slightly and wasn't sure if it was from the cool evening air or the conversation they were about to have. He considered making a joke to lighten her mood but it didn't seem appropriate.

Samantha turned her body enough to face him.

"Why? What are you thinking about?"

"I was thinking about you too and how much I'm going to miss summer. We had a lot of fun the last few months."

When there was no reply he knew he needed to bring up what was truly on her mind.

Lucas sighed. There was no getting around it now. He knew that Sam's thoughts were far away from idle talk and the conversation he had been dreading was slowly creeping up on them. If she wasn't going to initiate the conversation, then he knew he needed to do it.

"Sam, I saw the envelope on your kitchen table before we left." He paused, "And it was opened so I know that you know." He waited a moment before he continued. "So what did it say?" he tried to sound upbeat but his voice showed a hint of worry.

"I got accepted." Samantha said quietly and without turning to face him. She continued before he could say anything. "I know it's not what you were hoping to hear. I promise we'll find a way to work it out." Her words came rushing out before she could catch herself. She knew she sounded defensive but she needed him to know that she had thought everything through and that she wasn't making a rash decision. She stared straight ahead, not ready to see his reaction to her news.

"I *am* happy for you. I'm just sad too." He gave her shoulders a reassuring squeeze but instinctively moved away from her. He stared down at the sand and started picking at the random strands of beach grass that surrounded them. It was really starting to cool off and neither of them had brought a jacket. He wanted to make sure that they were both able to say what they needed to but time was running short on their evening. Lucas loved Samantha more than anything and he knew she felt the same. He also knew, though, that she wanted a lot of things that didn't include him. She was so damn smart. He knew she wanted to go away to college but it didn't make it easy. He would miss her and couldn't imagine finding enough things to do to fill his time without her.

Sam had grown up in what could only be kindly referred to as an unstructured household. An absent father and an alcoholic mother only fueled her readiness to leave the small town they lived in. Sam watched Lucas for a few minutes. She knew he needed to let the news soak in before she fed him more details. She bit her lip and silently searched for the right words to soften the blow.

"It's really not that bad, babe. Campus is just a little over three hours away so you can come and visit me anytime. I'll be home most weekends and every holiday." She leaned over and kissed him on the cheek. "I love you very much and there's nothing that can change that, especially just an address." She softly placed her hands on both side of his face and turned it towards her. She looked him in the eyes hoping to reassure him with a smile. "We'll just pretend that I have a really demanding job and will be working a lot." She waited for him to give in, knowing he would. There was no way either of them would end their relationship over her decision to go away to school. It seemed kind of silly that they were taking their upcoming separation so seriously.

Lucas stayed silent for a few moments longer and finally sighed. He had never been good at staying upset with Sam. It didn't matter what the situation was. She always had a way of putting a positive spin on things. This was no doubt from her life experience. When you are expected to become an adult at a very early age it becomes easy to naturally deal with big things in an adult manner. That was part of the reason he loved her so much.

Sam and Lucas had been together since her freshman year of high school. They were each other's first date, first kiss, and they both hoped they would one day have another first to add to that list. Although it was probably on his mind more than hers, complete physical intimacy was not something they talked about often. Based on how he knew Sam felt, Lucas didn't hold out much hope that it would be happening anytime soon. Sam had a different respect for intimacy than most people her age. She wasn't brought up like most of the girls in town. She had been raised by a single mother who was as unstable as she was promiscuous. At thirty-six Sam's mother Dorothy looked ten years older but acted fifteen years younger. She wore clothes that clung too tight and more make up than she needed. She was known around town as Hottie Dottie – and not in a complimentary way. Sam had always done her best to ignore the whispers and rumors that surrounded her mother. In truth, her mother had been the source of many bouts of bullying throughout her school years. Sam was always on the receiving end of the torture. Girls made fun of her and boys made lewd remarks. Most days she had ridden the bus home with her head buried in her arms to hide her tears and frustration. It had been difficult to deal with for so many years and was a big reason why Sam had so few friends.

It was difficult to watch her mother willingly be treated with such disrespect even now. Because of this, Sam had come to fear even the thought of sex. She knew that when it did finally happen for the first time she wanted it to be special. She knew Lucas respected that but could also feel the frustration he sometimes had with her reluctance to even discuss the topic. Ultimately, though, he loved her and would do anything she asked him to do - or not to do. After five years of waiting, Sam knew he was one of the very few people she could trust completely. That was why it was going to be so hard to leave him.

"So when do you go?" Lucas knew it needed to be asked, he just wasn't sure he wanted to hear the answer. He sensed her hesitation at his question.

She paused before responding.

"I actually leave this Thursday." She winced a little when she felt him release her hand. She knew she had surprised him with her answer so she gave him a minute before she went on. "Students on an academic scholarship have to meet for orientation a little bit earlier than everyone else." She paused before continuing, "And since I applied so much later than most students I think it's really important that I get focused right away." She hoped he could understand her reasoning. She could feel herself getting angry that he wasn't immediately supportive. "I don't think you understand how lucky I am to be given this opportunity. I'm a year out of high school and was just given a full ride scholarship to a great university. Do you have any idea how rare that is?"

Lucas groaned with each word. He stood and turned away from her, taking a few steps toward the edge of the water. He randomly started picking up stones and began tossing them into the water. He watched a few of them successfully skip into the darkness.

Sam watched him not knowing who would speak next. When he finally ran out of pebbles he turned to face her.

"Wow, I don't know what to say." He ran his hands through his hair. "I was expecting to have at least a *week*." He turned to face her. When he realized that he had an unconscious expression of disgust on his face, he quickly composed himself. He took a deep breath and searched for the right words that would best show his support. "Well, I guess first thing tomorrow I'll come over and help you pack." He needed her to know that he was going to be there for her, even if was the most difficult thing he had ever done. He sat back down next to her, clasped her hands in his and gave them a little squeeze.

Sam looked down at the ground and fought back the tears that threatened to appear. Her long hair fell forward, covering her eyes.

She should have expected him to eventually take everything in stride. He had always been that way.

"I promise that I will think of you every day we're not together."

She sniffled between words. "I love you so much and I can't imagine my life without you in it." She could feel her cheeks flush with embarrassment. They didn't normally talk with such depth.

Samantha wanted the awkward moment to pass so she lay back in the sand and pulled Lucas on top of her. Just the feeling of his arms around her and his scent above her made her close her eyes and thank God for the day she met him. Lucas always seemed too good to be true. They were an unlikely pair but whatever forces had brought them together, Sam was grateful for them.

Her thoughts were diffused by Lucas's kisses. He kissed her forehead, nose, and chin before settling in on her lips. She brought her hands up and ran them through his sandy brown hair. His eyes were a piercing green evident even in the moonlight.

"Come on." Lucas said. He kissed her once more and stood. He offered his hand to help her up. "It's getting late."

"Will you stay with me tonight?" Sam asked. "I hate staying home by myself at night." She looked over and gave him puppy dog eyes as they walked with their arms around each other back to his truck.

"Where's your mom?" he asked.

She rolled her eyes before answering,

"There's a men's league tonight at Al's."

Sam didn't need to explain to Lucas what that meant. Al's Alleys was the local bowling bar. Dottie spent most of her free nights at whatever joint in town was having some kind of male gathering. Some days it was golf leagues or socials at the local lodge. Tonight it was bowling leagues. These outlets gave Dottie the perfect opportunity to score free drinks and a hot ticket home. Although Sam trusted that Lucas would not be judgmental, it was always a little difficult talking to him about her family situation. It was embarrassing to know what a disaster her home life was. Sam had practically raised herself. Her father left them when she was two and she had virtually no memories of him. She had never even heard her mother mention his name. On occasion – and only after a few drinks – her father would be referred to as 'The Jerk' by Dorothy but that was the extent of it. When Sam was old enough to care for her own basic needs, Dottie went after the life she felt she was robbed of as a teenager. Sam had spent her childhood doing her homework alone, packing her own lunches and tucking herself in. She was used to it by now and she and her mother never acknowledged the unusual dynamic and role reversal between them.

Dottie had gotten pregnant when she was young and at the time getting married was the only way to make everything right. In the end, though, Dottie ended up a divorced nineteen year old single mother to a toddler. Now she was living life to the fullest and making up for being pregnant at seventeen and alone not long after.

This was why it was difficult to talk about her home life with Lucas. Compared to her childhood, his upbringing had been near perfect. The Benson's were like a family out of a movie in the fifties. They all had the same sandy colored hair and green eyes. His father Paul was handsome and successful. Della, Lucas's mother, was as beautiful as she was kind. They were both active at the school and members of many clubs and committees in town. Della was an English teacher at the local high school and Paul was the chief of police in Bradyville, where they lived. The Benson's had family discussions at the dinner table, took vacations together and they made sure they always knew what was going on in each other's lives. Sam loved spending time at Lucas's house, for her *that* was a vacation. There was always something cooking in the kitchen and noises coming from whichever rooms his three siblings occupied.

Sam thought about their differences and how opposite their upbringings had been as they rode to her house in silence. She watched out her window as they drove by the vast homes and manicured lawns that lined Main Street. Not far from some of the largest homes that Bradyville boasted, was the Benson home. Although you couldn't see it from Main Street it was not much different than the ones they were passing now. Sam lived on the outskirts of town and she watched as the houses got smaller and the street lights grew dimmer the further they drove. It was strange how two people so different could be so connected in the way that Sam and Lucas were. As they turned off into a small street at the edge of town Sam watched her house come into view. It's shabby, faded exterior was a far cry from the perfectly painted mansions at the center of town.

Lucas pulled his truck into the narrow gravel driveway that led up to the small garage of her home. He cut his headlights on the truck after putting it into park; leaving the engine running as he shifted his body to face her. He had been lost in thought the entire ride back to Sam's house.

"What do you want me to do?"

He looked at her with an expression that she was unfamiliar with.

"Uh, I want you to shut off your truck and come inside with me." She gave him a confused look. To Sam, the answer was as simple as the question and she wasn't sure what he meant by asking.

"Sam, you know what I mean," He looked down and started fidgeting with the hem of shirt. "I love you a lot and I want to - well you know…" His words trailed off.

She shot him a guarded look.

"You want to what? I can barely hear you." Sam crossed her arms and leaned back, waiting for his answer,

For Lucas it was now or never.

"Please don't tell me to wait; I have never loved anyone as much as I love you." His face grew hot and he found it difficult to use the right words; after all he *was* a guy. He wasn't supposed to be outwardly emotional. He knew he needed to get this out, though, before she went away for so long. It wasn't that sex was *that* big of a deal to him, but he couldn't help the feelings he had for her. He could feel the embarrassment creeping up his neck as he waited for her reply. Lucas knew what Sam was thinking. She had made it very clear in the past how she disapproved of her mother's choices. And it wasn't as if he was blind to the situation. He knew it was hard for Sam to see that intimacy wasn't always a bad thing. He wanted it to be just as special as she did and he really wanted her to see that.

"Lucas, seriously I'm just not ready. I don't know why I'm not; I just feel like I'll know exactly when the perfect time is when it happens."

She watched the hopeful look in his eyes fade to slight disappointment.

"Besides, it doesn't mean we can't do other things that are just as fun." Sam smiled at him deviously, poking him in the stomach with her fingers.

"Forget it." He mumbled, rolling his eyes as he shut off the truck. He jumped out and came around to her side. He reached for her hand to help her down, always the gentlemen.

In silence, they walked up the sidewalk and into the house.

Rubbing her eyes, Sam pulled her pillow over her ears and tried to block out the noise that threatened to wake her from her sleep. The clock on her nightstand read 3:39 a.m.

Sam could hear a sound that semi-resembled her name being yelled from somewhere on the other side of the small two bedroom house. The voice was familiar and it was persistent. She was quickly jolted from her slumber.

Sam slowly nudged Lucas's arm off of her waist and she quietly tried to slip out of bed. *Here we go again,* she thought to herself. She threw on a pair of boxer shorts with her t-shirt and walked out of her room, gently closing the door behind her. If she was lucky she would be able to quickly take care of the mess that was surely waiting for her. Then, hopefully she would have some time to jump back into bed for a while.

"Mom?" she whispered as loudly as she could. "Where are you?" Yawning, Sam walked down the hall. She glanced into the kitchen as she walked past it. Not seeing what she was looking for, she turned the corner and went into the living room and came upon a familiar sight. In a crumpled heap next to the front door lay her mother. With a sigh, Sam walked over and began cleaning up the mess that had long ago become a normal part of their routine. Grabbing Dorothy from under her arms, Sam dragged her mom into the living room. With a gentle maneuver of her foot she closed the front door completely so that they wouldn't again become the morning spectacle for the neighborhood. Sam laid her mother gently on the carpeted floor. Peering down at her mother Sam took in the sight and drew in a deep breath. It was painful to see Dorothy in such disarray. Sam couldn't help but wonder which special guy it was that booted her mother out of his car *this* morning. She stood there staring at the one person who was supposed to be her role model and guardian. Sam could feel her body fill with rage and sadness. She realized even more at that moment that she needed to get away from this place. No matter what cost it came with. Sam mentally pushed those feelings aside and decided to do her mother this favor one last time.

"Ok, you have to help me a *little* bit," she whispered in her mom's ear as she bent over to help Dorothy into a standing position.

"Oh honey," came the slur of barely recognizable words from lips smeared with a provocative color of red, "I'm so, so sorry. I promise, no more." Tears fell from her heavily made up eyes and landed on the thin leopard patterned material of her skirt. "I don't want to be this way anymore. I promise I'll get it together, please don't hate me." Dorothy's words were barely a whisper now and her eyes were closed.

Sam let her mother weep for a second as she held her up with all her strength. Biting her lip to keep from crying herself, she wanted to believe everything that she was hearing. Ever since she could remember this was the way her mother came home most weekend mornings. Her hair messed up, clothes smelling of smoke, and not a dime in her pocket. Sam gathered her bearings and threw her mother's arm over her shoulder and with a slight grunt got her to stand. It wasn't that her mother was a heavy person, she was actually quite small, but a drunken-dead weight was a difficult thing to maneuver on your own. Walking down the hall Sam tried to be as quiet as she could. She hated it when Lucas saw her mother this way. He never said anything negative about Dorothy, but it always gave Sam another reminder of how imperfect her life was compared to his. Opening the door, she dragged her mother who was half asleep by now over to the bed and dropped her onto the bare mattress. She could have been gentler but there wasn't much point. Tip-toeing out of the room, she closed the door behind her.

Sam slipped back into bed as quietly as she could, trying not to wake Lucas. Knowing she wasn't going to have many more times like this, she wanted to lay there beside him as long as possible.

"Where have you been?" he asked with his eyes closed and sleep in his voice.

"Ssshh, don't talk, just go back to sleep and hold me for a little while," Sam closed her eyes as she reached around and pulled his arm across her waist. "Just hold me." She whispered. Minutes later they were both asleep.

The alarm went off just after 7:00.

"*No*, I don't want to get up yet!" Sam tried to cover her head with the sheet as Lucas gave her shoulder a shake.

"Well too bad, you have to. We have a shitload of stuff to do today."

Being the morning person that he was, Lucas yanked the blanket back and started pulling at Sam's feet. Sam frantically tried to grab for the covers without opening her eyes. This only prompted him to start whistling some stupid tune right near her ear. She knew that there was no way she was getting any more sleep.

"Ok, ok, forget it, I'll get up. Just leave me alone." She pushed the hair out of her eyes, sat up and stretched.

Lucas walked over to her and rested his hands on her legs and stared her straight in the eyes.

"Awe, is someone a little crabby this morning?"

He was the image of perpetual happiness in the morning and it annoyed the crap out of her. In her opinion mornings weren't for cheerfulness and sunshine. In the morning all she wanted to do was sleep as long as possible, knock her alarm off of her nightstand, and gradually get used to the idea of getting ready for another day. Caffeine always helped the process. To Sam, it was the worst part of having Lucas stay overnight. She couldn't imagine what in the hell he had to be so damn happy about in the morning but the last thing she wanted was for any of it to rub off on her. Grumpiness was part of her morning routine and she didn't intend on breaking any rituals today.

"Get away from me." Standing up she left the room and walked down the hall to the bathroom. Shutting the door behind her she tried to drown out his cheerfulness. She took her time brushing her teeth and washing her face. After a few minutes to herself she felt awake enough to walk out and face her day.

They made breakfast together and ate without talking much. They both knew what they had to do today and packing was not going to be the easiest thing for either one of them. Sam knew that Lucas thought of her going away as just college and not a permanent move. She knew that to him they would just be packing enough stuff for her to live until she came home next. She, however, was thinking more along the lines of packing and throwing away enough stuff so that she would never really *need* to come back here. After she left, her mother would probably want to entertain more and have the space to do it. Sam understood that and wanted to clean house as much as possible. Even if she returned home for sporadic visits she didn't want to have to need this place or her mother. Even more than that, Sam didn't want her mom to be able to hang anything over her head or make her feel like she owed her anything. She was doing this on her own. Sam had gotten this far without the help of her mom or anyone else. She had applied for and received her scholarship, had gotten good grades in school, and had always stayed out of trouble. The only person she had to thank for any of that was Lucas. He went to every one of her academic functions and supported every decision she had ever made. This included her decision to take a year off to save money. During this time Sam had hung on to the hope that a good college would still want her a year later. He was her inspiration, her source of courage, and her means for determination. Leaving for college was the first thing she had ever done all alone. Lucas had always been involved in every part of her life in some way up until now. She was ready, though and looked forward to the future. She wasn't going to college for the parties, the boys, or the experience of being free for the first time. She was going solely for a good education and the opportunities it would present to her upon graduation. Sam had no interest in any of the other stuff. This was a once in a lifetime chance for her and she had no intention of blowing it.

They finished breakfast in silence while exchanging occasional glances and half-hearted smiles. It would be a difficult day for both of them.

Saturday went by quickly. They discarded as much stuff as she could bear to part with, and packed the rest. They had been working since breakfast and it was nearing five o'clock. Sometime that afternoon Sam had heard her mother fussing around the bathroom and muttering to herself. Without any acknowledgement to Sam or Lucas, Dorothy left the house with no mention of when she would be returning.

Sam let the sweatshirt she was folding drop to her lap as she slowly scanned the room. As anxious as she was to leave, it was still kind of sad seeing her memories and her childhood disappear a little at a time. Every hour they worked the walls became more and more bare. Every box that they moved out of the room made the space look just a little bit bigger. She couldn't wait to leave, she knew she couldn't, but something tugged at her a little and made her eyes tear up. She took it all in; the smell of the detergent she washed her clothes with, the burned piece of carpeting from a neglected curling iron and the bag in the corner filled with all of her stuffed animals. It was all a part of her, and she was leaving it behind.

Lucas walked in from taking a load out to the curb and noticed the look on her face right away.

"You don't have to go you know," He leaned against the doorframe and stared down at the floor. He used his foot to play with a snag in the carpeting.

"What other option do I have? Do you really want me to stay here and become a waitress or something? I *do* have to leave. I'm not unsure about that it's just seeing all of this stuff being thrown out makes me sad. A lot of these things were big parts of my life at some point." She walked over to one of the boxes that were half filled but still open. "Look at this," She said, holding up a plate with some colored macaroni noodles on it and one of her school pictures in the middle, "I made this, and it was probably really special to me." Sam could feel the jagged edges of dried glue coming away from the paper plate. She traced the outline of her younger face with her finger.

"Then don't throw it away, keep it." Lucas wasn't sure what she wanted to hear. He expected her to be sentimental but he didn't know what to say to make her feel better. He wasn't always the greatest with words.

"No, I don't want to keep it." She said as she threw her kindergarten-creation in the bag marked for garbage and turned to face Lucas. "This is exactly *why* I'm leaving. I made this project out of hard work and love, and it meant nothing to the person I gave it to. Why would *I* want to keep something *I* made? It wasn't for me."

Sam looked around the room.

"This whole place is full of things that were meant for someone who didn't want them." She paused before continuing, "The only good thing about all of this," she spoke softly, "is that it makes it that much easier for me to go away."

She handed Lucas the trash bag filled with her past.

"Can you please take this outside for me?" She turned away from Lucas and set off to finish erasing the life she was more than willing to leave behind.

Chapter 2

It was the fastest week of Lucas's whole life. They finished the bulk of the packing Saturday afternoon, leaving just enough clothes and necessities out for Sam to get through the next few days. It was short notice, but he was able to take the whole week off work from the grain factory he worked at to spend as much time with her as he could. On Monday, they stopped by the hair salon where she worked to give an abrupt notice and to say goodbye. Lucas just sat to the side and let Sam have her moment with one of the few real friends she had ever known.

Caroline Connelly was the owner of Caroline's Hair Design. It was the trendiest place to get your hair done in town. The only other choices were to go to the people who called themselves hairdressers based solely on the fact that they just happened to have a pair of scissors in their basement. Caroline's was the real deal, though, when it came to the stereotype of hair shops. It was a quaint building on the corner of the main cross streets in town. If the town had been big enough to have a stoplight, it would have been in front of Caroline's shop. The building was nestled between a bakery and the only bank in town and had a shockingly bright pink storefront. This was a cause of great distress among the socialites.

Caroline spoke with a thick, fake, southern accent and wore pants that were too tight and lipstick that was too red. She had miles of long blonde hair that was always worn up in a mess of curls. Her black rimmed glasses, which were without prescription, sat firmly at the end of her nose.

Caroline made it a point to know everything about everybody but made sure nobody knew anything about her. She was a mystery to everyone and it was one of the things that Sam loved most about her. Sam had never been much of a gossip but it cracked her up that Caroline could lend a sympathetic ear to Sally Johnson about her cheating husband when three hours later Mary Jo Welters would come in and share all of the details about having an affair with Sally's husband, Eddie. This all came with no protest from Caroline. It wasn't that she reveled in other people's misery; she simply enjoyed being the first to know everything. She also figured that the more dirt she gained on others, the less inclined people would be to search for any on her. In the seven years that she had been in town there had never been an ounce more of gossip about Caroline Connelly besides the initial curiosity upon her arrival.

Caroline took Sam into the break room and sat down with her at the lunch table covered in newspapers and snack items.

"Sam, honey, I am so proud of you." Caroline's sparkling blue eyes were teary. "I want you to know that I will always be here for you. And I want you to go out there and make the biggest success out of yourself that you possibly can. There's nothin' worth stayin' around here for. Well, except maybe for that cutie-pie out there that's always following you around." She gestured out to the waiting area where Lucas was very patiently leafing through magazines about the newest nail colors and lipstick shades.

Sam smiled at the patience Lucas was demonstrating.

"I know you're proud of me, and I can't tell you how much you've meant to me Caroline. And Lucas really is worth sticking around for, but I've got to at least try something new. I'll go crazy if I stay around here and become another high-school sweetheart, married young, poster girl for some damn country song."

Caroline chuckled at Sam's words. A truer picture could not be painted for what was expected of the women in their small town. Everyone assumed that it was normal to meet in high-school, fall in love, get married young, and then stay home and have babies. It was the way things had always been done and Caroline was so happy that Sam was going for something different. She knew Sam was too good for this town and her rough upbringing only made her more acclimated to leaving.

Sam, on the other hand was having a hard time saying goodbye to Caroline. She was really going to miss working in the little hair shop. Caroline had always treated Sam with more respect than anyone ever had, and for the last three years had been the only motherly figure she had in her life. Since coming to work for Caroline at sixteen years old sweeping up hair and folding towels for five dollars an hour, Caroline had never treated Sam any less equally than the hairdressers. Even though nearly everyone else only saw Sam as the girl who sweeps their split ends off the floor and does the laundry, Caroline took to Sam right away and knew that despite their age difference they would be great friends. They shared something special and she was going to miss seeing Caroline's bright smile each day.

"I have something that I want to give you," Caroline said to her as she walked into the rear entryway where the coats were hanging. She reappeared moments later holding a white envelope. "This is for you," She handed it to Sam and then sat down beside her.

Sam looked down at the blank envelope. "What is it?"

"Just open it and find out." Caroline smiled at Sam's bewildered look. When she opened the envelope she couldn't believe what she saw.

"I can*not* take this," Sam said immediately shoving the envelope back at Caroline. "There's got to be like, a thousand dollars in here! I can't accept it."

"It's your severance pay sweetie, you deserve it."

Sam was blown away.

"How did you even know I was leaving for sure? I just found out his week and only told you five minutes ago." She could barely close her mouth as she stared at the wad of cash that filled the envelope.

"You're little sweetheart called me this morning and gave me a heads-up about it. It's a good thing he did; I was booked solid all day. I wouldn't have had two seconds to say goodbye." Caroline looked away from Sam as her eyes started to glisten.

"Caroline, this is way more than I can accept from you. All I've ever needed, you always gave to me. Most of the time I just needed someone to listen to me or give me advice. I don't need your money." She thrust the envelope back at Caroline. "I've been a pretty good saver these last couple years. I've been waiting for this day longer than you can imagine so it was an easy thing to save for."

Caroline shooed Sam's hand away and then gave her a hug. "I don't accept returns. The money is yours to keep." She released the embrace. "However, it does come with stipulations."

Sam raised an eyebrow.

"Such as?"

"That money is not to be used for tuition, books, or any of that other necessary crap. It is for your personal pleasure. I want you to spend that money on stuff you don't need but really want. Things you've never let yourself buy." She gave Sam's hand a little pat.

"This has been much harder than I thought it was going to be." Trying to swallow the lump in her throat Sam stopped to stare into the face of one of the very few people who she could truly call a friend. Turning her back to Sam, Caroline tried to busy herself with folding the hair towels that just came out of the dryer, hoping to give her mascara the chance to dry.

"Well it's not like you're never gonna come back, right?" Caroline looked over at her with a look that was full of hope yet shy of pleading.

"Of course I'll come back. I'll only be a few hours away."

"Well isn't that just perfect, I'll have to come visit *you* to see what kind of college cuties you're gonna be surrounded by."

"Fine by me, but trust me, that is definitely *not* why I'll be there."

She shook her head. Sam didn't put it past Caroline to show up at her dorm ready for a college party.

"What I need is an education and a way out of this hellhole."

"Oh sugar, you make us small town folk sound so bad." Caroline stopped folding the towels and came back and sat by Sam. They sat side by side for a moment. When she finally gathered the right words, her voice took on a tone of seriousness that was unfamiliar to Sam.

"Just remember, God gives us only so many gifts in life. Rarely do we get anything for free, and I know you're willing to work for what you want, but don't take for granted the precious gifts you already possess. Because, take it from me, sometimes we have the most wonderful things in our possession and we don't know it until their gone."

Sam wasn't sure what had come over Caroline. She didn't know what had made her become so serious -or lose her accent for that matter- but she did know Caroline well enough not to ask about it.

"I'm well aware of what I have, but compared to the things I don't have I think I deserve better and that's exactly what I'm going to get out of this experience. The end result will bring about all of those things I have wanted my whole life."

Caroline stood and grabbed Sam. She hugged her as tight as she could. "You're a smart girl and you handle every situation you encounter with such grace, I trust you to do the right thing."

Those words stayed with Sam long after she and Lucas said their last goodbyes and left the shop.

By Wednesday Lucas was waking up in the morning praying that Sam had changed her mind. It was getting hard for him to breathe sometimes just thinking about being without her. It was like there was a constant battle of wills going on in his mind. He spent most of his time trying to convince himself that it was a good thing for her and that he would follow her to the ends of the earth after it was over. The other half of that argument, though, was trying to think of new ways to convince her to stay and be comfortable with a small town life.

Maybe he should propose to her? That might get her to stay. He sat up in bed as the thought came and went. He quickly lay back down as he realized it was one of the dumbest ideas he'd had so far.

For over an hour he stayed in bed and debated the situation. He supposed it was still possible that some horrendous natural disaster could rip through the university and knock the entire school down. Lucas knew though that Sam would just apply - and get in - somewhere else. And it would probably be even farther away. He should just count his blessings that she hadn't decided to go somewhere out of the state. He knew that part of the reason Sam had chosen this school was for their design program, and the other part was for him so that they would be close to each other. Lucas sat up in bed unable to lay there and think it over any longer. Walking over to his dresser to pull out clothes for the day his gaze came across a photo. It was taken last month at the county fair in one of those photo booths that spit out four tiny pictures on a narrow strip. He looked at the succession of pictures never having really paid attention to their expressions before now. The top photo was silly and they were both smiling into the camera. Each picture captured a different pose and by the time Lucas looked over the fourth and final photo he swore he could see traces of sadness in Sam's face. It caused Lucas to take a step back. Had there been other hints of unhappiness that he failed to notice in the past? While looking at the photo Lucas realized two things. First, that he could never remember in his life Sam looking more beautiful than she did in those pictures. And second, that he knew more than ever that she needed to leave him behind for something better.

It was just before noon when Lucas headed to Sam's house to pick her up. They were going to spend the afternoon having lunch, fishing and doing whatever relatively lazy activity they could think of. As he neared the small, faded yellow ranch house, he immediately knew that something was wrong. He slowed as he neared her street. Just then, an ambulance with its lights flashing passed by him in a blur. His breath caught in his throat as it stopped in front of Sam's house. He had no idea what could have happened but he cursed under his breath for not getting up early and coming right over. Unsure of what it could be, he swore to himself that if something had happened to Sam he would never forgive himself. He screeched to a halt in front of their sidewalk and left his truck running as he flew out of the driver's seat and ran up to the house. His shirt snagged on a stray nail in the railing as he reached the front door. He barely noticed the scraping of the rusty metal pierce his skin. The door opened before he could push his way in. Two paramedics rushed past him, taking someone out on a stretcher.

"What happened?" Lucas shouted, trying to grab at the sleeve of one of the two men. "Please tell me what happened!" He tried to stop them, but before either paramedic could answer he realized it was Dorothy being carried away, not Sam. He dropped to his knees on the cement porch as the front door tried to swing close. He took a ragged breath. After his heart stopped pounding, he realized he needed to check on Sam to see what happened and make sure that she was ok. He could see her in the kitchen through the doorway. She was seated at the table with her back to him talking to a police officer. Her face was buried in her hands. As he walked through the door and towards the kitchen, it took a moment to realize that the officer seated next to Sam was his dad. Lucas came up behind Sam and put his arms around her. "What happened? Are you okay? How's your mom?"

Paul Benson looked over at his son. "Just give her some breathing room, son." Paul patted Sam's arm as Lucas took a seat beside her. Sam didn't even look up at him.

"She just collapsed. We were m-making breakfast together because she didn't have to work today and, and she just collapsed." Lucas could see that she was on the verge of tears so he pulled her close to his chest and rubbed her back gently.

"She's going to be just fine babe." Not having the faintest idea if that was something appropriate to say, he directed his attention to his dad. "What did the paramedics say? What do they think happened?"

He could hear Sam taking deep breaths. Her body shuddered each time she exhaled.

"They don't know. Her blood pressure was really low and they were unable to get her to regain consciousness." Paul was clearly guarding his words. Besides the fact that he kept his gaze lowered, the furrow of his brow told Lucas that he knew more than he was saying.

"Oh God Lucas, she wouldn't wake up." Sam couldn't help the tears now. She was shaking violently and leaned over. He had to secure his arms around her waist to keep her from falling to the floor. Lucas felt useless. He kept rubbing her back but wasn't sure what to say. He gave his dad a pleading look.

Paul took the cue to step in.

"Sam, honey, your mama's gonna be just fine. And Lucas will make sure that you have everything you need. I'll go down to the hospital and talk to the doctor myself. Lucas will drive you down in a couple of minutes. Just give them time to get her situated." He gave Sam a reassuring nod and squeeze on the shoulder. And when he was sure Lucas could manage without him, he stuck his notepad in his shirt pocket and left the room.

When they were alone Lucas turned his attention back to Sam.

"I can't go now, Lucas. There's no way. She needs me to stay." She sagged back in her chair with a defeated look on her face. "You're probably pretty happy, aren't you?" She spoke bitterly and with unintended spite. Slightly stung, he brushed away her words. She was angry and needed someone to lash out at.

"You know that isn't true. I have supported you one hundred percent the whole time, so don't say something you don't mean. Besides, you can still go. I'm sure your mom's going to be all right. She would want you to go."

Lucas knew he could have taken this opportunity to convince her that she was right and that she should stay and look after her mother. It was a tempting but fleeting thought. He knew just by looking at her that she was torn between two vital things. Wanting to stay and do the right thing but needing to go and do what was right for her.

"Let's drive down to the hospital and find out what's going on. We shouldn't plan on making any decisions until we know more anyway." He helped Sam out of her chair and took her out to his truck. They didn't say a word to each other the whole way. He glanced over at her every few minutes but she never met his gaze. She stared blankly out the window likely wondering if this was all real.

Bradyville barely had a doctor's office let alone a hospital. They had to drive twenty five miles out of town to a hospital just outside of Charlotte. They arrived just after one o'clock. Lucas parked in the nearest space and walked around to help Sam out of the passenger side. They walked quickly up to the doors and through a waiting area full of screaming children with exasperated parents and other people that appeared to be generally annoyed with their wait to see a physician.

"Dorothy Weiler please, she was just brought in by ambulance." Samantha had the words out before she even reached the desk.

"Okay, just hang on a minute." The young nurse behind the desk looked like she had something better to be doing than helping them track down Sam's mother.

"Are you family?" It sounded more like an accusation than a question. She narrowly looked at the young couple. "Cuz' only the family is allowed to see a patient in the trauma center."

Sam spoke for the both of them before Lucas could argue with her.

"Yes, we're her kids. I'm her daughter Samantha and this is my brother Lucas." Sam nudged Lucas in the side before he could say anything.

The nurse looked at them carefully before waving them back to the room where Dorothy was being treated. They followed her down two hallways of depressingly bare white walls before reaching Dorothy's room. With a raised hand, the nurse stopped them short of stepping in the doorway and asked them to wait for a moment. She walked in and spoke to a doctor who looked to be somewhere in his mid-sixties. Sam tried listening to what they were saying but only caught bits and pieces. As the doctor spoke, the snippy young nurse seemed to soften as she looked over in their direction. She and the doctor both had grim expressions as they continued to whisper to one another. He gave the nurse a nod toward the door and walked over to where Lucas and Sam were waiting.

Extending his hand toward Sam, the physician introduced himself. "Hello, my name is Dr. Drexlin. You're Dorothy's children?" He shook both of their hands warmly.

Sam and Lucas exchanged looks. Once again, Sam spoke before Lucas could.

"Actually Dr. Drexlin, I'm sorry to mislead your staff but I'm Dorothy's daughter Samantha, and this is my boyfriend Lucas Benson. I didn't mean to lie to your nurse but I don't have a single other person in the world to be here with me so please, could you just let him stay with me for a while?" Sam searched his eyes for a sign that he knew what she was going through. She could see in his expression that he understood her hopeful plea.

"Of course it's all right. Why don't you follow me into the family room where we can sit and talk privately? After that, you can see your mother." He placed his hand on Sam's shoulder and gestured to a room across the hall and out of view of her mother's. They walked into the dimly lit room together. It had bright purple and red plush seating and largely framed art pieces on the wall. There was a table on one end of the room with coffee and a serving tray setting on top of it. There were boxes of tissues everywhere. This couldn't be a good sign.

Sam and Lucas took a seat on the sofa next to a window with the shades pulled. There was a massive oak sofa table in front of them with a variety of brochures on it; mostly dealing with grief and coping. It otherwise would have been a room that Sam considered comfortable and cozy but she had a sinking feeling in her stomach as to why they were there.

Sam's eyes filled with tears and she made no effort to brush them away. She and Lucas were seated across from the doctor. She searched his eyes as she said the first thing that came to her mind.

"Dr. Drexlin, I'm not a little girl and I don't need things sugarcoated for me. I don't want to be asked if you should call someone else in my family for me because there isn't anyone. And I don't want you to give me any false hope. I can see by the look in your eyes that it's bad enough to be sitting quietly in a room full of tissue boxes. So please just tell me," She took a deep breath, "Is my mother going make it?" With her shoulders squared, Samantha braced herself for whatever was coming.

"I believe in being honest too." He started, "Your mother's condition is not good, and it hasn't been for some time now. Based on the advanced stage of her disease I would give her a few days, maybe a week at best." He took Sam's fragile hands in his own. He felt a sudden surge of grief for this young woman whose entire family was sitting within this very hospital. "I know there's not much I can say that is going to make this any easier for you. Your mother is very sick and almost completely unresponsive. We've placed her on a pain control drip, so if it's any consolation, she's comfortable for now." He knew that statement wasn't going to make up for what Sam was feeling but it was all he had to offer her.

Sam's vision was blurred by a steady stream of tears. She couldn't believe all of the emotions she was feeling at one time. She hated her mother for doing this to her. Yet at the same time she hated herself for feeling the way she always had about her mother. She was angry for her mother not telling her she was sick. How could she keep such a major thing from Sam? Above all else Sam was the most upset about her own selfishness. Deep down she knew this compromised her scholarship and the possibility of her moving away if her mother needed to be cared for.

"Did she know what was wrong with her?" Sam felt she needed to know, even if it didn't change the outcome.

"You're mother has a very advanced stage of liver cancer. I spoke with her primary physician and he said that she was very aware of her condition but refused treatment. She was diagnosed last November." He gave Sam a moment before continuing. He knew it was a shock to hear all of this at once. "I can't speak for your mother, but I can speak as a parent. I understand if she wanted to shield you from all that was happening to her. Parents always feel like they have to be the strong ones. Your mother probably didn't want to burden you."

Lucas took Sam's hands in his own. Up until now she had forgotten he was with her.

"Babe, I promise you we'll get through this. We'll do this together." He wasn't sure what else to say to her. She looked as if she were the one in a comatose state. "I know this isn't what we anticipated. I know I promised that she would be all right but we'll figure this out." He pulled her to his chest and kissed the top of her head. He asked the only logical question he could think of. "What about a transplant? Don't they take the most critical patients first?" Lucas felt Sam stiffen underneath his arm at the suggestion but she didn't look up.

"I'm afraid that's not possible." Dr. Drexlin directed his answers at Lucas now. He realized that Sam was barely retaining a word he said. "Dorothy has been made aware of her condition. They will only place, and keep, you on a donor list if you discontinue any harmful lifestyles that could contribute to the worsening of the organ you need transplanted. If she would have, for instance, stopped consuming alcohol and smoking and if she would have taken her medication and started the recommended treatment that she was prescribed, then maybe she would be considered for a transplant. But she has consciously made the decision to lead a lifestyle that is in direct contradiction to her condition." He paused and gave them both a sorrowful look. "I'm afraid there's not much more that we can do for her but pray, control her pain, and wait." Dr. Drexlin rose from his seated position across from the grief-stricken couple. "If you need anything else please don't hesitate to ask." He pulled a white card out of his breast pocket and clicking his pen quickly scribbled something down on it. "This is my home number. Don't be afraid to call." He handed the card over to Lucas and gave Sam's knees a quick pat. He stopped at the door and turned back to face them. He wanted to offer some sort of consolation to them. He wanted to tell them that he had all of the right resources to make her mother perfectly well again. It was these cases that were the hardest on him as a doctor. In thirty-nine years of practicing medicine he never learned to become immune to the pain of a child. He left the young pair to resolve each other's grief as the door closed quietly behind him.

They sat in the hospital family room listening to the minutes tick by on the wall clock above them. After deciding that there wasn't much more they could do by sitting there, Sam and Lucas took the dreaded walk to Dorothy's room. The room was dimly lit and had a faint antiseptic smell to it. There was a faded yellow border around the top of all four walls that was peeling off in each corner. On the stand next to her mother's bed there was a plastic vase with faded pink tulips in it. It was the worst attempt at cheerfulness Sam had ever seen. However it was likely that those flowers would be the only ones that ever would be in that room during her stay. Sam knew that Dorothy didn't have many friends and was sure there would be no cards, flowers, or other gifts from anyone they knew. She took a seat in the chair next to the bed and carefully placed her own hand in the waxy, yellowish hand of her mother's. She leaned in close to whisper in Dorothy's ear that she was here and that everything was going to be all right. Lucas decided to give them a moment, and started to walk out. He hadn't quite reached the door when he heard the sudden, slow, monotonous tone of the monitor followed by a low whimper of despair. He knew right then that Dorothy was gone.

Chapter 3

The funeral was held on Friday. It was unusually chilly and overcast for a southern summer day so Sam grabbed a light sweater before heading out the door to go to the church. Lucas was waiting for her out in the truck with the wipers on low to dispel the light drops that were gathering on the windshield. She closed the door behind her and walked slowly to the vehicle. Everything had proceeded rather quickly. There was no health insurance to cover the medical costs so after Dorothy passed away the bills just "went away" like they always seem to do for people without coverage. There was no money, so there was no estate to settle and no banking to straighten out. And the Walken-Sloan funeral home in town donated it's time and all of the bare necessities to have a proper burial. Everyone knew that Sam and Dottie didn't have much and they all felt bad for Sam now that she really didn't have anyone to look out for her. It was overwhelming how in just two days lasagnas and other various casserole dishes could add up like they did. Everyone brought Sam something, hoping to be the one who could say that they helped this poor little girl the most. That's the kind of town Bradyville was. Sympathy and caring was measured in how much food you could make or how many good deeds you could do to show off to your neighbors. At least that was how it felt to Sam at that time. Sam was more determined than ever to get away from it all. The entire way to St. Stephen's Church she thought about how many dishes of food she had thanked people for and then promptly threw away and washed out. It was easier than letting them pile up and Sam had no desire to eat anything, anyway lately. Her figure, which was naturally willowy, seemed even more waif-like in the last two days. Her skin that was normally a golden tan seemed yellowed and her features looked permanently set in sadness. She kept her dark hair in a simple ponytail and wore large sunglasses over her eyes that were once a rich cerulean blue, but now seemed a faded watery gray. Lucas let her sit with her thoughts as he drove to the church. Once he reached the driveway he was saddened to see only about seven cars in the vast parking lot. He parked up front, close behind the awaiting hearse. He climbed out of the truck and walked around to help Sam down from her seat. He was worried about her. Since he had taken her home from the hospital on Wednesday she had barely spoken and hardly eaten. She looked thin and pale, as if the slightest touch would knock her over. They walked hand-in-hand through the front doors. Sam had opted not to walk behind the casket in procession to the funeral. This was usually done by the family of the deceased and Sam had no intentions of taking that walk alone. They seated themselves in the front pew. Lucas looked around and gave the few but familiar faces a weak smile. Two rows behind them was Caroline Connelly who was accompanied by an unfamiliar male companion holding her tissues. On the other side of the aisle in the front row were Lucas's parents. Paul gave his son a nod and took his wife Della's hand in his and gave it a small pat. Della tried to look over at them but couldn't overcome her own tears and didn't want to upset Sam any more than she already was. Behind his parents were Mr. and Mrs. Runley, who had been Sam and Dottie's next door neighbors since they had moved into town twelve years earlier. Seated next to them was crazy Gladys. Crazy Gladys was always in church even when there wasn't a funeral or a mass in place. The rumor around town was that she killed her whole family years ago and sat in church everyday repenting for her sins. No one spoke to her and she didn't speak to anyone. Most people didn't really believe the rumor, but they were too afraid to find out if it was really true so they just let her be. Today Gladys was in rare form. She looked as if she knew what she was here for. Instead of her usual drab, black dress she wore a large purple hat with a thin veil over the front and a bulky faux fur leopard coat. Her neck was adorned in multiple beaded necklaces and her fingers covered in gaudy fake rings. She frequently dabbed at her eyes under the veil as she quietly mumbled prayers and gripped her rosary. All the way to the back of the church, in the darkest and least noticeable seats were three lone figures scattered among the pews and sitting alone. Lucas recognized each one but couldn't recall any names. He did know that all three men had two things in common. First, that he had seen each of them at separate times skirting around town with Dorothy. And second, that they were each married. The latter fact was most likely the reason they sat so far in the back of the quiet church.

Without warning the organ piped up with a tune that somewhat resembled 'Amazing Grace'. Two volunteer ushers rolled the casket slowly down the aisle and applied the brakes when they reached the front of the altar. Everyone stood. There was faint participation in the singing amongst the crowd and it made the service seem that much more pathetic to Sam. She knew that everyone's gaze flitted frequently to her as if waiting to see some big meltdown, but she held her composure as best as she could letting the tears roll down her cheeks without making a sound. Pastor Thomas said a moving sermon and commented often on what a terrific family Dorothy had and how she will be incredibly missed by those around her. It was short, but probably more polite than was deserved considering the lifestyle and un-churchlike qualities of the departed. After the eulogy he asked the community of the church if anyone would like to come up to the altar and say a few words about Dorothy. Sam could feel everyone's gaze shift to the ground and heard throats being cleared and programs being shuffled around. No one wanted to be given the nod to take the initiative to speak. A few more people had trickled in after the funeral had begun but no one seemed to want to hold the spotlight. Without thinking Sam stood up and excused herself around Lucas's legs. She walked to the casket and said one final, quiet goodbye to her mother before turning to face the congregation.

She looked at each and every face of the now fifteen people that were seated in front of her.

"I know what you all thought about my mother," she choked back a sob as she continued, "but I'll tell you what you didn't know about her. I'll bet you didn't know that even though she didn't attend church she gave a small, anonymous donation through the mail each week." She could see out of the corner of her eye Pastor Thomas's head lift at the mention. "And, I'll bet none of you knew that she volunteered once a month at a women's shelter out in Kingsley. And although we didn't have much she donated all of our extra clothes to the families there." Tears were now streaming down her face as she turned away from the congregation, leaned over and laid her head on the grainy, pine box.

"You may all think that my mother was a cheap, trashy woman," she whispered "but she was still a person and she doesn't deserve to be remembered the way all of you are remembering her."

There were a few stifled sobs and mostly bowed heads. Lucas couldn't let her go on. He strode up to the altar and led Sam back to their seats. He kissed her gently on the forehead and put his arm around her shoulders. Pastor Thomas cleared his throat from the show of emotion before walking over and blessing the casket one final time. He stood before the parishioners.

"Let us go in peace." He said.

The two elderly ushers came from either side of the pews and rolled the casket back down the aisle. Each pew filed out behind them with Sam leading the way. When they reached the vestibule of the church Sam stood silently and received hugs from each person who came out. Everyone said the typical "I'm sorry for your loss" and quickly swept by her. When the last person hugged her, he held a little tighter and a little longer than the others. He whispered close to Sam's ear, "I knew what a great person your mother was." She looked up to see who had offered these kind words and found herself looking in the face of Carl Shepard. Carl had been her mother's boss for the last seven years. He was an accountant in town and Dorothy worked in his office part time.

"Please don't think badly about your mother for getting involved with me, it was six years ago and my marriage had been long over before your mother came into my life. She was the best employee and probably one of the best friends I ever had. I should have left my wife years ago for her." He gave a slight shrug and let out a slow breath. "You know, the ironic thing is that my divorce was just finalized on Monday. Regardless of all of Dorothy's problems or habits, I wanted to be with her. I should have told her sooner. Maybe she would have waited for me." He gave Sam's shoulder a light squeeze and walked out the door into the dreary afternoon. At first she was puzzled why he would tell her all of things he just had. It was such an intimate admission and something he could have easily kept to himself. Sam realized he likely just needed to get it off his chest and had no one else to disclose the relationship to.

"Are you okay?" Lucas turned to her and pulled her close to his chest.

"I'm fine. I just want to get this over with." She pulled away from him and placed the dark sunglasses back on her face and walked out to the truck. Lucas followed, helping her in and then took his position in line behind the hearse. There was a little flag suction-cupped to the hood, just in case anyone in town couldn't tell that the big, black, hideous vehicle in front of him meant there was a funeral in process. They traveled to the cemetery about two miles away. By now, the only people in attendance were Lucas, Sam, Pastor Thomas, and Lucas's parents. Everyone else had likely decided it wasn't their place to be there. They came to a stop in front of the cemetery and made their way to the freshly dug grave marked only by a plastic basket of flowers. Lucas helped Sam out of the truck and walked with her to the row of chairs that had been placed out for them. They sat in the two chairs on the right; his parents took a seat in the remaining two chairs. They all locked hands and watched as Pastor Thomas made a sign of peace over the casket that was now in place over the dark hole. He said a short prayer and asked God to accept His sister Dorothy into His Kingdom and keep her safe there for all of eternity.

It was finally all over. Paul and Della sat with the young couple for a few minutes wanting to console Sam for her loss but not really knowing what to say. After a while, they stood, leaned over to kiss Sam on the cheek and said goodbye. Sam was grateful for the Benson's comfort but was glad to see them go.

"Lucas could you give me a few minutes?" She didn't look at him as she made her request.

"Are you sure?" He didn't know if she should be alone right then. But he decided to let her be as she looked at him and nodded.

"This is the last time I am going to be this near her. Can't you understand that?" she whispered.

"Of course." He kissed her hand and walked back to the truck. He sat with the engine idling for a long time. He watched with sadness, the love of his life say goodbye to her entire family. He nearly intervened when he saw Sam leave her chair and lay down on the cool, damp earth next to her mother's casket. Lucas sat with silent tears as Sam stroked the dark box and said her last goodbyes. His heart wrenched when he saw her tiny frame heaving from the sobs. He couldn't let this go on any longer. It had started to rain and she was soaking wet and muddy. Lucas jumped out of the truck leaving the door wide open. He yelled her name as he ran towards her. It was pouring now and the trees around them shook with the loud claps of thunder. The workers who were there to fill in the grave were shaking Sam's shoulders when Lucas reached them.

"Ma'am you gotta go, the weather ain't too good out here and we got a job to do!" The one speaking to Sam was a bulking, gap toothed man who appeared to be about fifty years old. He was yelling over the thunder and lightning. Lucas shouted to the man over the large gusts of wind to let her go. He coaxed Sam up from the ground and covered her bare arms with his suit coat. They left the workers to their task of hastily trying to lower the casket and fill in the large gap in the ground with dirt.

Chapter 4

It was Sunday afternoon. Two days had gone by since the funeral and the house was all cleaned out. The furniture that was in good enough shape had been donated to a local charity that helps disparate families to get on their feet. All of Dorothy's clothes were given to the Kingsley Home for Battered and Abused Women, the dishes and appliances were either thrown out or given away, and what little valuable items there were in the house were packed away with Sam's things. Those items included a simple gold band that was Dorothy's wedding ring and an old tarnished silver jewelry box whose contents have always been nothing more than cheap, tawdry baubles. There was a sign in the yard placing the house on the market and there had already been considerable interest. Even if the buyer did not need a home, the people in town were surely not going to let an empty house just sit with over grown weeds and an unkempt yard. Whoever bought it would probably do it solely for the sake of salvaging the neighborhood's appearance.

Lucas hauled out the last box of trash and came back in the house to find Samantha wandering around its empty rooms.

"It's strange," she started, "I never really appreciated all that my mom did to keep this roof over our heads. It may not have been much of a roof, but it was always there." Samantha came up to Lucas and let him embrace her. "She was a good person deep down, Lucas, she really was." She tried to smile a little. "It was just hard to see under all of that make-up." She sniffled a little at the joke and felt Lucas's arms tighten around her.

"I know babe, I know. She *was* a good person and it's just important to remember that about her. Besides, after the funeral and your speech, I'm pretty sure everyone in town will keep pretty tight-lipped about your mom from now on." He kissed her forehead gently. Outside it had started to sprinkle. Within minutes it turned into a steady rain. They stood in the living room staring out the window with their arms wrapped around each other watching the storm. His lips wandered down to find her mouth but he was cautious and unsure if this was the appropriate time or place. To his surprise, she accepted his kiss fully. Her mouth parted to allow his to enter. They both knew it was one of the last times they would be able to spend an afternoon like this together. She knew what he wanted from her and her mind whirled with the uncertainty of what to do next. For a moment she felt shy and scared. She was dizzy with excitement and yet somehow that excitement was tinged with dread. She had always been positive about the choices she made. Up until now, that is. Sam let Lucas carefully lift her up. Their lips never left each other's as he walked down the short hallway to her empty bedroom. He laid her down on the floor and grabbed a quilt from one of the few remaining bags in the house. Spreading it out quickly and quietly he glanced over at Sam to see what her reaction was to his intentions. Sam raised herself up on her elbows and gave Lucas an eager look. Her hands came up to his neck as he started to unfasten the buttons of his shirt. She slid herself over to the blanket and stared up at him. The windows were slightly open and it was still raining. It was unusual weather for them, but today the change was welcome. It wasn't a dreary rain, it was a cozy shower and the scents and sounds of the outdoors surrounded them. Bare-chested, he let himself descend on her slowly. Lucas knew enough not to rush this. He couldn't if he wanted to. It was just too perfect the way it was. He could feel her heart racing through the white cotton shirt she was wearing. His mouth lazily wandered over hers and down to her neck. He was aching with what he felt for her. After indulging himself with the taste of her lips one more time he sat up slowly, and without taking his eyes off of her, lifted her shirt up over her head as gently as he could. Lucas let his eyes wander over her beautiful body. He knew that this was more than he deserved. And even as his hands tenderly undid the fastening of her belt buckle and the buttons below it, he knew that this was what his life was about. It was about Sam, and doing everything he could to keep her safe and happy. He knew he could die tomorrow and be satisfied that he was able to experience the love of a lifetime.

Sam had thought that being this undressed in front of Lucas would be embarrassing but she was wrong. It was beautiful, sweet, and completely worth waiting for. They lay next to each other for some time just taking in the sight of themselves. Neither of them spoke, they were both too wrapped up in the moment and each other. She let his hands wander and his mouth explore and when it came time to take that last leap Lucas looked her deep in her eyes, kissed the tip of her nose, and told her he loved her. He could read in her eyes how she felt and what it was that she truly wanted. Without going any further, he took her hands in his, lay down next to her and watched her fall asleep. Lucas and Sam spent their last night together knowing that he already had everything he needed from her without taking anything she wasn't ready to give. They drifted into sleep, listening to the rain.

Lucas groggily reached for his watch. He knew he had left it somewhere near his pile of clothing. When he finally grasped the leather band, he pushed the little button on the side to illuminate its face. It was nearly 2:00 A.M. He was surprised to look up and see a silhouette in the window.

"What are you doing awake? It's really late and you've had a really long day." He slowly sat up, his back cracking from the unexpected movement.

Sam responded without looking away from the window.

"It's still raining. Nights like these are my favorite because everything seems so peaceful and serene." She pulled the sheet tighter around her shoulders and walked towards him. "Thank you for tonight. I don't know how you knew...." She looked away. "But I'm glad you did."

He knew what she meant without having to hear the actual words. Something deep inside last night told him that she wasn't ready to take that step. He wasn't sure what it was, but he was glad for the intuition nonetheless.

He simply took her face in his hands and kissed her gently.

"You're welcome."

Sam looked at Lucas knowing there was no one else she'd rather share her life with. She kissed him back and brought him down to their makeshift bed. She traced his face with her fingers as she listened to him fall into a deep sleep. As softly as she could, she thanked him one last time for everything.

"There is no way I could have gotten through these last few days without you." She kissed his lips gently, trying not to wake him. "I love you and I'll never forget you." She whispered. She was surprised when he repeated part of her sentence.

"*Never forget...*"

Sam wasn't sure what had made her add those last few words or what had made him repeat them. She had no intention of ending her relationship with Lucas or ever being in the *position* to forget him. She just had some sneaking feeling that she should say as much to him just in case it was one of the last times he would hear it.

Sam was granted an extension by the college until Tuesday. The advisor she spoke with readily agreed to give her a private orientation and tour based on the circumstances. She decided to go Monday afternoon and Lucas said he would stay until the evening to make sure she got settled. It had taken some convincing but Lucas finally helped her realize that she couldn't sit around and mourn. She needed to get on with her life and with her original plans. They had spent all of Sunday lying around with each other, reveling in their new found interest and respect for one another. The day had been sweet and perfect and one that Lucas knew that he would never forget. He was sad to see her go, but he knew that they had solidified their relationship just that much more. He also knew that there was nothing that could keep the two of them apart.

On Monday morning they finished packing up Lucas's truck with the rest of Sam's things for college. They had slept in late so it was just before noon when they decided to grab something to eat. It was the last time Sam would ever sleep in the house she had spent most of her childhood in so she hadn't been in any rush to go anywhere. They agreed to meet Paul and Della at Lucinda's Café for lunch at Della's request.

Sam and Lucas pulled into the tiny parking lot off of Oak Street. The parking lot was shared between the café and a small antique store called Grandma Mary's Treasures. No one ever went into the antique store so when the lot was full, you knew the restaurant would be too. They parked and jumped out of the truck into the sticky, humid weather. Walking into the restaurant Lucas opened the door for them both and was annoyed by the bells that rung like a wind chime over their heads, signaling their entrance. Whenever you walked into any business in town there was usually a similar indicator. Just like any small town, everyone always wanted to know your business, even if it was as simple as walking through a doorway. As usual, today was no different. The café was full even for a Monday when it seemed everyone should be at work. Their entrance was received with several stares and a few whispers. Everyone looked but no one was brave enough to hold their gaze and acknowledge Sam or offer their condolences. Lucas took her hand and led her through the maze of tables. At the first big round table there was a group of middle-aged men discussing the upcoming season of high school football over coffee. The conversation was heated and there was an apparent division over the expected success of this year's prospects. Two tables over there were the Weston sisters. There were six of them all together. They were the matriarchs of one of the largest extended families in the area. Their children could do no wrong and their grandchildren were even saintlier. Each sister belonged to a different church and was a member of nearly every club and organization in Bradyville. Their collective knowledge of the goings-on of the town gave them much to discuss each week. Since none of them had ever worked they spent every Monday drinking tea and discussing the weekend's happenings with each other. They compared stories and discussed various versions of those stories. By the end of each gathering they had compounded their collection of gossip into chatter that would be spread among the town as first-hand knowledge.

The rest of the small dining area was peppered with older couples having a light meal and town professionals conducting business lunches.

Sam and Lucas squeezed past the crowded tables, said hello to all the Weston women who each gave Sam a look of forced sympathy, and finally made their way to the rear of the room where Paul and Della were seated with menus and ice waters.

Paul was concentrating hard on the decision between a turkey club sandwich and a meatball sub when they approached the table.

"The government should hire you to make all of its difficult choices for them, Dad." Lucas grinned as they sat down across from his parents.

"Huh?" Paul didn't get the joke so Lucas just let it go.

"How are you doing sweetie?" Della laid a hand over Sam's and gave it a light squeeze.

"I'm okay. It's still quite a shock, but I'm getting better. Lucas has been such a help to me. I wouldn't have known what to do without him." Sam looked over at Lucas and smiled.

Della picked up her menu and pretended to scan its content. Without looking up she spoke to Lucas.

"I noticed you didn't come home last night. It would have been nice if you had called."

Della paused before continuing, finally setting her menu down in front of her. Della was watching them intently with an obvious expression of worry mixed with a touch of anger.

It became clear to Lucas that his mother had some agenda for this farewell meal and he could see she was wasting no time in getting to the point.

"I'll be honest with you both. I realize that you two are very close but you still are only teenagers."

She stopped to make sure that they both realized where the conversation was going and looked around to be sure no one was eavesdropping. Della didn't normally have a problem with Lucas spending a lot of time over at Sam's. She just had this suspicion that something had changed recently and she wasn't sure how to deal with it. Her mother's intuition was telling her to intervene.

"I'm not trying to butt in, but the two of you are very young yet, and I wanted to discuss the arrangements for while you're away at school, Sam. That's partly why we asked you to lunch today." Della tried hard to take the edge out of her voice. She wanted to be understanding and supportive of her son but she couldn't stand by and allow him to make a big mistake.

"There is no *we* in this conversation. I just came here for a good sandwich." Paul interjected. "I think you should stay out of their business Della." He looked back and forth from Sam to Lucas. "They're smart kids." Paul shook his head, dismissing any ownership of the conversation and went back to scrutinizing the menu.

"I'm just saying-," Della started.

"Saying what?" Lucas was started to get angry. He had never known his mother to be distrustful of him and the feeling was unfamiliar and unwelcome.

"I just want you two to be careful!" Della had raised her voice to a level that made the occupants of the surrounding tables to quiet down.

"Go ahead mom. Just ask." Lucas could hear the snide tone of his own voice but couldn't force himself to remove it. "Ask us if we've had sex." He put his fists on the table and was prepared to leave.

Beatrice Weston had her ears perked right up and there was not a mite of conversation going on at their table.

"Lucas, this is no one's business!" Sam whispered loudly.

She begged him to stop. Her life had been enough of a spectacle the last few days she didn't need this to continue.

"Well, I'm just curious where all of this suspicion is coming from all of a sudden?" He ignored Sam's pleading looks and the fact that she was tugging on the bottom of his shirt, silently imploring him to be quiet. "We've never been bad kids. We've dated since our freshman year of high school and we've always stayed out of trouble. Why do you suddenly doubt our behavior?" Instead of letting his mother answer he added, "Not that I personally think it's any of your business."

Della had her napkin to her lips and her eyes were to the floor. Her cheeks had colored a deep red. She looked around to see how many people were staring at them. This was not going as she had planned.

"Lucas please lower your voice. No one needs to be a part of this discussion." Della was sorry she hadn't asked them to lunch at home instead of in public.

"I'm sorry to embarrass *you* mom." He wasn't sure what the sudden cause for concern was but he was also realizing how many people around them were likely eavesdropping.

Della relented a little, and sat back in her chair. "I just-," she let out a breath and lowered her eyes. "I just don't want the two of you to become the object of gossip." She wasn't quite sure how to explain herself. She knew she was being overprotective.

"I think I understand." Sam said slowly. "You don't want Lucas's reputation ruined for getting involved with 'Hottie Dottie's' daughter." She paused to let Lucas catch her meaning. "You're afraid that I'll turn out just like her. You think I'm going to get pregnant and keep Lucas from making something of himself and we're going to end up in the same trashy little house that I was raised in."

Sam turned to Lucas.

"I think I should go." She stood to leave the table.

"Wait." This was the first word Paul Benson had uttered since the argument began. "Sam, sit down. That most certainly was not what my wife meant." He reached over and grabbed Della's hand to help show a unified front. "You of all people should know that we have never had a problem with you and Lucas being....friends."

"But that's just it dad," Lucas interrupted, "we're not just *friends*. Are you kidding me?"

Lucas grabbed Sam's wrist before she could walk away. "I don't know what's going on here, or what started this conversation, but we all need to get on the same page. Sam and I have been dating for over five years. When exactly did this become a problem to the two of you?" He looked from his dad to his mom. They in turn exchanged glances.

Della's expression softened and she brought her hands up to her cheeks.

"Oh Sam, honey, I didn't mean to make you feel that way. Of course this has nothing to do with your mother or how anyone may have felt about her. Please sit down."

Sam looked over to Lucas. He clearly wanted her to stay. She sat back down and folded her hands in her lap. She couldn't help but feel uncomfortable and unwelcome after their heated exchange but knew Lucas needed to keep peace with his family.

"I agree with Lucas. We all need to be the same page. Let's just be adults about this and be honest about how we feel." Sam looked at everyone at the table. "Can we all do that?"

Everyone nodded their heads in agreement. Della let out a breath and started first.

"I am so sorry Sam. It really has nothing to do with you in particular. I'm sorry if that's the way I came off to you, I should have had a little more control. I just don't want the two of you to get so caught up in each other that you forget that there is a whole other world out there. Sweetheart, I am so proud of you for wanting to go away to college. It takes a lot of courage." She stopped for a moment. "You always handle yourself with such grace despite your circumstances. Just promise us that you will respect each other's needs and wait a little while before making any big decisions about your relationship. There is so much for you to experience out there." She reached across the table and placed her hands over Sam and Lucas's. "We love you both very much and just want what's best for you." She smiled and looked at Paul. "Is that what we meant to say?" She asked with a chuckle.

"I think that is *exactly* what we wanted to say." He turned to the kids. "So, no hard feelings and we're all in agreement?" He looked from Lucas, to Sam, to Della. Once again everyone nodded at the same time. "Thank God, because that poor waitress has walked halfway to our table and back about ten times waiting for all of this nonsense to end, and I am starving." Paul signaled to the waitress that it was finally okay to come over to their table. The tension was gone and everyone became more relaxed.

A tall girl with long, red hair came bouncing over.

"So ya'll know what you're going to have?" She looked at everyone with a smile and with her pen and pad ready to go.

When everyone finally ordered and their lunch was served, they relaxed and enjoyed one another's company. After almost two hours of laughing and sharing memories they all walked out into the parking lot where everyone hugged each other goodbye and said another round of apologies. Sam promised to stay in touch with the Benson's and agreed to let Della know if there was anything at all she needed. Paul and Della got into their SUV and Sam and Lucas climbed into his truck. They waved to each other and parted ways.

Chapter 5

The afternoon went wonderfully slow. Lucas took Sam down to the park in town where they sat on a bench carved with the names of all of its past visitors. They passed the time talking, laughing, and lying sprawled out on a blanket while enjoying the late summer day, despite the heat, neither wanted to the day to end. It was like they were characters in their own favorite movie and each wanted to continually press the pause button with each passing moment. They watched the kids playing on the monkey bars and the mothers chaperoning the play with babies in their arms and in nearby strollers. They made their way down by the edge of the water and found a spot in the sand near the one they occupied the night Sam shared her news with Lucas. That night seemed like only moments ago and years away all at the same time. They were both still a little shell-shocked at the recent events that happened in their lives. Between her mother's passing and the funeral, and the unexpected ambush from Lucas's parents it had been an exhausting week. It was nearly four o'clock when Lucas brought up hitting the road.

"We should get going. It's getting late." He looked at Sam and kissed her softly. When he pulled away he was surprised by her expression. "What's wrong?"

She looked terrified.

"I don't want to go. At all, I mean." She let go of his hand and gazed out at the water shaking her head slowly. Closing her eyes, she took it all in. The feel of the warm breeze on her skin and the familiar sights surrounding them reminded her of all of the fun times they had shared in this small town she was trying so hard to get away from. "Can I tell you something?" She finally turned and looked at Lucas.

"Of course, babe, you can tell me anything. What's up?" He tried reaching for her again but she stood and turned her back to him.

"I'm scared-"

"Well, that's natural, of course you're scared."

She cut him off before he could say anything else.

"No, just please let me finish." She paused before continuing. "I'm scared of going back to school. I'm terrified of who I might meet and what I'm getting into. I'm worried that I'm going to hate it and that I'll get stuck with a roommate that I don't get along with." She took a breath. "And I'm *so* scared that you and I are not going to work out." She looked into his eyes hoping to find something that would reassure her that everything would be fine. "I know we've been over and over this but what can you say that will completely convince me?" She waited for an answer.

Apparently he paused too long.

"Nothing! That's what. There's nothing you can say that is going to make me sure of the fact that you'll still be there for me."

She was close to being hysterical. She felt like someone had squeezed all of the air from her lungs, leaving her breathless. She was pacing back and forth in front of Lucas, kicking up flecks of sand at him,

"I thought you were excited. And since when do you not have any faith in our relationship?" He asked with obvious exasperation.

Lucas was dumbfounded. Up until now he tried to be calm about her leaving and did his best to be supportive of all of her decisions. Suddenly it felt like everything she was throwing at him was just to push his buttons. Nothing he could say was right.

"Are you trying to make me *want* to leave you? Is that it?"

He got up and strode over to where Samantha was standing with her arms around her waist. He hugged her close to him. He knew she was just confused.

Samantha sighed and looked at him, putting some space between their bodies. She knew she sounded unreasonable and that Lucas was probably tired of having this same argument again and again.

"Of course that's not what I want. But you have no idea what it's like to have no one." Sam ran her fingers through her long dark hair and looked up at Lucas. "I don't mean that to offend you. I just mean that you don't know what it's like to go away for this long and know that you don't have a family at home wishing you well, or waiting for you to come home on the holidays. You've always had this, like, wonderful family supporting you and just being there for you when you're hurt or scared. You've always had that so you don't know what this is like for me. It's really, really scary." She shrugged her shoulders. "So sometimes it just seems like it would be even easier if I had no ties to this place at all."

She regretted the words as soon as she said them. She sounded ungrateful and knew that he was feeling as if she was disregarding his feelings.

Sam could feel him loosen his grasp on her, and she knew she had upset him.

"Lucas, I'm sorry."

"No, its fine I understand." He jammed his hands into his pockets and looked away.

He knew this would be difficult but he couldn't help but think that people went away to college all of the time and it shouldn't be this dramatic.

"I don't think you do…." Her voice trailed as she lost the words to say that would take back all of the hurtful things that had already been said. He turned and looked at her blankly.

"You tell me what you want then. Whatever it is, I'll do it." He took a step closer to her.

Lucas knew he sounded harsh but it was important to know now before she left what she truly wanted, especially in light of all of the recent events in their lives. "I will walk away right now if that's what you want. If I thought that it would make your life easier or help lessen the pain of losing your mother, I would do that for you. But don't think for a second, that I could ever love you any less than I do now. Doubting me is the worst thing you could do, so if you want to put an end to us then now is the time to do it." He threw his hands up in the air and began to walk away.

Sam was stunned by his words. He had always been honest with her but never to the point where he sounded uncaring. She was suddenly sorry for her thoughts and her words and she realized how selfish she was being. She ran after him and desperately tried to come up with the right way to apologize.

"I'm so sorry." She caught up to him and threw her arms around his waist. She could feel his breathing and his muscles tightening with anger. Sam brought her face to his and pulled him toward her. She kissed his cheek and kept repeating how sorry she was. It immediately became clear to her that he was truly meant for her. She was obviously very lucky to have someone like Lucas in her life and there was no way she was letting him go.

After a tiring conversation, they accepted one another's apologies and decided there was no point delaying the inevitable. She had somewhere she needed to be and so he helped her into his truck as they started the journey to her new life away from him.

"Why are you so quiet?" he asked.

They were about forty five minutes into the trip.

She had been mentally going over everything she had packed to see if there was anything that she may have forgotten.

"Huh? I'm sorry what did you say?" She tried not to seem as nervous as she felt but she hadn't even realized that neither of them had spoken since they left home.

"Nothing, it wasn't important." He reached over and gave her hand a quick squeeze. "Don't be nervous. I bet you'll love your roommate, your classes, and your professors." He gave her a reassuring smile. "You'll see."

"I hope you're right. I mean, I had a few friends in high school and everything but I definitely didn't win any popularity contests." She bit her thumbnail nervously. "What if I don't make *any* friends?"

"Then you'll just be that much more excited to see me when I come to visit." He flashed a wide smile trying to keep her spirits up.

He figured keeping the conversation light would be best considering how dismal their lives and discussions had been in the past week.

They were about halfway there when Lucas's stomach started to rumble.

"Do you mind if we grab something to eat real quick? I'm starving." He had already put his turn signal on and was exiting the freeway before she could respond.

"I guess not." Sam gave a quick wave with her hand since obviously he had already made his mind up to stop before waiting for her answer. "I just don't want to get there too late. It's already almost six."

"I'm just going to run through a drive-thru; I promise I'll be fast. Do you want anything?"

"No way. If I eat something now I'd probably get sick. My stomach is way too nervous to eat." She shook her head at the idea of eating anything.

Lucas eyed her cautiously. Sam hadn't eaten much since her mom passed away. At least not that he had seen and he had spent just about every moment with her since then.

"Are you sure?"

"I'm positive." She said. He could sense her annoyance at his questioning. "Please just decide where you're going, get what you want and let's get back on the road. I feel like this trip is already taking forever."

"Okay, okay." He pulled into the nearest fast food joint off the ramp. "Geez I was just asking." He was only semi-joking at this point.

Sam said nothing as she listened to him order his food and wait for the worker to repeat it back. On the third attempt at confirmation, the drive-thru attendant finally got it right.

"Holy hell…how un-educated do you have to be to work here?" She was saying this to no one in particular, but loud enough for the worker to hear her.

As they rounded the curve to get to the window – waiting behind a pickup truck full of young teens – Lucas was about to again ask what Sam's problem was but decided against it. He chalked it up to nerves and drove ahead to pay for and collect his food. He could only pray that the young women who had had such a difficult time taking his order would not still be at the window. As he stopped parallel with the window he knew he had no such luck. Behind the glass he was sarcastically greeted by a toothless, overweight woman with a snarl on her face. She had obviously heard Sam's comment. He handed the lady an exact amount for his food, grabbed the bag she thrust at him, and gave a weak smile as he drove away.

"Thanks a lot Sam. I probably have spit in my burger now."

"Oh stop, I bet our words were too big for her to understand anyway." She kept facing the window as she let the snide comment slip out. She chewed at her thumbnail as she stared off into the distance.

He still didn't know exactly what her problem was but didn't dare ask. Chalking it up to nerves once again, he turned the corner and got back on the road.

Just over an hour and a half after their stop they passed a sign indicating that Fremont Technical University was only seventeen miles ahead. They both took a deep breath, staring straight ahead as they watched their future approaching them from the distance.

Chapter 6

The whole house shook from the music blasting from the speakers. The entire place was crowded with people drinking, yelling, and doing lots of other things that Jessica tried hard not to pay attention to. She eased her way down a hallway of unfamiliar faces, unwanted touching, and occasional whistles. This was definitely not the scene she was used to and she was quite certain that this was not the building she meant to be in. She had only arrived on campus that day and had not found anyone to really ask for help with directions. Jessica was amazed at the fact that school hadn't even started yet and it seemed as if everyone here knew each other. Everyone, that was, except her.

She finally reached an area of the house that had only a handful of people in it and decided to be brave and ask someone to help her find what she was looking for. Scanning the room she saw a tall red-headed girl coming down the stairs in a short white sundress and sandals. The girl appeared to be approachable enough so Jessica decided to stop her.

"Umm….excuse me," Jessica managed to get out as she tried to reach the girl before she walked away from her. Approaching strangers, or anyone for that matter, was not one of her strong points.

With what seemed to be a forced smile, the girl turned toward Jessica and responded.

"Can I help you?" She was clearly itching to walk away.

Reaching out her hand, Jessica introduced herself. "Uh...hi, my name is Jessica Carlisle and I'm not sure how I ended up *here*, but I am looking for the Kappa Phi Delta Sorority House. Do you happen to know where that might be?" She tried to sound confident but the girl staring at her squarely in the eyes seemed like the type of girl Jessica had spent most of her life trying to avoid. She was tall, pretty, and from as far as Jessica could tell, fairly popular.

"Well, honey you found it." The girl started to walk away but on an impulse, Jessica reached out and took hold of her wrist. Realizing her mistake too late, she released her grip.

"I'm sorry for doing that. It's just that I don't know if you heard me correctly. You see..." Jessica reached into her bag and unfolded a piece of paper. "The brochure says that Kappa Phi Delta is a warm, friendly environment where girls can get to know each other and help one another navigate through their college experience." Jessica looked up from the brochure and around the room again. She noted the beer bottles on the floor, the bead necklaces hanging from the doorknobs, and the random people running around. "This just doesn't sound like the brochure at all."

The girl, who still hadn't introduced herself, seemed to be growing impatient. She snatched the brochure from Jessica's hand and held it to her face. "If you want to find a group of people who will do all that for you then maybe you should join another club." She started to walk away when she noticed Jessica starting to tear up. With a sigh, she decided to take pity on the girl. "Look, this is what fraternity and sorority houses are like. It's Welcome Week on campus and it's not unusual to host a party like this. Our sorority is top of the line as far as sorority's go at this school and so we have to have the best parties. It's expected of us."

Standing as straight as she could, Jessica quickly wiped her eyes and apologized. "I'm really sorry for wasting your time. I'm a freshman this year and at orientation my advisor told me that joining a sorority would be a good way to meet people." She looked down at the floor. "I don't really know anyone and I'm not very good at introducing myself. I guess it was pretty stupid me to think it would be like this. Thanks for your help." She offered a weak smile to the red head and turned to leave.

The girl watched Jessica walked toward the door. She couldn't help but notice that even though Jessica was kind of pretty, she wore awful baggy clothes and no make-up. Her shoes didn't really match her outfit and her hair hung too long and too straight. Torn between wanting to get back to the party and feeling sorry for this freshman who was so clearly lost, she remembered what it was like to not know anyone. She decided to act like the sorority sister that she was and take pity on the lost girl.

"Wait!" She called out, half-jogging to the door before Jessica could walk out. "My name is Taylor and I'm a senior this year." She took the brochure from Jessica's hand and turned it over. "Let me give you my number here at the house and you can call me once all the craziness of Welcome Week is over. We can get together and I can talk to you a little bit about the sorority to see if it's something you'd be interested in." She looked around at the disaster that had become of her house. "Besides, it'll be much quieter then." She let out a sparkling laugh and Jessica thought that this might possibly be the nicest "pretty girl" she had ever encountered. Taylor was certainly a far cry from the girls she had known in high school.

Letting out a relieved sigh, she smiled and gave Taylor a hug.

"Thank you so much!"

"Whoa, whoa. It's no biggie, really." She pried Jessica's arms off of her to end the embrace. Blushing at what she had just done, Jessica stammered another quiet thank you and turned to leave.

Out on the sidewalk, Jessica couldn't help but start to tear up. No one had ever been that nice to her in any kind of social situation. She especially wouldn't have expected such friendliness from someone who was as seemingly popular as Taylor. In any event, she wasn't going to question the girl's motives. Jessica knew enough to accept Taylor's graciousness and be grateful for any help she extended to her. With a little extra pep in her step, Jessica started on her search for Perkin's Hall where she hoped to meet her new roommate and start her life as a new and improved college freshman.

It took some driving around and few stops for directions but at last Jessica finally reached a weather-worn brown brick building. The sign above the massive double doors looked like it at one time read the words 'Perkins

Hall'. She couldn't be positive, but Jessica was fairly certain she had reached her intended destination. She pulled into the nearest parking space and got out. She didn't mind parking a ways from the dorm. Her car was nothing short of a rusted mass of metal and rubber and although it got her where she needed to go she didn't care to show it off. She decided to only take a few small bags and her purse with her to search for what was to be her home for the next year. She'd save the heavier suitcases for later. When she reached the front of the building she breathed in the warm fresh air and let out hefty sigh. "Here goes nothing." She muttered to herself. She just about had her hand on the handle when the door flew open, nearly knocking her off the steps.

"Watch out!"

The warning came from a tall brunette who was bounding down the steps with a whole slew of friends. The girl didn't give a second glance at Jessica as she continued laughing with the crew that surrounded her and proceeded down the walkway.

"I'm s-sorry!" Jessica tried to call after the group. The only response she heard was someone mocking her for stuttering. They disappeared around the sidewalk before she could say anything else to them. "Great." Jessica mumbled to herself. "Way to go." She bent over to pick up her purse that had been knocked to the ground when someone else's head collided with her own.

"Sorry!"

Jessica looked up at another dark haired girl who had retrieved Jessica's purse from the ground before she could get it herself.

"Th-thank you." She took her purse from the girl and wiped off the leaves that were stuck to the material at the bottom.

"Those girls are assholes. Don't let them get to you." The girl gave Jessica a warm smile and stuck out her hand. "I'm Samantha. It's nice to meet you."

Jessica slung her purse over her shoulder and returned the handshake. "I'm Jessica Carlisle. It's nice to meet you too." She smiled back at Samantha not really knowing what to say next. "Uh…are you in this dorm too?" It was probably a stupid question considering that Samantha was coming out of the building she was going into. "Sorry that was probably dumb of me to ask."

Samantha let out a small laugh.

"Yes I'm in this dorm too. I'm up on the second floor in dorm 26-B."

"You're kidding! Me too!" Jessica was relieved that not only had she met someone so nice but that she was fortunate enough to be her roommate as well. She felt like giving Sam a hug but then she remembered how awkward her last impulsive embrace was.

"Let me help you with those." Samantha took one of the bags that was slipping from Jessica's arm and held the door open for her.

"Thank you." Jessica walked through doorway and waited for Samantha to enter so that she could lead the way.

"And by the way, you can call me Sam. Everyone does." She gave Jessica another warm smile and walked past her towards the stairway. "There's an elevator in this building but I guess it's broke." Sam nodded toward the sign on their right that indicated as much. "It doesn't sound like they're in any hurry to fix it either. I heard some of the maintenance men talking about it yesterday."

They both started up the stairs, maneuvering around the people coming and going.

"Besides the shabby look of the outside of the building, I guess a broken elevator is another way to know that you're definitely in a freshman dorm."

Jessica giggled at Sam's joke and decided in that moment that the two of them were probably going to be fast friends. "I think they wait to give you the nicer places to live once you've spent more money. Every year you pay tuition you get upgraded." They were both laughing when they reached the second level.

"How long have you been here?" Jessica thought that Sam knew an awful lot about the campus for being a freshman. "You seem to know quite a bit about what goes on around here."

"I got here on Monday night." Sam had to catch her breath as they reached their room. "My boyfriend drove me here from home so I've had a few days to settle in. "I was supposed to be here last Thursday since I'm here on an academic scholarship. There were some extra tours that I was supposed to go on and meet-and-greets with some of the professors. There was also an extra orientation for students who were interested in some AP labs and after hour's courses."

"So how come you didn't get here until Tuesday then?" Jessica wondered why someone would miss that kind of an opportunity. She would have jumped at the chance to ease into the campus and get to know things around the area before the other thousands of students showed up.

"Umm…I had some personal things to take care of at home."

Jessica watched as Sam grew quiet and started messing with her key ring. She got the feeling that whatever personal thing it was, Sam didn't want to talk about it. Instead of taking the risk of hurting her new friend's feelings, she decided not to press the issue.

"Well I'm just glad you're here at all." She gave Sam a wide smile and a little knock with her elbow. "Now why don't you show me our palace for the next year?"

Jessica could tell that Sam appreciated the change of subject.

"Oh it's beautiful *dah*-ling. I bet you've never stayed in a place as charming as this." Sam gave Jessica a sly smile as she opened the door and entered their room to begin their adventure as college freshmen.

The first few weeks of school flew by for Jessica. She had even managed to make a few friends in some of her classes. She spent most of her time studying but still tried to make an effort to become more outgoing. Taylor had kept her promise to Jessica about getting together to talk about becoming a member of the sorority. And although Jessica appreciated Taylor's help, in the end she decided that sorority life was not for her. She was glad she had that accidental run-in with Taylor that first day though. It presented her with the opportunity to be introduced to a lot of new people and it helped bring Jessica out of her shell even further with Taylor introducing her to some of her friends.

By mid-October Jessica was attending parties regularly and meeting up with people for lunch all while keeping up her grades. If someone would have told her that this is what college life would be like for her she never would have believed them. Jessica did, however, wish that she could become closer with her roommate Sam. She had tried to coax Sam out of the dorm on a few different occasions to go to a party but Sam never seemed interested. In fact, the only time Jessica even noticed Sam leave their room to do something even semi-social was when Sam's boyfriend came to visit.

Jessica had met Sam's boyfriend Lucas a few times in the beginning of the year, but they both always declined Jessica's invitation to go out for the evening so she didn't really know too much about him. He seemed nice enough, but he definitely was not pushing Sam to have an active social life on campus. Jessica just figured that it was because Lucas was afraid that Sam would meet someone new and forget about him.

The last day of mid-terms had Jessica nearly skipping up the steps to Perkins Hall. She felt she had done well on all of her tests and was incredibly glad they were all over. She was also excited about the party that was being held that night. It was going to be hosted by one of the campus fraternity houses and Jessica was planning on just letting loose and forgetting all about studying.

By the time she reached her door she was starting to think about what she should wear. Her wardrobe had improved considerably in the last few weeks thanks to some of her new friends. When Jessica pushed the door open she bent over to pick up the backpack she had set on the ground while digging for her keys. She looked up to find a teary-eyed Sam sitting on her bed with the phone in her lap.

Shutting the door behind her, Jessica put all costume thoughts away as she made her way over to Sam's bed.

"What happened?" Jessica grabbed a tissue from the nightstand. "Are you ok?" She handed the tissue to Sam and waited for her to answer.

"Oh....I'm fine." The words caused her voice to crack. Taking the tissue from Jessica she blew her nose and sighed. "It's nothing really. I'm totally overreacting." She took a ragged breath and gave Jessica a faint smile. "Really…it's something totally stupid."

"Well…you can tell me you know." Jessica reached over and grabbed another handful of tissues. "Seriously, what's wrong?"

"Promise you won't tell me I'm an idiot for getting so upset."

"I promise." Jessica made an 'x' over her heart and waited for Sam to continue.

"It's just that I studied really hard for all my mid-terms and I don't think that I did that well on my Psych test."

Jessica was about to tell Sam what an idiot she was for crying over *that* when she remembered her promise moments ago.

"Well that isn't the end of the world you know." Jessica took the balled up tissues from Sam's hand and threw them in the trash can next to the bed.

"It's not just that." Sam had calmed down enough to talk in a normal tone again. "Lucas called. He was supposed to come down for the weekend but he called to say he can't come all of a sudden." Sam bit her lower lip before saying what was really bothering her. "I think he might be seeing someone else back home."

Jessica wasn't really sure what to say. She hadn't spent much time with Lucas so she couldn't really vouch for his character. Knowing what she did about their relationship though, Jessica tried to convince Sam that there was no way Lucas would do such a thing.

"Come on. Do you really think he would do something like that?" She met Sam's gaze and persisted. "I've heard you guys talk on the phone to each other. You sound like you're married already. I've never met a couple that has as mature of a relationship as the two of you."

Sam could hear Jessica but was too busy rationalizing her assumption in her head to agree with her.

"Think about it though. I don't have any family back home and hardly any friends. If Lucas were cheating, who would call and rat him out?"

"What was his excuse for not coming?"

"That's the worst part!" Sam bent over and buried her face in a pillow. Before she could get upset all over again, she continued. "He said he is going camping! He has never gone camping in his life!"

"So…maybe he started. What's the big deal?"

"The big deal is that his family members are the *least* outdoorsy people you will ever meet. His dad's idea of camping is staying in a two star hotel. Lucas doesn't even like to skip a shower when he *hasn't* been sleeping in the dirt. I doubt he would go a whole weekend without one."

"That doesn't mean anything. You guys have been apart for two months now. Maybe he's taken up some new hobbies." Jessica was trying to be supportive but her mind was starting to wander back to what her wardrobe choice would be for the party that night. "Look maybe he is and maybe he isn't cheating, but I wouldn't draw my conclusions based on one missed visit." Jessica gave Sam a sly grin and interrupted her before she could respond. "Come with me to the party tonight." She gave Sam a bright smile and a light shove on her arm. "It'll be s*ooo* much fun."

"No way. You know I'm not much of a partier." Sam sniffled a little and turned to throw her last tissue into the trash can.

"Not usually. But that's because your little boyfriend is always here on the weekends monopolizing your time." Jessica was thrilled with the idea of taking Sam out for the night. "Come on, you just said you were upset with him and you think he's cheating on you. The best way to take your mind off of him is to go out for the night." Jessica shook her head up and down when Sam started to resist.

"I don't think so but maybe some other time." Sam let herself fall back on her bed. She stared at the ceiling trying to get the image of Lucas and another girl out of her head.

"I'm not giving up that easily." Jessica grabbed Sam's hand and pulled her back up into a sitting position. "You have no studying to do since midterms are over and there is never anything good on television on a Friday night. You're coming out with me."

She could tell that Sam was starting to give in. Jessica stood and bounded over to her closet.

"You can even wear something of mine."

Sam started to smile and finally conceded.

"Only if you mean the black and silver tank top that you bought the other day."

Jessica gave an emphatic sigh.

"I *guess* so!" She was thrilled that Sam had relented. "I promise you will have a good time." She turned around and started digging in her closet for the shirt that Sam was talking about. "I've never been to a party at this fraternity but I heard they can get pretty wild."

Sam's smile faded when she heard those words.

"I – I've never been to a really big party before." She was about to say she wasn't going to go when Jessica interjected.

"I promise I won't leave your side. I'll introduce you to some of the girls that I met through Taylor." She turned back around and continued digging though her mass of clothes. "You remember me telling you about Taylor right?" Jessica said over her shoulder.

"She's the sorority girl, right?" Sam was still hesitant but felt a little better knowing that she wouldn't have to wander around alone at a party where she knew no one.

"Right." Jessica stood. "A-ha...success at last!" She turned to face Sam, holding the shirt that Sam had requested. "I think it even still has the tags on it." She threw the shirt to Sam who held it up to see if it would fit.

"I still don't know if I..."

"Mmm...Nope you can't back out now. You agreed to go and I'm holding you to that. Jessica gave Sam a reassuring look. "Now let's do something with your hair." She grabbed Sam's hands and pulled her toward the bathroom they shared.

"What's wrong with my hair?"

"Nothing is really *wrong* with it. It's just that you could use a little more style. You always wear it long and down."

"I like it that way." Sam was not thrilled with the idea of a makeover but she could tell what was brewing in Jessica's mind. She decided to relax a little and let Jessica do what she wanted.

"Just please let me take over and I promise you'll love it." Jessica sat Sam down in a chair facing away from the mirror and got to work.

Sam decided to just close her eyes and let Jessica work her magic. She figured Jessica couldn't do any real damage. Anything she did to Sam would either wash off or comb out.

Forty five minutes later Jessica had to nearly wake Sam up to show her the results.

"*Voila!*" Jessica turned Sam to her left so that she could see the outcome for herself.

Sam was speechless. She looked at herself in the mirror and brought her hand up to touch her curlier and much shorter hair.

"Holy shit." It was the only thing Sam could think to say.

"You don't love it?" Jessica frowned a little, showing that her feelings had been hurt.

"I-I-I don't even know what to say. It's not that I *hate* it. I just need to get used to it." Sam peered at herself closer in the mirror and took in all of the makeup that was usually foreign to her face. "I just don't normally wear this much makeup. I actually don't really wear any makeup at all."

"I know you don't. And you're super pretty and everything, I just thought you could use something different." Jessica turned away to start putting her makeup back into her cosmetics bag. "You can wash it off if you want…it's no big deal." She gave Sam a shrug to emphasize her indifference to the matter.

"I'm not going to wash it off. I'm already getting used to it." Sam didn't want to hurt Jessica's feelings so she plastered a large smile on her face.

Jessica brightened a little at Sam's words.

"Are you sure you don't hate it?"

"Positive. In fact, I'm going to go get dressed in the other room so that you can finish getting ready and we can leave." Sam gave Jessica a quick hug on her way out to show her appreciation.

It was after nine o'clock when Jessica and Sam left their dorm.

"Are you sure I don't look too…I don't know….slutty in this get-up?" Sam was biting her lip as she gave herself a quick glance in a passing window.

"I'm going to pretend I'm not hurt by that." Jessica elbowed Sam as they made their way down the sidewalk. "Considering that you're wearing my clothes and I did your hair and makeup, I don't think you look slutty at all. Besides, you've never been to one of these parties before. You're dressed like a nun compared to some of the girls you'll see tonight."

They both giggled a little as they turned the corner.

"How far is this place?" Sam asked after they'd already walked almost five blocks.

"Not far. We're almost there actually." Jessica linked arms with Sam. "Trust me; you'll know when we're there.

The music was blaring when Jessica and Sam walked in the front door of the frat house. Jessica gave a quick wave and a smile at the first people she recognized. Sam was trying to tell her something but she couldn't make it out and really wasn't trying that hard to. In fact, although she was happy her roommate had decided to come out with her, she was a little agitated at the way Sam was grasping onto the bottom of her shirt.

"What?" Jessica called back to Sam as loudly as she could as they made their way to the back of the house where the drinks most likely were.

"I *said* please don't leave me by myself!" Sam shouted back to make sure that Jessica heard her.

Jessica wasn't paying much attention. She freed her shirt from Sam's grip and pranced over to an incredibly good looking guy who shared a class with her. Sam watched as Jessica whispered something in the guy's ear and the pair giggled a little as Jessica pointed at Sam. Feeling her face redden at being talked about, Sam turned to look around her. She brushed her hair behind her ear and sighed, noting the fact that she knew not one single soul in the room. It shouldn't have surprised her. Most of her friends – or the people that could be somewhat considered her friends – were all classmates from one of her AP courses or after hours study groups. They wouldn't be caught dead at one of these parties for fear of getting in trouble and jeopardizing their scholarships. Lost in her thoughts, Sam got turned around and lost track of where Jessica had gone. She tried shouting Jessica's name over the crowd but found it useless when she realized she couldn't even hear her own voice. Fighting back tears and the foolishness she felt for even considering coming to the party, Sam tried to make her way to the front door using any sense of direction and memory she had from when they entered. She blindly pushed her way through the throngs of people that crowded the room. She was stopped short by someone grabbing her elbow.

"Hey, what's wrong?"

Sam looked up to see what may have possibly been the most gorgeous face she had ever laid eyes on. She tried to push her way past the strange guy without answering, but his grip on her arm was steadfast.

"Could you please let go?" Sam whispered without looking him straight in the face. Luckily someone had dialed the volume down a little on the music but even then she spoke too softly for him to understand.

"Come on. Let's go somewhere we can talk."

She wasn't sure why, but Sam allowed herself to be led away from the noisiest portion of the house. Before she knew it they were both walking up a staircase lit only by a strand of holiday lights adorned with beer cans. They were at the landing at the top of the stairs when Sam was able to twist away from him.

"What do you think you're doing?" Sam backed away from him and frantically looked for the exit. Although she had to admit to herself that this boy did not look at all threatening, she was uncomfortable with being near him and wanted to get away.

"Hey, hey, chill out. I'm not trying to hurt you." He flashed Sam an impressive smile complete with perfectly straight, white teeth. He motioned to a sofa that was a few feet from the stairway. "You want to sit down?"

"No thank you." Sam couldn't believe how arrogantly the guy was acting for not knowing her from a hole in the wall and she decided to tell him as much. "Why would you possibly think that I'd want to sit up here with you? I don't even know you're name."

"I'm sorry. You're totally right." He genuinely looked apologetic, so Sam reached for the hand he extended to her as an introduction. "I'm Josh. I'm a junior here, I am twenty one years old, my favorite color is blue, and I live about five feet from where you're standing." He gave Sam that smile again and she actually started to feel bad for being rude. "Now will you sit down?" He gestured toward the sofa again.

Sam smiled a little, shook his hand, and sighed. She was still cautious, but she actually felt a little relieved to have someone else to talk to.

"I guess I can sit for a minute."

"Why only for a minute? Is there another party that is funner than this one? If so, then you are totally taking me with you." He laughed and leaned back in his seat completely unaware of his grammatical error. Sam gave an uneasy laugh in response, unsure of what to say next.

Sam knew all about the things that happened on college campuses. She had read magazine articles and news stories about girls who met strange guys and were able to be talked into a bedroom or some equally remote place. The girls were usually naïve and either drunk or on drugs. The all claimed that they were smart enough to not get into situations like that and swore it was something that would never happen to them. In spite of a small nagging doubt, Sam was confident that those occurrences did not apply to her or this situation. She decided to take a little of Jessica's advice and just let loose and relax a little. She was even starting to forgive her roommate for abandoning her.

"No, no. I don't have anywhere to be that is *more fun* than this." She relaxed into her seat as well. "I hope you're not an English major because in case anyone hasn't told you 'funner' is not a word." Sam gave a small chuckle, hoping she hadn't offended him.

"Ooh, sorry miss smarty pants. I didn't know we were in class." Josh got up from the sofa and Sam started to think that he really was offended at her correcting his grammar.

"I'm sorry. I didn't mean to make fun of you." Sam frowned and got up to leave.

"No, no. Sit back down. I'm not mad." He made sure she sat back down before turning around again. "I was just going to get us some drinks from the other room."

"Oh…okay I guess." Sam tried to decide if she should just make her exit now or stay awhile and visit with her new friend. "I'll have something diet if there is anything." She called out after Josh, suddenly aware that she had just made the unconscious decision to stay.

"What do you want in it?" He poked his head out from around the corner.

"What do you mean 'in it' "? She was confused.

"I mean do you want vodka, rum, or tequila?" She watched him quickly peer into the room to his left. A moment later he stuck his head back out. "I don't think there's any whiskey left."

"I just want a plain diet soda, but if there's caffeine in it that's ok." She ignored his comments on which alcohol she wanted in her drink and heard him laugh at her request.

Moments later, Josh returned to the sofa with two opened cans of beer.

"Here you go. Sorry no soda, it's strictly shots or beer. I figured this would be easier on you. It sounds like you don't drink much." He gave her the can from his left hand and sat down beside her. He was sitting quite a bit closer to her now than he had been before he left to get their drinks. He leaned back and set his hand on her leg. "Look on the bright side though. There's no caffeine in it." Although his tone was friendly and she didn't feel threatened, Sam thought she had better leave.

"I think I should get going." She turned to set the drink on the table that sat in front of the sofa.

"Oh, come on. It's just one drink. You're not driving are you?"

"No. My roommate and I walked here." Sam tried to get up but Josh still had his hand on her leg.

"Well….then just sit down and have one drink with me." He persisted. He made no move to stand and did not put any more pressure on her leg with his hand. Rather, he just gave her another smile and took a drink from his beer.

Sam was torn between knowing she should do the right thing and wanting to stay.

"Ok, but just a few more minutes and then I really have to go." Sam took a drink of her beer and gagged slightly at the bitter taste that was left in her mouth. It wasn't that she had never had a drink before. She had, but only a glass of wine or a wine cooler and even that was on the rarest occasions. She wasn't sure why, but something made her take a second swallow of the harsh liquid.

"See! Now we're having a good time." Josh gave her leg a quick squeeze and finally removed his hand. He took another large gulp from his own drink.

Sam could feel herself relax with each sip. Her mind briefly allowed her thoughts to include Lucas. Was he doing the same thing she was right now? Could she imagine him sitting in some remote room with another girl that was trying to win over his affection and keep her company? Sam's thoughts kept her preoccupied. Too pre occupied. She only half-heard Josh's contribution to their conversation and she missed all of the warning signs. She didn't see the thumbs up that Josh gave to one of his buddies. She didn't notice that her drink was opened prior to Josh bringing it into the room and handing it to her. She was a smart girl making some stupid choices. She was tired though. She tried hard to focus on Josh's face but everything was so fuzzy. The music sounded like it was fading and her head was swimming. Maybe she should just lie down for a few minutes. Sam rested her head in her hands and soon after, everything went dark.

Chapter 7

Hearing whispers somewhere in the distance, Sam tried her best to open her eyes and lift her head. She had a pounding headache and her eyes felt as if there were lead sinkers attached to them. She gave one last attempt to sit upright and finally opened one eye to look around. The blanket that lay across her stomach was itchy and didn't feel anything like the one she usually slept with. For a moment she wondered if she had crawled into Jessica's bed by mistake. That still didn't explain the whispering though, which Sam now realized were definitely male voices, and why they were in her room. Her hand fumbled around for her alarm clock which was usually on the night stand next to her bed. When she realized there *was* no nightstand next to whatever she was lying on, her eyes finally snapped open. Sam looked up to see two guys standing at the foot of the bed. Their hands were in their pockets and they were both staring at her and whispering to each other. She looked around in a panic, realizing that not only did the blanket that was partially covering her look unfamiliar, but the entire room did as well. She was even more horrified to look down and notice that she was entirely naked. She didn't even think to ask where she was, her only concern was finding her clothes. Struggling against the tears that were falling rapidly down her cheeks, Sam did her best to cover herself with the itchy blanket.

"Where are my clothes?" She started hyperventilating as she tightened her grip on the blanket.

"Hey calm down…I don't know where you're clothes are or why you're even in my room to begin with." One of the guys that had been whispering moments ago started to walk towards Sam. He had dark brown hair and a surprised look on his face. He bent over to pick up one of his own shirts off the floor and threw it to Sam. "Here, take this. You can wear it until you find your own stuff." He carefully sat on the edge of the bed. "So do you mind telling me what you're doing in my room?"

Sam scrambled to put the shirt over her head. Her mind was whirling with what was happening. She struggled to remember where she was and who this person was that was claiming ownership of the room. Luckily, the shirt was too big and so it covered a good portion of her body. Sam covered her face with her hands and started sobbing. She had no idea who this guy was or what had happened the night before. Suddenly a name popped into her head.

"Josh!" She looked from the guy standing in front of her to the one standing behind him. Neither of them looked anything like the guy she had met the night before. Josh had been tall with dark blonde hair and blue eyes.

The two guys looked at each other and then back at her.

"Who is Josh?" The one seated on the bed asked her.

"You've got to know Josh. He said he was a junior on campus and a member of this fraternity. H-he has blonde hair, blue eyes and was wearing a red shirt." That last fact abruptly came to her but she was talking so fast neither of the two guys caught most of what she was saying.

"Hold on, hold on. Slow down for a minute." He got up from the bed when he spotted a silver tank top laying on the floor next his dresser. Retrieving it, he also located what he assumed were the girls jeans and underclothes. "I think these are yours." He brought the items over to Sam but when he tried to give her a reassuring squeeze on the shoulder, she flinched and backed away from him. He could tell she was obviously upset and wanted to find out what had happened the night before. "Um, I'm not sure who you met last night but we don't have a Josh in this fraternity." He could tell that she was starting to lose it again. "Why don't Paul and I leave the room and let you get dressed." He motioned to the guy who had been standing behind him not saying a word. "I'm Mike by the way." He considered extending his hand but remembered how she had recoiled moments before when he had touched her. "I'll just go grab you a glass of water." Without asking for an introduction in return, Mike gave Sam a small nod and left the room, closing the door behind him.

Sam took a ragged breath and looked down at the clothes that Mike had handed her. She was grateful for him being so nice but barely gave it another thought when she remembered that just moments before she had been completely naked in front of him. He had to be wrong though. Of course there was a Josh. She had found out all kinds of things about him. Sam bowed her head and tried to remember everything that she and Josh had talked about the night before. With a sinking feeling, she realized that she hadn't gotten any real information from him. He never said what he was majoring in or where he was from. In fact, she suddenly realized, he hadn't even told her his last name.

She put her feet on the floor and took a shaky step, trying to stand. She could hear people milling around the house, talking and laughing. She bent over to put her underwear on first and then her jeans. She started to remove the shirt that Mike had given her but looked around cautiously first to make sure that there really wasn't anyone else in the room. When she was positive she was alone, she removed the shirt and grabbed for her bra and the tank top she had borrowed from Jessica. Once she was fully dressed, she instinctively turned around to start making the bed. When she pulled back the covers, she almost fainted when she saw the large stain on the sheet. With her hand shaking, Sam leaned down to get a closer look. Her breath caught in her throat when she realized that it was blood. Her mind raced as she tried to remember the events from the night before. In a rush it all came back to her.

"Where are we going?"

"You'll see."

Sam tried her best to keep her eyes open. She heard him give out a small grunt as he kicked the door closed behind him. She could feel his hands under her but for some reason her mouth would not let her form the words to tell him to stop. Seconds later he was laying her down on the bed. For a while she had been having a good time talking and laughing with him but now all she wanted to do was get away. When she heard the lock on the door click she started to panic. Her arms felt too heavy to move; it was if her brain could not remember how to signal the rest of her body to function. Within moments he was on top of her. She could feel his breath in her ear; it smelled of alcohol and smoke. She hadn't even remembered him smoking. She tried to protest when she felt his hands reaching inside and up her shirt. She started to panic when she realized what was about to happen. Her mind raced with thoughts of how she let herself get in this situation. She couldn't believe that someone who seemed so nice only minutes earlier could be doing something like this to her. She was finally able to let out a weak objection to his actions.

"P-please stop..." Sam could hardly hear her own words but she knew for sure she had spoken loud enough for him to hear. She felt a sharp sting on her face as he slapped her as hard as he could with the back of his hand.

"You know you want it." He let out a noise that reminded Sam of large animal ready to feast on its prey.

His face was near hers again and her breath caught in her throat as she felt her jeans being pulled down. She knew this was it. She had been warned about things like this happening and she had been stupid enough to believe it would never happen to her. She was a smart girl though. This wasn't supposed to happen to honor students. This happened to girls who were promiscuous and like to party and get attention from boys. This didn't happen to people like her. And yet, somehow it was. Her thoughts were broken as she heard him whispering in her ear that she had asked for it. Warm tears were rolling down her cheeks as she tried to bring her arms up between his body and her own. She did her best to push on his chest but did not have much success. She couldn't understand why she had no strength. She only remembered taking a sip or two of her drink. She couldn't possibly be drunk. Sam heard a small tear as he pulled her underwear away from her waist.

"Please, please stop." Somewhere within her, she gathered the ability to get out a few words. Her face was hot and the pillow she had her head on was wet with her tears. She couldn't seem to stop her legs from shaking. "Don't do this to me...please don't do this."

"Shut up!" He whispered loudly through gritted teeth into her ear. She could feel the sweat on the side of his face rubbing up against her cheek

Sam felt his hand clamp down on her mouth at the same time as he used his other hand to spread her legs apart.

"No, no, no." *Her words were muffled under his hand. She let out a wail as she felt him push himself inside of her. She tried to scream underneath the palm of his sweaty hand. His fingers were tightly pressed into her jaw. With a few thrusts, Sam felt him take away everything she had held sacred. Her innocence was diminished with the forceful motions of this stranger.*

In moments it was over. She could hear him panting as he hovered over her.

"You asked for it and you know it."

She couldn't believe what had just happened. It was even worse to hear him try and justify it.

"How could you?" *Sam whispered. It was the only thing she could think to say as she lay there damp with her tears and his sweat. Her body started to shake violently and she was certain she was about to get sick .Somewhere in the darkness she heard the flick of a lighter and could see the burning end of a cigarette. His features were shielded by the shadows in the dark.*

She was positive she heard him laughing right before she felt him approach the bed and give her one last back-handed smack across the face. And then she blacked out.

Sam lifted her head as the realization of the previous night's events sunk in. Her eyes were swollen from crying; her cheek from the assault the night before. She didn't even hear the door open or Mike come in and sit next to her on the bed.

"Here, I brought you some ice too." Mike gently reached over and placed the cold pack on Sam's left cheek. "Look, I don't know what happened last night but it didn't have anything to do with me." He picked up Sam's hand, putting it on the ice and replacing his own. "I passed out downstairs after the party."

Sam could only give a slight nod.

"I asked around to see if anyone knew somebody named Josh in this house. I mean, I'm new to the fraternity so I could have been wrong about there not being anyone by that name here." He looked down at the floor. "I was right though. No one knows anybody named Josh." He was quiet for a moment. "Do you know what his last name was?"

Sam shook her head no.

"Well, um…" Mike let out a breath "What do you want me to do? I don't want to be a jerk or anything but if we call the cops we're all going to get in a lot of trouble." He looked away from Sam and his eyes widened as he noticed the blood stain on his sheets. He turned away from the sight, sickened, and tried to figure out what to do. He wasn't sure who had done it but he could pretty much determine what had happened. He was queasy at the thought of it happening in his room but he was also afraid that he was going to somehow get in trouble for it. "I mean, there was a lot of underage drinking going on here last night. Probably even some drugs." He knew he sounded like a jerk. "I'm on the football team…so are a lot of the guys that were here last night. We could all lose our scholarships and get kicked off the team." He was doing his best to ignore the fact that he sounded like someone he never wanted to be. He knew he was a better person than this but the thought of jeopardizing his entire future because some girl did something stupid didn't sit well with him either.

Sam couldn't believe what she was hearing. She was still trying to come to grips with the fact that she had been raped and this guy was trying to make her feel bad about it. She decided that all guys must be this way. Between what Josh - or whoever the guy who claimed to be Josh was – and this guy today had done and said to her she was certain that her reasoning for not being actively social was accurate. All guys were pigs trying to take advantage of girls in some way. All guys that is, except for Lucas.

"Lucas…" Sam whispered. She couldn't believe what she had let happen. How would she ever explain this to him? She had kept limited physical contact with Lucas their entire relationship solely because she wanted their first time to be in the right place at the right moment. She wanted intimacy to be special and had constantly made him agree to understand her need to wait.

"I thought you said his name was Josh?" Mike looked questioningly at Sam. He figured if she couldn't even get a guy's name right then she probably didn't deserve much sympathy. "Look, you can do what you want but I guarantee you that no one here will back you up." He stood up and strode over to his door and opened it, motioning for her to leave. "Just think hard about it before you start making accusations." Mike couldn't believe how horrible he was being to her or that these words were coming out of his own mouth. He knew deep down something awful had happened and his conscience told him that he should report it and help her in any way he could. His fear of getting in trouble and of being disliked in a fraternity that he was new to won over in the end. He stared at the floor and asked her to leave one more time.

Sam got up and left the room. She could feel the eyes of strangers on her as she walked through the hall, down the stairs and out the front door. She didn't even bother to take another look at the place where her virtue had been stolen and her entire life had been changed.

The hospital walls were stark and the curtain that surrounded her examination bed hung shabbily, not doing much to ensure the privacy it was meant to. Sam rested her hands on her stomach as she leaned back and stared at the ceiling. In the room with her were an older male doctor, a young nurse, and a female police officer. She had already given the officer her statement that morning when she arrived at the station. After giving the best detail she could, she was whisked away in a police cruiser to the nearest hospital in Fremont for a rape examination. Sam did her best to hold back tears as she was undressed and photographed multiple times. After an incredibly uncomfortable and mortifying exam, the doctor confirmed what she already knew to be true.

"You can sit up now. I'm all done." The doctor told Sam as he removed his examination gloves and threw them in the trash receptacle next to the bed. "There's extensive bruising surrounding the area and you have a small tear on the left side. Based on the physical evidence, I would be confident in saying that the damage is concurrent with rape." He gave Sam a pat on the leg and a sympathetic look. "We should have your lab results back shortly and the nurse will bring you some medication that you will need to take for the next week."

The officer left the wall and walked closer to the bed. "I'll need your statement for the report doctor."

"Of course; let me just see a few more patients while you finish up here and I'll come back to give you everything in writing." He started to leave and then stopped when he was near the door. Turning he felt obligated to give Sam some consolation. "I'm very sorry this happened. Is there anyone we can call for you?"

Sam didn't even look up. "No. There's no one."

The doctor gave a small nod and he and the nurse left the room.

"Ok, let's go over this one more time." The officer took a seat on the stool that had been previously occupied by the doctor and flipped open her note pad.

"I don't have anything else to say. I told you everything I remember." Sam's words were hollow. She couldn't cry anymore. Her throat was raw and her head was throbbing. There was a small ache in her gut and she wanted nothing more than to go home, shower and crawl into bed.

"I just have a few more questions." The officer's voice held barely a shred of sympathy. She sat ram-rod straight and talked in a methodical tone. "First I need to know where the rape occurred." She looked up from her pad and waited for Sam to answer.

"I don't know." Sam was staring at the floor, dreading having to go over the details again.

Sighing, the officer closed her pad and pinched the bridge of her nose with her fingers. She was obviously exasperated. "That's right, I forgot. You don't know *anything* do you?" Her sharp tone made Sam wince with each word. "You don't know where the party was. You don't know this 'Josh's' last name. You don't even know if he is actually a student on campus, isn't that right?"

Sam nodded in agreement. She couldn't believe how everyone was making her feel like this was her fault.

"I'm sorry. I wish I could remember something else." Sam wrapped her arms around her middle and continued to stare at the floor.

"Look, I can't do my job if you don't do yours. I understand you're a victim and everything; that much has been made clear. But there are real crimes out there that need to be solved. If you can't remember anything else I'm going to have to close this case."

"Fine." Sam whispered.

"What?" The officer didn't look up from her scribbling.

"I said fine!" Sam finally started to get angry. "Just close it ok?" Her voice was shaking. "I don't' want to ever think about what happened last night ever again. We're never going to find this guy and I can't help you anymore so just close the case and leave me alone." Her whole body shook with anger and sadness.

Without an ounce of compassion, the officer flipped the notepad closed and clicked her pen shut. "Ok. Case closed then." She turned to retrieve her jacket from the wall hook and started walking toward the door. She turned back to Sam who was still sitting on the examination bed trembling. "Keep in mind that this is where promiscuity gets you. It might keep you out of trouble in the future." She gave Sam a narrow look and then left the room.

The remainder of the semester went by as if nothing had ever happened. Sam wouldn't talk about it with anyone and since the only people that knew what happened were herself, a doctor and two guys in some fraternity, she wasn't too worried about it getting out. She especially wouldn't talk about it with Jessica. In fact, she didn't really want to talk about anything with Jessica. Although she blamed herself for what happened, she partially blamed Jessica for leaving her at the party with no one else to talk to. If it hadn't been for that, Sam never would have met Josh and she never would have spent the time with him that she had. Sam sensed that Jessica knew something had gone on at the party but she never pressed the issue. She figured that Jessica probably assumed something happened and felt a little guilty about abandoning her. They only spoke when needed and it was usually during the few times that Jessica stopped by to shower or get her books. She rarely slept in their dorm room anymore and Sam didn't bother to ask where it was she spent her nights. In the last few weeks, Sam had become reclusive and withdrawn. Her days consisted of the same routine that included waking up, going to class, studying and going home to bed. She barely fit in time to eat anymore. Besides Jessica, the only person that attempted to speak to her was Lucas and she was doing her best to avoid his calls. At one point, about a week after the frat party, Sam was walking home from class and caught a glimpse of Lucas sitting on the steps of her dorm hall. She turned around and ran as fast as she could in the other direction. She ended up spending the majority of the night sitting at a pizza parlor down the road. When she was certain that Lucas had given up and made the trip back home, Sam went up to her dorm room and locked the door behind her. She didn't know how long it would take but she knew that she was too embarrassed to face him right now. Whenever he would call she either wouldn't answer or she would ask Jessica to tell him that she was in class. She knew that he was probably starting to get suspicious, maybe even worried, but she just couldn't deal with talking to him yet. She felt like the moment he saw her he would know what happened. She still felt used, dirty and humiliated. Not only had she basically cheated on Lucas, but she had disappointed herself as well. There was no way they could stay together after what she had done. She couldn't even forgive herself, let alone ask for his forgiveness. Their relationship was over.

By Thanksgiving, Lucas had made three more trips to the university to see her. Each time, Sam had found a way to avoid him. The day before Thanksgiving there was a knock at the door and when Sam opened it to see who it was she was astonished to find a police officer staring back at her.

"Are you Samantha Weiler?"

"Yes. What's this about?" Sam was curious what he wanted with her. She was certain that they were no longer investigating the rape but a small part of her was hoping that Josh had been caught and they wanted her to come and identify him.

"Look, tell your boyfriend to invest in a phone or to take the hint." His expression conveyed sincere boredom.

"What are you talking about?" Sam wasn't sure what Lucas could possibly have to do with this visit.

"Your little boyfriend Lucas has been begging my department for weeks to come and check on you. He's certain that you've been abducted or murdered." He lifted the radio that was attached to the left shoulder of his uniform and brought it to his lips. Speaking to the person on the other end of the radio, Samantha wasn't sure what the officer said since he spoke mostly in numbers and abbreviations. She wasn't sure what a 10-17 or an ATL was.

" Look, if you're going to break up with the guy just make it clear to him. We have better things to do then to hunt down cheating girlfriends."

The way the officer said the word 'cheating' made Sam's ears perk up. "I appreciate the obvious concern." Sam said dryly. "But why would you assume I cheated on him? Or that I even broke up with him to begin with?"

The officer narrowed his gaze at Sam. "I read your file."

"I have a *file*?" Sam was in disbelief.

"Yeah, you've got a file. That was a pretty sketchy claim, don't you think?" He snorted a little under his breath.

Sam's face paled at the mention of the rape. "You didn't-didn't say anything to Lucas about that did you?" Sam was horrified at the thought of Lucas finding out about what happened. Especially from this officer and the way he talked about it. He was obviously one more person that blamed her for being assaulted.

"Don't worry I didn't rat you out." He was speaking to her like she was a child who was hiding something from her parents. "Besides, that information is confidential and I have better things to do then to get in the middle of a love spat between two college kids." He said something else into his radio that Sam couldn't decipher before tipping his hat in her direction. "Have a nice day. And please, call your boyfriend and tell him to stop bothering us." The officer gave her another fed up look and walk away.

Shutting the door behind her, Sam leaned against it and breathed a small sigh of relief. She still hadn't dealt with everything that had happened or how she was going to tell Lucas, but she was thankful that the officer hadn't told him about it before she had the chance to. She walked over to her bed and flung herself facedown. She stayed there for a while with her head buried in her arms contemplating on what to do next. She missed Lucas terribly and wanted nothing more than to go home and spend Thanksgiving with his family. She knew she couldn't though, and the longer she avoided him the worse the encounter would be when she did have the courage to face him. It had been almost five weeks since the party and the attack and she still wasn't ready to deal with it all. She was most afraid of the way that Lucas would treat her after he found out about it. Would he think that it was her fault? Everyone else seemed to think so. She was almost starting to believe it herself. She was sure he wouldn't want to date her anymore. She had made him wait five years without being intimate and then she goes off to college and gives herself to the first guy that pays any attention to her. How could Lucas see it any other way? Although it broke her heart, Sam knew that the best thing for the both of them was to stop seeing each other. She couldn't imagine her life without him but knew it was best for his sake. She had betrayed him in the worst way possible and she knew he deserved better than what she had left to give him. Sam sat up in her bed and brought her knees up to her chest. Wrapping her arms around herself and leaning her head forward, Sam tried to determine the best way to end her relationship with Lucas. She wanted him to hurt as little as possible but she was certain that if she saw him in person she would give in. Knowing that she could no longer give him the partnership he deserved, Sam decided the best way would be continued avoidance. She hoped that the officer who had paid her a visit earlier would relay back to Lucas that she was indeed alive and unharmed. That would leave one less thing for him to worry about. And although she knew it would take a considerable amount of time, Sam trusted that eventually Lucas would move on with his life. Wishing him nothing but the best, Sam said a silent goodbye to her best friend, laid her head down on her pillow and cried herself to sleep.

Chapter 8

Lucas stared at the phone long after the conversation had ended. He was sure that something terrible had happened to Sam, yet the police officer he just spoke to told him she was just fine. Although he wasn't able to get any details from the officer, he had been told to stop worrying and to please stop calling the Fremont campus police. He was out of ideas. If nothing bad had happened to Sam, why was she avoiding his calls? And why was it that every time he went to visit her, she was never in her dorm? Each visit had been on different days and at different times. Lucas knew that Sam wasn't going to class seven days a week and twenty four hours a day. Something had to be wrong and he knew it. He couldn't believe that Sam would just ignore him for no reason. He was afraid something like this would happen when she left for school he just couldn't have imagined her leaving him in this way. He vowed to do his best to get to the bottom of whatever was going on, no matter how long it took him.

Thanksgiving Day came and went. Lucas was feeling sad and still a little confused about Sam. He wanted nothing more than to spend the holiday with her. He was positive there weren't classes being held during the holiday so he wasn't sure what Sam could be spending her time doing. Since she had no family to come home to he was worried that she was alone in her dorm. The Sunday following Thanksgiving brought clouds and a light rain. Lucas sat on the back porch of his home watching the leaves blowing around the yard. It was cooler than usual so he zipped up his sweatshirt and shoved his hands into the pockets. He could sense that someone was standing behind him before his mother even spoke.

"How are you doing?" She came up beside him handing him a mug of coffee.

Lucas let out a sigh. "Fine I guess." He took the mug from her, grateful to have something to warm his hands. They weren't used to it being this cool until January. Normally the average temperature was around sixty degrees in November. Lucas figured it couldn't be much more than fifty out. "I'm just still trying to comprehend everything. He took a sip of his coffee waiting to hear what his mother had to say. He knew she had a strong opinion about the seriousness of his relationship with Sam.

She set her own mug on the table next to Lucas and took a seat in the chair on the other side. Wrapping her sweater tighter around herself, she contemplated what to say. "I just think you should have been a little more practical about the situation." She pressed her lips tightly together to keep from saying too much. She didn't want to hurt his feelings. She just wished he would have been a little more realistic about the situation. "These things fall apart all of the time. I know you and Sam thought that what you had was the most special thing in the world, but honey, young love rarely lasts forever." She picked up her mug and took a sip, waiting for him to respond.

"You and dad were high school sweethearts. Didn't you assume at our age that you'd be together forever?" He still couldn't get over how unsupportive his parents could be. They had known Sam for five years and knew what her home life was like. If anything, he thought they should be pushing for him and Sam to stay together. At least that would give her the stability she badly needed.

"Your father and I were very much in love. And yes, we always assumed we'd be together forever. But don't get the impression that our relationship was always perfect." She stared out at the darkening sky, breathing in over her cup and feeling the warmth on her lips. "Your father didn't always feel the same way about me as I did him. Things – and other people – got in the way more than once."

"Are you saying that dad had an affair?" Lucas could feel his face getting hot. He wasn't sure if he could stand one more betrayal in his life right now.

"No, I'm not saying he had an affair. Anything that happened, happened before we were married." She turned to face him. "But it doesn't hurt any less either, and staying together doesn't always make it better."

Lucas was mulling his mother's words over in his mind. Could his father really have been unfaithful to his mother? Their relationship always seemed so perfect to everyone, was it possible that it was all a sham?

Della could tell that her son was deeply upset by what she had just revealed to him. Reaching over and taking his hand in hers, she tried to soothe him. "Don't take what I've told you the wrong way."

Lucas quickly stood, pushing his mother's hands away. "How am I supposed to take it?" The chair he had been sitting in tipped backwards to the floor. "The relationship that I've been in for the past five years is over and now I have to find out that my parents don't love each other and regret staying together."

"Now just wait a minute!" Della was on her feet and she had her hand tightly grasped on Lucas's arm. "I only told you what I did to help you realize that overcoming obstacles isn't always as easy as it sounds. You may think that you have the ability to forgive anything that might happen while Sam is away but it isn't always that easy. Maybe Sam is trying to protect you from finding out something terrible that she's done. Don't assume that you can just *get over* it." She released her grip on his arm. "I'm sorry for raising my voice, but I don't want you to think that I don't love your father because I do. I only told you about this for your benefit." She sat back in her chair and looked up at him. "It wasn't a mistake for us to stay together." She brushed a tear away from her cheek and cleared her throat. "I'm just saying that some memories can be as painful as they are wonderful."

Lucas didn't want to hear anymore, all he wanted to do was get away. He brushed past his mother and walked to his truck.

Following Thanksgiving, the days turned into weeks. Christmas was fast approaching and Lucas still had not heard from Sam. All of his calls went unanswered and his attempts at visiting her were unsuccessful. He was tempted to call the police department one more time just to make sure that they had indeed spoken with Sam and not someone else. He stopped himself when he remembered the officer's harsh warning to stop contacting them. By the middle of December he became more miserable and despondent. He was tired of answering his father's questions about Sam and when she was going to come home for a visit. He didn't have the heart to tell him about her avoidance because he was afraid if he said it out loud it would mean his relationship was truly over. He knew that his parents would try to convince him to move on and that he should have expected this to happen. They had never really believed that he and Sam could have a successful long distance relationship and he was in no hurry to listen to them claim that they had been right all along.

When Christmas arrived, Lucas knew in his heart that it was over between him and Sam. He swore that he would still try and contact her but he knew that there was no other explanation for all of this time passing and two missed holidays. On the first day of the New Year, Lucas sat out on the front porch of his home and decided to write a letter. It would be a goodbye letter to Sam. He did not want to be angry with her. He knew that if she no longer wanted to be with him then she must have a good reason for it. He would not try and find out why she was avoiding him, he wouldn't ask her if she was seeing someone else. In fact, he wouldn't even ask her to respond. He just needed to say goodbye for his own peace of mind. If the letter ended up being returned then he would still know that he had done everything he could to get in contact with her. For two hours, Lucas sat outside and poured out his heart to her on paper making sure by reading and re-reading that he told her everything that was needed to say goodbye.

Dear Sam,

First, I want to say that although I don't understand why you did what did, I respect your decision and have come to accept it. Since you won't speak to me over the phone, I wanted to take this opportunity to write to you and tell you how I feel.

I have never loved anyone the way that I love you. I know that even though we are young, the time we were together was more special than anything else I could ever hope for. You taught me how to love, and how to be loved. You taught me to enjoy life and that especially through the bad times I should appreciate all that I have. I am writing to you knowing that I gave you my whole heart every day that we were together and I know that you gave me the same in return.

If I die never feeling this way about another person, I will be happy because I will know that I was able to one time in my life experience the greatest feeling in the world. I am certain that you will go on to do great things and I can only hope that you will save a small piece of your heart to hold the memories of us.

Now, all I have left to say is 'Goodbye'. I want you to know that I will never forget you or everything we've been through together. I'll look for your name in the headlines because I know that you are destined for something bigger than this small town, and I, could ever offer. And although I would have happily moved across the country or even walk through fire for you, I understand the choice you made and want nothing more for you than the happiness you truly deserve.

I love you. I miss you. Goodbye.
Lucas

Lucas leaned down and kissed the bottom of the page before gently folding it and placing it in an envelope. He addressed it to Samantha Weiler, followed by her dorm information, and put a stamp in the corner. He drove into town and dropped it into the blue mailbox at the corner of the post office parking lot on his way to work. With his truck idling, he sat in the driveway exit for a while reflecting on what he had written to Sam. He knew that he had said everything that there was to say. He was satisfied that even if she didn't feel the same about him anymore, she would know that he had always been honest with her and loved her more than anything. Putting his truck into drive, he pulled out of the parking lot and started toward a future he could not have comprehended only months earlier.

At the end of the semester, Sam had gone to her Resident Advisor and asked for a dorm re-assignment. By the start of her winter classes, she was already settled into a single room. She didn't share any classes with Jessica the rest of the year so she was pretty easy to avoid. And since it didn't seem as though Jessica had any intention of reconnecting with her, Sam assumed their short lived friendship was over.

By the time spring arrived, Lucas was starting to feel like he was a little bit back to normal. He never received his letter back or any response to it, but time had allowed him to become more at peace with the situation. Even though he wasn't quite ready to date anyone else, he had been spending more time out with friends and was even starting to enjoy it. He still missed Sam, but it was obvious to him that he needed to move on with his life and he hoped she had been able to do the same. He tried calling her one time in early February, since Valentine's Day had been coming up, but he found that her number was disconnected. He never tried contacting her again after that.

It was the worst feeling she could have imagined; as if her insides were all being compressed. The pains made her want to vomit and cry at the same time. The nurse by her bedside tried to hold her hand and she could hear someone else telling her to 'just breathe'. She had spent the last ten hours curled up on the hospital bed with her arms clutching her middle. She hadn't asked for this. All she wanted was for it to be over. The drugs they gave her were a joke. They barely touched the pain. The closer she came to having to push, the worse the pain got. When it was time, the nurse helped bring her legs up. It was supposed to help her 'bear down'; whatever that meant. She strained through each push, sobbing from the terrible pressure she felt. She pushed with every ounce of energy she had left, feeling herself tearing. Finally, after almost two hours of pushing, she felt the baby being ripped from her body. She didn't even bother to look up. She was afraid that if she saw the baby she would want to keep it. The doctor was telling her what was happening as he finished the delivery and then started on the stitches. She kept her eyes closed and let herself sink into the bed, relieved that it was all over. She couldn't understand the words that were being spoken around her and she didn't notice the nurse who walked to her bedside. The only thing she heard was someone lean down and whisper to her, "Would you like to meet your baby girl?"

She squeezed her eyes closed, furiously shaking her head and began to sob.

Part 2

December 2012

Chapter 9

Matt rubbed his eyes and yawned. It had been a long day and it was turning into an even longer night. He stared out the window and looked seventeen floors down to the bustling street below. Even at nearly midnight, the streets of New York City were busy with traffic and the sidewalks were crowded with people. He had always loved living in the city. The commotion and liveliness was most of what he adored.

Matt had grown up in New York and couldn't imagine living anywhere else. That is, until his girlfriend recently started talking about wanting a change of scenery. He couldn't fathom why anyone would want to live anywhere other than here. If you want Chinese food at two o'clock in the morning, you just pick up the phone and it's delivered within thirty minutes. You can walk down any street in Manhattan and buy a hot dog on any corner. Who would want to leave all of that? *Especially to move to some hick-town in the south.*

Matt knew that this was not what he should be thinking about. He should be working on the project that was sitting in front of him and had been for several hours now. It was Friday night and his deadline was eight o'clock Monday morning. If he didn't nail this advertisement for the clients coming to view his presentation, he could very well kiss his job goodbye. He knew his boss would be watching him closely. Their firm desperately needed the boost in clientele and he sorely needed the bonus that would follow a guaranteed sale. That, Matt supposed, was the downside of living in the city. Rent for his apartment was already outrageous and he just got a notice that it was going to be increased by the first of the year. If he could produce a winning presentation, he could live comfortably knowing that he wouldn't be evicted anytime in the near future. He turned away from the window and sat back down at his desk. The project he was working on was for a major soda company shopping for new representation. They were hoping to ring in the New Year with a refreshed logo and new image. He had to knock it out of the park or he knew his head would be on a platter.

Matt Creighton was new to Preston & Myers Advertising Agency. He recently graduated from college and was trying to work his way up from the bottom of the company. It was harder than he imagined it would be. He hadn't started college until he was almost twenty-five years old and now that he was approaching thirty, he was finding it hard to deal with being the low man on the totem pole. Almost all of colleagues were his age, yet it seemed that although his title wasn't 'secretary' he was the one getting their coffee and running their office errands. He guessed it was the price he had to pay for spending so many years after high school partying and carousing around the city. If he had gone to college right out of high school like his father had wanted, he would be much higher up on the corporate ladder by now.

Matt returned his thoughts to the half illustrated presentation board in front of him. He decided he was only going to work for another hour and then he would call it a night. If he still wasn't finished by then, he would just have to come in on Saturday. Just as he picked his pencil up, his office phone rang.

"Hello?" His tone was short. He knew he sounded irritated to whoever was on the other end.

"Wow! You sound pretty grouchy."

The voice belonged to his girlfriend and he instantly felt bad for sounding rude. He should have known it would be Jessie. No one else would be calling him this late.

"Sorry babe. I'm just stressed out over this presentation coming up. What's up?"

"I was just wondering when you were coming home. It's pretty late, but I haven't eaten yet and so I wanted to know if you wanted to bring us both something home for a late dinner."

Matt knew that Jessie loved the perks of the city as much as he did. It wasn't uncommon for the two of them to go out for dinner as late as nine or ten o'clock at night. Most restaurants were still busy at that time and since it was a Friday night, he was sure he would have no problem ordering something this late. "Sure. No problem. I'll pick something up on my way home. Does sushi sound ok?"

"Oooh…yum. That sounds great. I still have a hard time adjusting to the fact that you can just run out and get sushi at midnight." She laughed a little in the phone.

Jessie had come from a pretty small town. Where she used to live no one served food this late and sushi itself was not an easy thing to track down no matter what time of day it was. "Ok. I promise I won't stay much later." Matt looked at his watch. "I should be home within an hour." Matt placed a call for some takeout from a little Japanese place near his apartment and then spent the next half an hour finishing the sketch he had been working on.

At eleven thirty he turned his computer off and stood up. Grabbing his suit coat from the chair in front of his desk he walked out of his office, flipping the light switch off behind him. He walked to the bank of elevators and pressed the down button. He leaned against the wall and sighed, wondering how it could take so long for an elevator to arrive when there couldn't be more than ten people in the whole building.

When he finally heard the 'ding' that signaled the arrival of the elevator car, he picked his briefcase up off the floor and trudged inside. He was dog-tired. When the elevator reached the main level, he stepped out onto the freshly waxed marble lobby and walked to the front door. Saying a quick goodbye to the two janitors that were still mopping, Matt swung his coat around his shoulders and braced himself for the chilly night air. Signaling a cab, he gave the driver his address and asked to make a quick stop at Sushi Haven just a block before his apartment.

Just after midnight he put his key in the door to his apartment and walked inside. It was pitch black except for a few lit candles on the sofa table in the living room. Jessie was sitting on the sofa waiting for him in the dark.

"Hey babe, what took so long?" She was sitting there in her bathrobe with a mischievous smile on her face.

Matt could tell right away that she probably wanted to fool around but he was not in any mood for it tonight. "Sorry. I worked a little later than expected." He set the food on the table in the entry way so that he could hang up his coat. "I am so exhausted." He let out an exaggerated yawn, hoping she would take the hint and he wouldn't have to actually reject her. He brought their dinner over to the table and turned the overhead light on. He figured if he could slowly destroy the mood she had set, then he would be able to get to sleep quicker.

Clearly taking the hint, she frowned a little and blew out the candles. "Ok. I'm sure you're probably really tired and want to go to sleep but tomorrow is *my* day." She gave him a kiss on the cheek and walked to the refrigerator to get them each something to drink.

"What do you mean?" He could tell she meant that she had something planned. "I have to work tomorrow and I'm sure I'll be there late again." He heard her slam the door to the refrigerator.

"This is such bullshit. You have backed out on plans with me for the last two weekends." She dropped herself heavily into one of the kitchen chairs. "Can't you get out of it?"

"You have no idea what kind of pressure I am under." He was angry with her for being angry at him. "If I don't do well on this presentation I could lose my job." He sat down across from her and opened the soda she had set in front of him. "It's not like we can all work only two days a week and screw off the rest of the time." Matt knew he was being unkind, but he was tired of her telling him to not take his job so seriously. He felt like he worked a lot harder than she did and so she had no way of appreciating the amount of dedication he had to put into his job.

"You know," Jessie threw her napkin on the table and stood up, "I'm not really that hungry anymore."

Matt kept chewing his food as he heard the door to their bedroom slam shut behind her. "Well," He said to himself quietly, "At least I got out of having to *do it* tonight." He took his time as he finished eating. He was in no hurry to walk to their bedroom and find pillows and a blanket outside of the door. He was positive he would be sleeping on the sofa tonight.

By eight o'clock Saturday morning, Matt was back to the office. He was surprised to see the light on in his boss's office. He poked his head into James Preston's doorway to say a quick hello.

"Good morning Mr. Preston." Matt gave him a wide smile, hoping that he didn't look too eager. He heard the white haired man grunt a response not even bothering to raise his head from his reading to acknowledge Matt. Turning on his heel, Matt quickly left the door of the office. He didn't want to be known as a pest. When he got to his own office he shut the door behind him and got to work. He spent the next five hours completing his presentation, opting to skip lunch and get it one hundred percent finished. When it was nearing two o' clock he looked over everything that he had done and felt satisfied that Monday morning would be a success. He decided that he should try and call Jessie and make amends for the conversation the night before. He had, indeed, slept on the sofa which didn't bother him at all. If he would have slept in the bedroom there would have been the possibility of make-up sex and he probably wouldn't have gotten any sleep. Out in the living room he was able to get a full six hours of much needed rest. Picking up his desk phone, he dialed Jessie's cell phone certain that she would be out shopping or doing something in town. She picked up on the third ring.

"Are you still mad at me?" He wound the cord around his fingers waiting for her answer.

"That depends. Are you still acting like a total asshole?" She tried but wasn't able to sound totally mad at him. Her voice depicted a hint of playfulness. "You know, you really hurt my feelings last night."

"I know, I know. I'm really sorry for what I said." He put his feet up on his desk. "Do you forgive me?"

"I'm not sure if I'm smart enough to know how to forgive. That is, since I'm just a brainless hairdresser who only works two days a week."

"I never said you were brainless."

"You implied it. Besides, it doesn't matter now. You're at work and the weekend is just about shot."

"How about if I come and meet you right now? Where are you?" He was already standing and putting his coat on. He had dressed more casual than usual since it was the weekend and he wasn't actually required to be there. "I'm dressed for anything." He looked down at his sweater, jeans and loafers. "Well, maybe not the opera." He laughed a little, hoping to keep her mood light.

"Oh good, I just gave away my tickets to the opera." She laughed back. "I'm down on Fifth just about to go into Saks. Call me when you're close. You can just meet me here."

"I *knew* you'd be shopping!" He grinned at how well he knew her. They both hung up after agreeing where to meet. They had only been dating for about a year but their personalities were so similar they were able to read each other very well.

Matt was sure he didn't know everything about Jessie's background, but what he did know made him marvel at how alike they were. Like Matt, Jessie had been somewhat of an outcast in high school. After she graduated, she went off to college expecting her experience to be just like the previous four years. What she hadn't expected was to be befriended by a few popular kids and turning into a socialite herself. And even though she dropped out of school in the middle of her sophomore year, she credited those two years as the turning point in her life. She spent a lot of time after that trying to find out what she wanted to do with her life. That time included odd jobs, a lot of partying, and starting, and stopping, beauty school classes at least four times. Finally, by the time she was twenty eight, Jessie completed the courses required to get her cosmetology license. She wasted no time in packing up her stuff and moving to New York City. A year later she met and started dating Matt, and she was working at a high class salon in lower Manhattan. Although Matt didn't start college right away, he did move to Virginia for a short period of time after high school to attend The Criminal Institute of Technology, an advanced securities institute in a town in Virginia just outside of Washington D.C. Shortly after enrolling, he found that he didn't have the discipline needed to do any kind of law enforcement work, so he dropped out and moved back to the city. Working as a bartender, he spent his days in bed and his nights on the town. He knew he was searching for what he wanted to do with his life, but it took several years to nail down a specific career path. Once he had decided what he wanted to do, he applied to NYU and by the grace of God, was accepted. He figured it was only because his father was a fairly high-powered city official, but he had been accepted nonetheless and made it through the next four years. He even managed to graduate with honors. With the same recommendation that had gotten him into college, he was offered a position at Preston and Myers, and the rest is history. His relationship with Jessie was going well; he just wasn't sure exactly *where* it was going. They talked about marriage from time to time but never really decided anything specific. He didn't think his life was stable enough right now to support a wife and kids, and he wasn't sure that Jessie was mature enough to commit to that kind of life. So for now, he decided it was best to just enjoy life and apply his dedication to his job.

It was almost three o' clock when his cab pulled up in front of Saks Fifth Avenue. They had agreed to meet at the west entrance. Jessie swore that she would be done shopping by then. However, just as Matt had anticipated, it was almost a full twenty minutes before he saw Jessie strolling his way. Her arms were loaded with bags. It made him wonder if she had cleared out an entire department of the store.

He gave her a kiss on the cheek when she reached him.

"I knew you couldn't be on time." He grabbed some of the bags from her as she struggled to get her sunglasses out of her purse. "Where do you want to go for lunch?" He opened the door for her as they made their way out into the chilly afternoon.

"I don't care." She paused for a moment. "As long as it's someplace nice; you owe me big time for last night *and* today." She gave him a smile over her shoulder as she walked ahead of him, but he knew she meant it.

He chose a little bistro on twenty first. It was classy, yet not ridiculously priced – which was almost unheard of in Manhattan. He would never tell Jessie this, but it was where he used to take girls on a first date. He found that girls were usually so impressed that he had good taste they would be more "affectionate" on the date. Plus, he didn't have to spend a ton of money to get them into bed. For a moment he reflected on his former lifestyle. It wasn't that he so much missed it; he just wouldn't trade it is all. They were seated at a table near the window. Thankfully there was also enough floor space for all of Jessie's shopping bags. The hostess gave them their menus and assured them that their waitress would be right there. He pretended to glance over the menu as if he had never seen it, but he already knew what he was getting. He watched Jessie contemplate the many choices, knowing he could recommend something for her if she just asked. He was afraid, though, that if she asked if he had ever been here he wouldn't be able to lie to her. And that was just not a fight he was willing to get into today. When the waitress came over Jessie ordered a Mediterranean salad and an iced tea, he chose the Cuban sandwich and tuna salad with an iced tea as well. After the waitress left, Matt covered Jessie's hand with his and tried to apologize again for the previous night.

"Jess, I am really sorry for last night. I shouldn't have bailed on our plans." He gave her hand a quick peck and watched her blush. "I just really wanted to do well on this presentation. You know it could mean really good things for us if I get promoted."

She gave his hand a squeeze and smiled. "I know. And I'm sorry for being such a bitch." She leaned across the table and gave him a kiss; a kiss that was probably too intimate for daylight. Now it was his turn to blush. He looked up at the waitress as she set their drinks in front of them and Jessie returned to her seat. There was an awkward silence as she looked out the window and he took a sip of his tea.

He broke the silence when he remembered something he had forgotten to tell her. "Hey, did I tell you I got a call from one of my old buddies?" Matt watched Jessie shake her head. "I guess he's going to be in town this week for some conference."

"Where do you know him from?" Jessie looked up and thanked the waitress as their food was set on the table.

"He was my roommate when I lived in Virginia." Matt watched her giggle a little when he said that.

"Oh, was that during your attempt at being an 'agent'?" She brought her napkin to her mouth to stifle another laugh.

"Hey, I don't make fun of your past."

"That's because you don't know anything about it." She grinned at him over a forkful over her salad.

"*Anyway*, although I didn't live there long, we got to be pretty good friends. He's a really nice guy. I wish we would have stayed in touch more." He bit into his sandwich.

"Don't you have to, like, be a cop or something first. I mean, not just anybody can decide they want to be a federal security agent, right?"

Matt finished chewing and wiped his mouth. "To tell you the truth, I don't really know. It was one of those things that just sounded like a good idea at the time and I think my dad knew one of the instructors at the institute and pulled some strings for me." He took a sip of his drink before continuing. "I'm sure there are rules that I was supposed to follow but didn't. My dad really just wanted me to be successful at *something*, and he would have done anything just to get me into a valid career. He was so grateful by the time I applied for college that he paid for the entire four years up front. Now that I think about it, I'm pretty sure it was guilt money."

"Oh, you poor little rich boy." Jessie feigned sympathy for Matt and even pouted a little for him.

"Quit it." He knew she was just joking around with him. "Besides, I'm not a rich little anything. My parents are the ones with money, not me. Once I got a decent job, that gravy train came to a screeching halt."

"So when is the last time you talked to this guy?"

He was grateful that the topic had changed back to his friend and off of him. "I don't know, probably four or five years. He called me to invite me to a small graduation thing he was having but I didn't really want to go. I guess I was too embarrassed to see what I wasn't able to accomplish."

They finished eating and Matt paid the bill. After they had gathered all of Jessie's purchases from off the floor, they walked outside to hail a taxi. Once they were able to flag one down, they got inside and gave the driver directions to their apartment.

"You should ask him to dinner one night."

"Who?" Matt almost forgot what they had been talking about.

"Your friend dummy. We should take him somewhere really nice since he's not from New York." She braced herself on the door to the backseat as the driver made an unexpected lane change. "Let's do it Monday night. I'm sure we'll be celebrating your promotion anyway." She elbowed him playfully. "Is he going to be in town by then?"

"I think so. I'm pretty sure he said he'd be here Sunday evening because the conference starts Monday morning."

"Great! I'll call and make reservations somewhere."

The driver came to a quick stop, jerking them both out of their seats. Matt paid the fare and got out of the car, holding the door open for Jessie and swearing he would never ride in another taxi again. Although he knew living in New York City would be impossible without doing just that.

They made their way inside and up the stairs to their apartment where Matt spent the rest of the weekend making up to Jessie.

Chapter 10

The weather was almost unbearable that winter in the south. It was the second week of December and it was turning out to be one of the coldest winters that anyone could remember. Lucas sat on the front porch of his rental home with a cup of coffee. He knew he should be inside packing, but he was dreading the trip. He hated to fly and hated reunions even more, which is exactly what this trip would turn out to be. The purpose of the trip was to attend a conference about terrorism and how to be prepared in the event of an attack. He knew, though, that it would just be a reunion among his fellow graduates and he would be the butt of all of the jokes. He was, no doubt, the only graduate who had not gone on to the academy to be a federal agent. Instead, he had chosen to return to his small hometown and work in the local police department for his father. Last month, after a couple of years of working together, his father retired from his post as chief after an unfortunate accident left him unable to perform his duties.

Paul Benson had been chief of the small town police department for nearly twenty two years when he was shot during a routine traffic stop. The event had shaken the town. Nothing like that had ever happened in Bradyville. It was supposed to be a safe place to live. Which is exactly why Lucas thought it was a waste of his time to attend a conference on terrorism. He was quite certain that if there was going to be another terrorist attack on the United States, it wouldn't be in South Carolina. He was going, though, to appease his father and the townspeople. After Paul had been shot, someone called a meeting at the town hall to talk about what happened and how they could restore safety and peace of mind to their community. Lucas had made the mistake of mentioning an upcoming conference that was being hosted by the New York City chapter of the security institute he had graduated from. When someone insisted that he should go and bring back anything that he learned to train to the rest of their department, his father agreed and everyone had cheered. Lucas tried to convince them that the conference was on *terrorism* and not general public safety, but no one would listen. Everyone seemed so relieved that there was going to be some kind of action taken to make sure that their town would remain secure and protected that Lucas didn't have the heart to protest.

Lucas's father had been so proud of him when he had graduated first from the police academy, and then a few years later from The Criminal Institute of Technology. He had tried to get Lucas to accept a position somewhere in a big city for a major government agency, but finally relented and agreed to hire Lucas as a deputy in his department. Lucas always thought that his dad was secretly happy that he had decided to return home instead of moving away, but Paul would never show that emotion. When it came to the job he only wanted the best working for him and he agreed that Lucas was one of the best. The only time Paul had broken down on the job in front of his son was after the accident. Lucas had been the first to respond to his father's distress call over the radio. When he arrived on the scene, Paul was laying on the ground next to the driver's side with the door open and the radio in his hand. He wasn't moving and his eyes were closed. During all of his training, all of the drills he had performed, and all of his time as a police officer Lucas had never lost his cool. He always executed the job with precise judgment and a collected attitude. Seeing his father on the ground in that state, though, had caused him to lose it. He ran to his father's body and started screaming his name. It was Lucas's partner Jeff that had to pry him away and call for an ambulance. Before the ambulance arrived, Paul awoke for a brief second to tell Lucas that he was proud of him and wanted him to take the place of chief if something should happen. After an extended sick leave and some extensive therapy, Paul resigned his position and gratefully accepted the early retirement that was offered to him. At fifty four, he should have been too young but in light of the situation everyone agreed that he should be able to collect full retirement benefits and enjoy his time with his family. Not long after, Lucas accepted the position as police chief and found himself sitting at a podium in front of a whole crowd of people promising to go on a trip to New York City to be trained to keep their town safe. To the people of Bradyville, the man who had shot their beloved law enforcement leader could be called nothing other than a terrorist. So in their eyes, this conference was the best thing to reset order to the town.

    Setting his coffee down on the table next to his chair, Lucas decided to head inside to start packing. It was almost ten thirty in the morning and his flight was leaving at four out of Columbia. He still had to drop his dog off to his parent's house and make a quick stop to the post office to have his mail held for the time he would be away. The conference only lasted until Thursday but he thought he would hang around the city for a couple of extra days to spend some time with an old friend of his.

Lucas hadn't spoken to Matt Creighton in about five years. Matt was Lucas's roommate during the brief time that Matt attended CIT. Lucas was pretty disappointed when Matt dropped out. Although they were only roommates for about five or six weeks, they had actually become pretty close to one another. Lucas didn't have too many guy friends in high school because he spent most of his time with his then girlfriend. After they stopped seeing each other, Lucas focused on getting through police training and getting his Bachelor's Degree in Criminal Justice. After that he applied to, and attended, CIT for intensive criminal investigative training. By the time he was accepted and had entered the school, he realized that he had never really spent any time on making any real friends. It was surprising to Lucas that he and Matt hit it off as well as they did. After all, their personalities were very different. Lucas always knew what he wanted to do with his life and then there was Matt who kind of just drifted along trying new things every once in a while. Matt had never been real serious about the program and when Lucas found out that he didn't even have any police background or training prior to arriving, he knew Matt would never be able to stick it out. You had to be pretty dedicated to complete the rigorous training the institute put you through. The drills were difficult and sometimes even downright terrifying. The first year focused primarily on physical endurance and mind skills during hostage, kidnapping, and other intense situations while the second and final year focused mostly on labor intensive forensics and crime scene investigation. Lucas knew that Matt wasn't made for that line of work. And besides their education and career goals, they also had very different views on dating and relationships with women. Lucas liked being in long term, committed relationships where Matt liked to bounce from girl to girl. One night after a killer round of mid-term exams, Lucas and Matt went to a local bar and got pretty lit up. Lucas ended up spilling his whole story about his relationship with Sam and how it had ended. And although Matt had sympathy for him, he had no real advice to give. He had never been in love and at the time couldn't understand why anyone would want to be that committed to just one person. They never talked about it again and it was the only real deep conversation they ever had the whole time they knew each other. Sometimes Lucas still felt a little embarrassed that he dumped his whole sappy story on a guy he just became friends with, but Lucas figured by now there was no way Matt would still remember what he had told him.

It was noon when he reached his parent's home. Lucas reached for the handle and held open the back door to his parent's house so that his four year old St. Bernard could walk in ahead of him. Oscar stood almost three feet tall and tipped the scales at over one hundred and forty pounds. He looked like a monster, but Oscar was one of the gentlest animals Lucas had ever known. Lucas bought Oscar as a graduation present to himself when he graduated from CIT and he soon became the best friend Lucas had ever had. His mother pretended as though she detested him, but when she thought no one was looking she was quite friendly with the dog. She even kept a secret stash of treats for him that she thought Lucas didn't know about. As soon as they were both in the kitchen, Lucas bent down and whispered in Oscar's ear to "Go find grandma!" Oscar responded with enthusiasm and took off running as fast as his large body would allow him. He grinned when he heard a loud shriek coming from somewhere in the back of the house; a sure sign that Oscar had indeed found "grandma". Soon after, Oscar came bounding back in the room to let Lucas know that he had done as he was told.

"Good boy!" Lucas bent down on one knee and petted the dog generously.

"That *thing* almost knocked me right into the bathtub!" Della came storming into the room behind Oscar holding a scrub brush in one hand and spray bottle in the other. "I was leaning into the tub to clean the walls and this monstrosity of an animal almost pushed me right in." She pulled on the bottom of the shirt she was wearing. "Do you see this mess? I've got shower cleaner all over me and I'm pretty sure this stuff has bleach in it!" Della was trying to sound as mad as she could, but she never seemed to be able to stay angry with Lucas or his dog for very long. They both had the cutest set of puppy dog eyes she had ever seen.

As if Oscar knew she was talking about him and what he had just done to her, he lay down on the floor and put one paw over his nose.

"Aw ma, do you see what you did? You've hurt his feelings." Della relented and set down her cleaning supplies. She let out a sigh and gave them each a small smile. "Oh alright." She turned to face the dog. "I'm sorry Oscar." She looked back at Lucas. "There, are you happy now? I've apologized to him."

Lucas leaned down and told Oscar that she apologized to him, as if Oscar could understand him. He stood up and looked back at Della and shook his head. "He doesn't seem to accept your apology. I think you might need to give him a kiss too."

"Ha! I'm not giving that thing a kiss." She looked down at the dog's giant mouth and the large pool of drool that had begun to collect beneath him.

"Alright boy, come on. I guess we're going to the kennel for the week."

Oscar understood the word and rolled onto his back in the 'play dead' position. This was no easy feat for a dog his size.

"Ok, ok. I'll give the stupid dog a kiss!" Della bent down, intending to give Oscar a small pretend kiss on the top of his head. When she was close enough, Lucas shouted "Get her!" which prompted Oscar to take his large tongue and mop Della's face with it.

She jumped up to face Lucas. "If you don't get out of here, I just may kill you." She wiped her face with the back of her hand and looked very serious about her threat. Lucas gave his mom a kiss on the cheek, patted Oscar on the head and strolled out the door.

On the drive to the airport, Lucas tried to mentally go over everything he had packed. He didn't travel that often and was worried that he may have forgotten something important. He glanced over to the passenger seat of his truck to assure himself that his plane ticket and wallet were all in tow. After he was convinced that he hadn't forgotten anything, he shifted his thoughts to his old friend Matt that he was planning on meeting up with. Lucas was curious what Matt's life would be like now. He wondered if Matt was married or had any kids. During the phone call that Lucas had initiated when this trip was planned, Matt hadn't said much about his life. They pretty much spent the entire conversation chatting about old times, not catching up on their lives now. Lucas was semi-hoping that Matt would still be the bachelor that he used to be. It would be strange to hang out with him at his home if he had a family. It's usually awkward enough to meet up with someone you haven't seen in a while, let alone be surrounded by a bunch of people you've never met or know nothing about. His thoughts consumed him so much that before he knew it, he was at the airport. He followed the signs pointing towards long-term parking. After at least twenty minutes of circling the massive parking lot, Lucas finally found a spot in Lot G. He scribbled the letter down on a piece of paper and shoved it into his wallet. He knew that if he didn't take a reminder with him of where he parked, he would never be able to find his vehicle once he returned. He was glad that he had arrived with plenty of time to spare before his flight departed. He could count the number of times he had flown in his life on one hand, and no matter what he was always afraid the plane would take off without him. It took almost two hours to go through the check-in process, travel through security, and find the gate he would be leaving from. By the time he got there, the sign on the wall showed they would be boarding in the next fifteen minutes. He contemplated running to the restroom before boarding but since he had upgraded his ticket to first class he knew he would be one of the first to board and decided to wait. To Lucas's delight, the plane arrived at their gate on time and did not take off without him. The flight went smoothly and by the time he was awakening from his nap, the flight attendant was on the loud speaker announcing that they would be making their descent into JFK airport and everyone needed to follow the proper procedures for landing. He was now in New York City.

Chapter 11

Samantha noticed the note on her desk when she returned from lunch. It was a blue sticky note with words written in terrible chicken scratch. She knew right away that the note was from Alexis Marshall, her boss. Samantha knew it must be important if the president of Prestige magazine personally walked down to her office to put it there. Then again, maybe Alexis just wrote it and then sent one of her many assistants to bring it down to her floor. Either way, if it was important enough for Alexis to write, it was probably not something Samantha should be looking forward to. With a sigh, Samantha set her coat and purse down on one of the overstuffed chairs lining one wall of her office. She had been hoping to come back from having lunch with her editing staff, and just lock herself in her office to finish her work for the week. Being the Senior Editor, though, did not always allow her the alone time she needed to get her own job done. She was usually being called to oversee someone else's work or to make revisions on articles and stories that did not meet Alexis' approval. She walked over to her desk to read the note and see if there were any clues to what Alexis wanted. The note simply read the words "my office, a.s.a.p." Gathering her planner, Samantha walked out of her office and made her way to the elevators on the other side of the building. She pushed the button and waited for the next car to arrive. Knowing that Alexis would be getting impatient, Samantha pressed the button about twenty more times hoping that it would make the elevator arrive sooner. Finally the doors parted and revealed a space that could barely fit another briefcase, let alone one more person. Weighing her options, Samantha decided to try and squeeze into the group instead of taking the chance on waiting for the next elevator to arrive. When she finally made it to the eighteenth floor, Samantha almost leapt out before the doors were all the way open. When an elevator was that full, you couldn't help but feel as if you were being touched in places that made you uncomfortable. Samantha made her way down the marble hallway to the very last office. It was the largest office in the magazine's portion of the building and it commanded half of the floor. The other half was divided among Alexis' assistants, a public restroom, and two large conference rooms. The closer she got to Alexis' office, the louder the shouting became. Samantha could tell that someone was either being majorly scolded for something they did wrong, or someone was being fired. It was a common commotion to hear on this floor and after having worked for the company for over six years, making it up a few notches during that time, Samantha was pretty used to it. She just did her best to do her job well and stay under the radar. She was happy with her position and wanted nothing more than to keep her job for as long as possible. Once she reached Alexis' office, she took a deep breath before knocking on the door frame and walking in through the open door. She had to keep herself from putting her hands over her ears, but instead of interrupting the yelling she quietly took a seat in the corner of the massive office. She tried not to stare at the poor defenseless girl who was doing her best to keep her composure while enduring the wrath of Alexis Marshall.

"If you come to me with this crap next issue, your job will be eliminated!" Alexis took a seat behind her desk and focused her attention on the papers in front her. When the girl she had been berating didn't budge from where she was standing, Alexis looked up at her from over her glasses and asked her what she was still doing there. The girl whispered an apology and turned on her heel, quickly exiting the room. When everyone was gone, Samantha watched Alexis open her bottom drawer and pull out a small, silver flask. She averted her eyes as her boss popped a couple of pills in her mouth and took a swig from the flask. She knew better than to ask if everything was alright. It was common knowledge that you didn't question anything about Alexis; even if your intentions were good. Alexis was tall and thin, yet had a powerful look about her. She wore her hair short and spiky and in a color of blonde that Samantha was certain hadn't been her natural hair color in a good twenty years. No one was really certain of Alexis' age, and although she claimed to be in her late forties most of the time, Samantha was one of the few who knew what the real number was.

"Can you believe the garbage that some of these columnists turn in and call a finished product?"

Samantha also knew that no matter what you should agree with whatever Alexis says. "I know. I'm amazed some of them call themselves writers." She felt a little guilty saying this. It was as if she was betraying some of the people on her team. She had become pretty good friends with a lot of the people at the magazine from her fellow editors all the way down to the front desk receptionist and security personnel.

"I mean, we only hire the best and still I get handed pure trash!" Alexis stood and almost threw the copy of what had just been turned in to her at Samantha.

She turned it over and read the first line of the article which was to be the title. It read, "Confronting my Rapist…" Samantha almost dropped the pages to the ground when she read the first few words. "Maybe…maybe this article wouldn't be so bad to run?" She scanned the story and felt a lump form in her throat when she read the words of a college student who had been brutally raped and then contracted the HIV virus from her attacker.

"Are you joking?" Alexis stared hard at Samantha. "This is primarily a fashion magazine. We do not have room on our pages for sappy, human interest junk like this." She sat back down and brought her fingers to her temples. "We write about sex, make up and the latest trends in clothing. Our features are about celebrity fitness secrets and spring colors." She slowly pointed to the copy in Samantha's hand. "This is not Prestige material. This kind of journalism makes you feel depressed…it certainly doesn't make you want to go shopping." She sighed heavily. "Our numbers have not been good this past year. If we don't make a serious jump in sales soon, we could be forced to end publication." Alexis rubbed the sides of her head, trying to make her headache disappear. The two pain pills and sip of whiskey she had slammed earlier were doing nothing to relieve the pounding that was resounding in her ears.

Samantha felt a sudden burst of courage and decided to take the opportunity that was presenting itself to change Alexis' mind about the article. Just by briefly scanning the article, Samantha could tell it was a well written piece and definitely could appeal to a number of women. Samantha was well aware of the impact this topic could make on a person.

"I know the magazine hasn't been doing the greatest this year in sales. Maybe we need to take this opportunity to shift the face of the company and appeal to another audience. If we start running more human interest pieces, it may help us boost our numbers in the coming year." Samantha gave Alexis a hopeful look. She was trying to convey her support for the change but didn't want to step on her boss's toes. She watched Alexis contemplate the risky proposal. It was almost a full minute before Alexis said a word.

"Do you really think this could help our image to the general public? Because I'm not willing to take such a risk unless you are one hundred percent sure it will work."

"I definitely think this could do us some good. You know I always have this company's best interest in mind and I want nothing more than for us to remain one of the oldest and highest selling magazines around. Times are changing and we need to change with them." Samantha tried to sound as confident as she felt. "I'll talk to my editing staff and to some of the writers. We'll set up a meeting in the next few days to go over the new ideas and get some feedback on how to make this change a success." Samantha stood and walked over to Alexis' desk. She reached down and gave her boss's hand a quick squeeze. "Don't worry, everything will work out just fine I promise." Samantha was certain she was the only one at the magazine who could speak to Alexis in such an informal manner but she also knew there were limits to what she could say.

"Thank you. I know I can trust your judgment." Alexis put her glasses back on and picked up the sample issue in front of her. "Although I'm sure you know, if this idea of yours fails, your job will be no more." She spoke without ever making eye contact with Samantha; her words riddled with threat.

Samantha knew this was the warmest good bye she would receive so she just nodded and walked out of the office.

The whole way back to the elevators she replayed the conversation she had just had with Alexis and tried to squelch the nagging doubt she had about her idea to refurbish the magazine's image. She wasn't sure she could actually pull off what she had promised. She would do her best though, because without her job she pretty much had nothing.

It was near the end of the day when Samantha finally tracked down Toni. She found the girl in an almost catatonic state, sitting on one of the sofas in the ladies restroom. Toni was a fairly new writer to the magazine and the one who had just received her first tongue-lashing from Alexis. Samantha sat down next to Toni and tried to comfort the girl who was no doubt scared shitless to return to work and write anything else that would be reviewed by Alexis. Before Samantha could say anything to her, Toni blurted out an apology.

"I-I'm so sorry for turning that article in." She was almost hyperventilating. "I thought it was a good piece. I mean, I graduated top of my class last year with a journalism degree from *NYU* for God's sake. Doesn't that mean anything to her?"

Samantha sighed and grabbed some tissues from the table next to the sofa.

"I should be the one apologizing. Apparently you were never warned about Alexis." She handed Toni the tissues. "She sounds like a horrible old witch, but you have to understand that this magazine was her dream. She literally built it from nothing. So when someone brings her something that is anything other than exactly what she wants, you have to be prepared for some pretty harsh criticism." Samantha gave Toni a sympathetic look. This was not the first bright young mind that she had seen shattered by the wrath of Alexis Marshall.

"No, no. Criticism I can take. This was *not* criticism. This was like I had just taken her only child and sold it to the devil!" Toni wiped her nose with one of the tissues that had been crumpled up in her hand. "I don't know if I'm cut out for this job. I thought I would be able to write about anything I wanted. I know Prestige is a fashion magazine, but it still needs more depth than two hundred pages of the latest colors and fabrics."

"You most certainly are cut out for this job." Samantha had taken the time to review some of Toni's writing and recognized her talent immediately. She really didn't want to lose her. "I think I have some news that might make you feel a little better." She gave Toni a bright smile. "Alexis decided to use your piece! Isn't that great?" She waited for returned exuberance from Toni.

"Why all of a sudden?" She was still guarded and wanted to know why the crazy lady upstairs had changed her mind.

"Well, actually we're going to be changing the entire face of the magazine. As you may have heard we've been in a bit of a sales slump this year and unless we make some dramatic changes, we could all lose our jobs." She gave Toni's knee a small pat. "I really need you to stay on board. You're a fantastic writer and I'm going to need all of the ideas you've got." Samantha watched as Toni took a deep breath. She could read people really well and already knew that the girl had decided to stay.

"Is there any chance that I can use this opportunity to barter for more money?" She gave Samantha a sly look.

"I'm pretty sure that this isn't the best time to be asking for a raise." She had to laugh a little at Toni's gumption. "But I'll tell you what, if you can write some more amazing stuff for me and the magazine starts to do better, we'll talk about it." Samantha stood and gave Toni her hand. "Come on, let's finish the day and go out for a drink. Are you free?"

Toni gave her a grateful look and let Samantha help her to her feet. "Sure." They both walked to the door of the restroom, briefly checking their appearances in the full length mirror on their way out. "Are you sure you don't have something better to be doing?" Toni couldn't believe that Samantha had nothing better to do than take her out for a drink.

"Trust me, this magazine is my life. I rarely have something better to do." She gave Toni a smile to assure her that it was no trouble. "It's already almost five. Why don't you just go shut down your computer and grab whatever you need and we'll take off a little early."

"Can we do that?" Toni didn't want to get in any trouble. She was still new and although she had threatened to quit, she desperately needed this job and didn't want to jeopardize it twice in one day.

"Honey, I may not be the president of this company but I'm up there enough to make my own schedule. I promise you won't get in trouble. I'll meet you downstairs in ten minutes." Samantha watched Toni grin and walk back to her cubicle.

Satisfied with herself for keeping such a promising writer on staff and happy with the upcoming changes to the magazine, Samantha walked back to her own office knowing she would definitely enjoy her weekend.

Samantha met Toni in the lobby at ten to five. They agreed to go downtown to a place called The Smoking Olive. It was a martini and cigar bar that regularly attracted young hot professionals on any given night. They walked in the door of the dimly lit establishment and quickly found a table near the back. There was soft jazz music in the background and Samantha was familiar enough with the place to know that she should enjoy the music now. By six o'clock the background noise would be full of various conversations about major lawsuits won and important deals made. Everyone in the place would be dressed in stylish suits and trendy professional wear. It was a natural breeding ground for affairs to be started among coworkers and inappropriate attraction between unavailable people.

They each ordered their drinks; a dirty martini for Samantha and a cosmopolitan for Toni.

"So why does Alexis listen to you and no one else?" Toni took a sip of the drink that was brought to her.

"I don't know. I guess because I've been there so long I've got a lot of dirt on her." Samantha laughed. "I wish it was because she knows what an intelligent person I am but I'm pretty sure it has mostly to do with the fact that I know what a raging alcoholic she is." Samantha gasped at what she had just blurted out and covered her mouth with her hands. "I cannot believe I just said that! Please don't repeat that to anyone!" She was horrified that she had admitted knowing such a personal thing about Alexis.

"Are you kidding? You saved my ass today. I wouldn't get you in trouble." A smile played at the corners of her mouth. "But now you have to fill me in. Does she really drink that much?"

Samantha wasn't sure how much she should say to Toni. It wasn't as if they were great friends or anything and Samantha valued her job much more than she valued any new friendship with one of her subordinates. Deciding she could trust Toni with a few secrets, Samantha leaned forward and spoke in a more hushed tone. "She drinks like a fish…even during the *workday*. Plus, no drink is complete without a painkiller or two for dessert." They both giggled. Samantha didn't usually like to talk about people. She had to admit, though, that it felt strangely powerful to know so many dirty things about her boss and then be able to decide who to let in on them. "Not only that, but she gets weekly de-wrinkling injections *and* annual mini-facelifts!" Samantha was now giddy. She was glad that she had decided to come out for a few hours with Toni. Normally she would just go home at night and spend her evenings and weekends waiting to go back to work in the morning. She slowly stopped laughing and dabbed at the corners of her eyes. "Seriously though, you have to promise not to repeat any of this. I could lose my job…and Alexis would probably have me killed." She smiled at the joke, but knew it may not be that far from the truth.

Toni signaled the waitress to bring over another round of drinks. Turning back to Samantha, she assured her that she would not say anything to anyone.

They spent the next few hours talking about the job and about Toni's background. When the conversation turned to Samantha and where she had gone to school, Samantha did her best to change the topic. "Oh you know, grew up in a small town, went to college, moved to New York. Blah, blah, blah…nothing too interesting." She smiled back at Toni and tried to ignore the puzzled look on her face. She cleared her throat and moved the conversation in another direction. "So, where did you get the idea for that article you submitted? I read it when I went back to my office and I have to say that it was pretty powerful. You did a wonderful job writing it."

Toni looked at the ground and brought her hand to her mouth. Biting her thumbnail, she responded in a muffled voice. "The article was about me." She couldn't bring her eyes to meet Samantha's. She had responded without thinking about the consequences to such a confession. She finally looked up as Samantha did her best to hide the shock that was clearly written across her face. "Well, I guess now you know that you can trust me with a secret. I'm pretty good at hiding them."

Samantha tried to choose her words carefully. She knew she should admit that she had experienced something similar to Toni's story when *she* was in college but she just didn't have the guts to talk about it. What had happened to her was not nearly as tragic as what had happened to Toni. Obviously Samantha's life had been dramatically affected by her own rape, but it was not as bad as having to live with an incurable disease as a constant reminder. "Toni, do you want to talk about this? We don't have to if you don't want to." Samantha scooted around the table to sit closer to Toni.

"You know most people move *further* away from me when they find out that I have HIV, not closer." Toni dug through her purse to search for a tissue. She refused to let Samantha see her cry twice in one day. As soon as the full realization of her admission hit her, Toni looked up at Samantha with pure terror on her face. "Am I going to lose my job now?" She finally allowed her gaze to meet Samantha's.

"Of course not." Samantha could tell that Toni was trying to determine whether or not she should have said anything, just as she had been moments earlier regarding Alexis and all of her secrets. "Besides the fact that it's illegal to discriminate against someone with an illness, you are too talented to let go of." Samantha knew that she had just formed a bond with Toni based solely on trust. They had each gone against their initial judgments and told the other something personal. Samantha felt badly that she wasn't able to admit her own story to Toni but she knew that she could make up for it by just being there for her. "If there is anything you need or you ever just want to talk, I'm here for you." She tried hard not to look as though she pitied Toni; that was the last thing this poor girl needed. "I've already told you that my work is pretty much my life so you know I don't have anything better to do."

Toni sniffled a little and gave Samantha an appreciative smile. Samantha nodded back, knowing that nothing else needed to be said.

There was an awkward silence for about thirty seconds. They both sat at the table sipping their respective drinks and taking in the noise around them. A small smile spread across Toni's face. She had been dying to ask Samantha one more thing about Alexis. "So how old is she *really*?"

Chapter 12

Matt woke up almost two hours early for work on Monday morning. He hadn't slept much the night before. He laid awake most of the night worrying about the presentation he was due to give the next day. He had tried to convince himself that he needed to sleep or else he wouldn't be well rested and prepared, but nothing he did made sleep come. It was almost three o' clock in the morning when his body finally gave in and now that it was five, his alarm clock was blaring with the morning news and the local disc jockey's annoying blabbering. He was sure that most radio stations did their best to find the people with the most irritating voices to work the early morning shifts. He threw the covers off of himself and tried to bring himself to a sitting position. He knew he wasn't in the best form to be giving a life changing presentation, but he knew he still had to do his best. Trying not to wake Jessie, Matt tiptoed to the bathroom and turned on the shower. Instead of blasting it on the near scalding temperatures he was normally accustomed to, he opted for a cold shower. He was hoping it would give him a more awakened appearance. While he scrubbed himself, he went over the advertising pitch in his head. He knew he couldn't blow it. Jessie had made reservations at an incredibly swanky French restaurant for later that night. She undoubtedly had used Matt's father's name as a way to get in on such short notice as it was almost unheard of to get into such a nice place without making reservations months in advance. He was looking forward to having a nice dinner and catching up with his old buddy Lucas later that night *while* celebrating his professional victory.

By five-thirty he was completing the knot in his tie and giving his appearance a once-over in the hallway mirror. Staring at his reflection he mentally tried to pump up his confidence. Repeating to himself that he would "knock 'em dead", he flashed his reflection a bright smile and walked out the door.

The only people occupying the lobby of the building were himself and the security guard behind the desk. He flashed his company pass at the burly guard, who he knew was named Edward and proceeded to walk to the bank of elevators. It was always strange to be in a near empty building that early in the morning, but Matt knew he needed it to be quiet in the office so that he could use the conference room to perform a dress rehearsal of his presentation. He was relieved to find it still dark on the floor of Preston & Myers. He turned the light on in his office and quickly gathered his proposal materials off of his desk. Walking to the conference room, he turned the light on in there and shut the door behind him. He would be embarrassed if anyone walked in and saw him giving a speech to an empty room but he was going to have to take his chances seeing as how the conference room was made entirely of windows and anyone else who came in early would be able to see his performance.

By nine o' clock Matt was wiping the sweat from his brow and shaking hands with the marketing executives from the soda company he had just pitched to. Everything had gone smoothly and he could already see his big fat bonus in his bank account. James Preston, who was normally in the office during all advertising proposals, was surprisingly accompanied by his counterpart Winston Myers during Matt's presentation. The two men had sat in the back of the room with their eyes fixed on Matt. They may as well have been wearing signs that read 'Your job is on the line' on their foreheads. Luckily, the clients liked Matt's worked and signed a contract to begin a new campaign. Matt had to keep from pumping his fist in the air. He did his best to keep his poise until he could close the door to his office and celebrate by calling Jessie with the good news. His happiness was short lived when he heard mention of dinner plans being made by Preston, Myers and the clients. He knew if they were to ask him to come along he wouldn't be able refuse and that could cause quite a problem between him and Jessie. It had taken him all weekend to make up for breaking their plans on Friday plus he was really looking forward to meeting up with Lucas. Just as he had anticipated, they invited him to come along. Luckily James already had dinner plans so they decided to just go for pre-dinner drinks at five o'clock. Matt made the rounds of shaking hands and thanking everyone once more. He agreed to meet for drinks and then excused himself to his office to make a phone call.

He dialed Jessie's cell number since he wasn't sure if she was working or not. She picked up on the first ring.

"Well, what happened?" She spoke with a hint of caution. She didn't want to seem too excited just in case things hadn't gone well.

"It was a knock out!" He had contemplated messing with her by pretending that it hadn't gone well but couldn't contain his excitement. "I have to meet James, Winston, and the clients for drinks after work."

"But what about..." She interrupted.

"Don't worry, I'll be at dinner. I'm just going to have to meet you there instead. It's just drinks and I'm sure we'll be done well before eight o'clock. That is what time the reservations are right?"

She tried not to sound disappointed. He had broken so many of their plans lately that she was worried if they agreed to meet instead of riding together, he would end up being a no-show. "Yes eight o' clock, but you better be there or I swear I won't forgive you this time."

"I'll be there. Eight o'clock sharp, I promise." He was already flipping through his planner. "In fact, I'm going to call Lucas right now to tell him where we're meeting." He could tell she was hesitant to agree. He couldn't blame her though; he had cancelled many of their recent dates.

"Ok, I guess." She sighed. She didn't want to argue with him or spoil his good mood. "What does this Lucas guy look like in case he is there waiting? I mean, is he good looking? Tall? Short? Fat? I should probably know who I'm looking for."

"Are you seriously asking me to tell you if one of my old guy roommates is cute? How in the hell should I know if he's good looking?" Matt tried to draw on his memory for a way to describe what Lucas looks like. "He's got short blondish-brown hair, he's pretty tan, and I think he might have brown eyes." Matt thought for a moment. "Or wait, maybe they're green. Oh hell I don't know, I don't usually look into the eyes of any of my guy friends. Plus it's been years since I've seen him. He could look totally different."

"Well, you're a lot of help. Don't worry, I'll figure it out when I get there."

Matt hung up after saying goodbye. He found the number Lucas had given him the last time they had spoken and dialed. After three rings, a voice came on prompting Matt to leave a message. He figured Lucas must be in part of his conference and unable to answer his phone so he left the information on where the restaurant was and what time they would meet. He also left a description of what Jessie looked like in case, just as Jessie thought, he would be late. After leaving the message, Matt decided he should go back and see Mr. Preston in case there were any loose ends to tie up with the advertising deal that they had made that morning. He figured now that he was on the good side of both of his bosses that he should take it one step further and show he was in fact committed to the whole process. Sucking up to people was not one of his favorite things to do, but now that he was on the fast track towards a guaranteed promotion, Matt was determined to do whatever he had to do to get there.

Sitting in the back row of a large lecture hall, Lucas tuned out the speaker and glanced around the room for any familiar faces. He thought he recognized one guy sitting two rows in front of him but he couldn't be sure. It had been so many years he wasn't sure if anyone would even recognize him. After all, he had grown his hair to just below his ears and he wore it in a bit of a messier style than the short, clean cut he used to have when he was at the institute. He also spent a lot of his spare time –which was considerable - using the free weights he kept in his basement so he figured he was probably more muscular than he had been five or six years ago. He thought if he could avoid being asked any direct questions out loud where he would have to introduce himself, he might just be able to escape this whole conference without any embarrassing run ins. Lucas was not in any hurry to receive the ribbing he knew would come from his fellow graduates who had gone on to be big city agents. There were a few hundred attendees who had graduated from The Criminal Institute of Technology at some point, all with the intention of becoming a federal agent. Lucas was sure he was the only who had settled for being chief of a small southern town police department. The truth was, after getting his degree the only reason he had furthered his training was to fulfill his dad's dream not his own. Paul had always wanted Lucas to follow in his footsteps of law enforcement and then go on to graduate from the FBI academy or some other major government agency. He told him it was the best way to ensure that he had as many options as he wanted and to be able to work wherever he wanted. And now, sitting here listening to a bioterrorism expert drone on about the steps they would need to take in case of an attack through the United States food system or postal service, he had to remind himself why he was there. He tapped his pencil on the small fold up desk that was in front of him and tried to follow along with the booklet that had been provided to him. He pulled out his phone to check the time and saw that he had one missed call and a new voice message. Debating on whether or not he should take the chance of being seen on his phone, Lucas slouched down as far as he could in his tiny seat and pressed the button to retrieve his message. It was almost noon and the message was from Matt telling him where they were meeting for dinner and what his girlfriend looks like in case she got there before him. At hearing the word "girlfriend", Lucas figured that took care of whether or not Matt had a wife and kids at home. He sat up straighter and shoved his phone back in his pocket. He hadn't realized that during the time it took for him to listen to his message, the speaker had stopped to wait for him and now all eyes were turned his way.

"Would you care to introduce yourself?" The instructor spoke loudly into the microphone to make sure that he caught Lucas's attention.

Lucas figured he should stand to reply. He had already embarrassed himself this much; he might as well try to be somewhat respectful. "Um… hello. I'm Lucas Benson and I apologize for the interruption."

"You should introduce yourself as Agent Benson. And I hope the call was important enough to cause us all to stop and wait."

The stern voice of the speaker made Lucas wince a little. He hadn't meant to cause a disruption and he certainly hadn't asked the guy to stop talking. "Actually, I'm not an agent. I graduated in 2007, and now I'm the chief of police back home in South Carolina." He heard a few snickers and some mumbling from the people seated around him. "Oh, and the call was from my wife. Sorry, she's at home and due to deliver twins any day now. She just called to let me know how her doctor's appointment went." He gave the instructor his most apologetic smile and started to sit down but then thought to add one more thing. "But thank you for asking." He smiled and gave a small wave with his hand. He sat back in his seat satisfied with himself. He figured it couldn't hurt to tell a small lie like that. He didn't plan on seeing any of these guys again after this week and it was the best way he could think of to shut the guy up.

"Well, apology accepted." The speaker stammered. "And I hope your wife is doing well. Feel free to excuse yourself if needed." He quickly turned his attention back to the rest of the attendants and continued with his speech.

Lucas gave the guy a nod in response and smiled a little to himself.

"Psst, hey!" A woman who was sitting four seats down from Lucas leaned over his way.

"Hmm?" He turned to face her, trying not to draw more unwanted attention to himself. He didn't want to get in trouble for being on his phone *and* talking in class on the very first day.

"That was a nice little lie you told." She whispered, smiling at him.

Lucas hadn't even noticed that there was anyone else in his row, let alone someone as beautiful as this woman.

"Now how do you know I was lying?" He was curious how she had read him so well. He waited for her response but she was interrupted by the thunder of clapping that had just erupted around them. Everyone was standing and the speaker was taking a bow, offering to answer any questions after lunch.

They all filed out of their seats and walked through the doors at the back of the room. To Lucas's delight, the stunning and mysterious human lie-detector was there waiting for him.

"Are you following me?" He tried to look serious but his mouth gave way to a smile. He couldn't help but feel instantly attracted to her. It was a strange feeling, he didn't even know this woman but he was pretty sure he wanted to.

"Would you mind if I was?" She started walking and gave him a nod to come along. "Anyway, like I said, that was a nice lie. It shows what a quick thinker you are."

"Now how are you so sure that I don't have a big fat pregnant wife at home?"

She stopped walking and grabbed his left hand. "No ring." She dropped his hand and started walking again.

"So? A lot of men don't wear their wedding rings. That doesn't necessarily mean anything."

"Not small, southern town happily married men. Those men all wear their wedding rings because usually finding a wife to settle for them is one of their biggest accomplishments. It's like they're own little way of bragging." She turned to look at him. "Isn't that right, 'ya'll?"

"Oh, so not only are you making fun of me but now you're picking on my accent?"

"Sorry, I couldn't help myself." She flashed him a large smile.

They walked in silence for a few minutes. He wasn't sure where they were headed but he was enjoying her company. She still hadn't introduced herself, so he tried to learn as much as he could just by her appearance. She had short dark brown hair styled in a very trendy way. Between that and the well-tailored suit she wore, Lucas figured she must be from the city. He noticed that she didn't wear any rings on her own fingers, and he found himself hoping there was a reason for that. She had bright green eyes and full lips. Even without much make-up she was striking.

Feeling his eyes on her, she stopped and turned to him. "Well, well. Now who's following whom?"

"I'd at least like to know your name." He couldn't take his eyes off of her. She had a great figure and from their brief conversation he thought she had a personality to match.

Her cheeks flushed a little. "I'm sorry. I totally forget to introduce myself." Without saying anything else she kept walking. Smiling to herself, she knew that she had him intrigued.

He had to jog a little to catch up with her. "So what do I have to do to get your name?"

"You could take me to dinner. That is, if you don't have to rush home to your wife and twin babies." She smiled at him again.

"Dinner it is." He stopped walking when he remembered that he had already made plans to meet up with Matt. "Shit. I forget I already made dinner plans with a friend."

She shrugged her shoulders. "No biggie, some other time maybe." She gave him a wave and walked through the set of double glass doors they had come upon. He watched her walk through the lobby of the building and head toward the exit. Deciding he didn't want to let her get away that easy, he shoved his way through the doors and sprinted after her. He caught up to her just before she made her way outside.

"Ok." He paused to catch his breath. "Why don't you just come with us?"

She seemed surprised at the offer. "You mean you really are meeting a friend of yours?"

"Trust me, although our conversation started with me lying, I generally don't make a habit of it."

"Are you sure your friend won't mind the intrusion?"

"Not at all. In fact, his girlfriend is going to be there as well."

She looked a little relieved. "Oh, so by 'friend' you meant a guy. I assumed you were meeting another woman and were just letting me down easy."

Lucas grinned at her. "See, you don't know everything."

"I'm Julie." She stuck her hand out.

He grabbed her hand and shook it. "Hi Julie, I'm Lucas."

She smiled. "I know. You already gave us all quite the introduction earlier, remember?"

It was his turn to blush. "Oh yeah, I forgot about that. So are we on for dinner then?"

"Well that depends. Are we going someplace nice?"

"Wow, you're pretty demanding for a first date!"

"So this is a date then?" She gave him a sly look, trying to catch him off guard.

He hadn't realized that he had even used the word "date" until she said something. "Well, not like a *date*, date." He fumbled his words and tried to find a way to recover from his assumption.

She squeezed his hand and laughed. "I'm totally kidding! I was just joking around with you." She kept laughing and it caused his face to redden even more. "You don't do this much, do you?"

"Do what?"

"Date, I mean. You don't ask women out much do you? I say that because you don't seem to be very good at it." She tried to stifle another laugh with the back of her hand.

"Isn't there somewhere we need to be right now?" Lucas looked around as if he was trying to get away from her.

"Nope. It's our lunch break right now." Julie looked down at her watch. "Which, by the way, we've almost completely wasted it by standing here and talking."

"Oh I see. Talking to me is a complete waste of your time is it?" He was just teasing her now; trying to pay her back for all of the poking at him she had just done.

"Man, I just can't seem to stop sounding rude!" She gave him a wide smile, showing off perfectly straight, white teeth. "I'll totally understand if you don't want to take me to dinner now."

"Wait, I didn't say anything about *taking* you to dinner. I agreed to *go* to dinner with you. You make it sound like I'm buying." He crossed his arms and tried to look serious.

"Ok, ok. This conversation is going nowhere. Are we really still on for dinner?"

He gave in as well. They *had* pretty much spent their entire lunch break joking with each other. He had to admit, though, that it felt good. He hadn't dated anyone in a really long time and even more than that, he hadn't met anyone in a while that he even thought about trying to date. Julie fascinated him, though, and he knew he wanted to get to know her better. "Ok, you're right. Meet me at a place called Claude's at eight o'clock. It's somewhere on Forty-Seventh Street." He wrote the directions that Matt had left him on a piece of a paper and handed it to Julie. "The reservation is either under Creighton or Carlisle. Matt didn't know which name his girlfriend had listed it under."

"So we're meeting Matt and…?"

"Jessie, I guess. I've never met her. In fact, I haven't seen Matt in years. We're only having dinner because he's an old roommate of mine and he's lives here in the city."

"He's a roommate from where, college?" She scanned the scribbling that was on the paper Lucas had handed her. She put the directions in her planner, figuring she'd be able to find her way there.

"No, actually you'll love this. He was my roommate at CIT in Virginia but he only made it a couple of months. Not even, I don't think."

She was interested in that fact. "Ooh, so he's a law enforcement dropout?"

"Yup."

"And you're just his lowly roommate who couldn't cut it as an agent?"

He knew she was teasing him again. "If that's the way you want to look at it, I guess. I love my job though. It's great being able to work in the small community you grew up in."

"Well you'll have to tell me more about it later." Julie glance back down at her watch. "I've got another session to get to in about three minutes. It's called 'Terrorism and Our Borders'. I'm sure it will be fascinating." She laughed. "How about you, where are you off to?"

Lucas looked down at his own itinerary. "Uh, I guess I am going to learn how to 'Develop a Disaster Plan in the Event of an Attack'. Sounds fun, huh?"

"Sure does. Look, I've got to run but I'm really looking forward to tonight." She flashed him another bright smile and headed off to her next workshop.

Lucas couldn't get over how enamored he was with Julie. It had been a long time since he had felt anything this strong for another person. He turned and went in the opposite direction, whistling as he walked. He hadn't been looking forward to this conference at all, but he had to admit that he was really glad that he came. This trip was definitely getting better.

At ten minutes to eight, Lucas was walking in the front door of Claude's. He gave his name at the front desk and found that the reservation was under Matt's last name. The hostess led him toward the back of the restaurant and Lucas found himself searching for Julie more than he was Matt. He hadn't asked if any of his party had arrived yet so he didn't know if anyone would already be at their table. They finally reached a table in the back corner of the room near a group of men playing various classical instruments. Lucas was sure that there was even someone playing a harp. He had never been in a restaurant as nice as this one. He was also hoping that he had enough room on his credit card to pay for two meals. He was pleased to see that Julie was already at the table, along with another woman he didn't recognize. He assumed she must be Matt's girlfriend. Julie stood and leaned in while Lucas kissed her cheek. He didn't think it would have been possible, but she was even more stunning than she had been earlier. She wore a slim fitting black dress that came just above her knees. It was sleeveless and cut low enough to be sexy but high enough to still be classy. She had on a darker shade of lipstick and if it was possible, her lips looked even fuller than before. It took a minute for Lucas to even acknowledge Jessie. Remembering his manners he reached over, shook her hand and introduced himself.

"I'm sorry. You must be Jessie." He tried to keep his eyes on Jessica but they kept wandering Julie's way. "I'm Lucas, it's nice to meet you."

"And you as well." She gave him a warm smile, pleased with what she saw.

Lucas waited for both women to sit back down before taking his own seat. "So have you two gotten acquainted?"

Julie and Jessie looked at each other and nodded in unison.

"We both got here early so we've had a chance to chat." Jessie spoke before Julie could respond.

"Do we have any idea when Matt will be here?" Lucas looked over the drink menu that was in front of him.

Jessie sighed. "Hopefully he'll be here soon. He was having drinks with his bosses because he got some big contract today for an advertising campaign. I'm hoping he won't be too late."

"That's right. He works in advertising now." Lucas tried to sound interested but he found himself wanting to just find out more about Julie.

They made idle chit chat with each other for the next twenty minutes. The waitress was just about to bring them another round of drinks when finally, Matt arrived.

"I'm so sorry I'm late." Matt leaned over and kissed Jessie on the cheek.

Lucas stood, unsure of what kind of greeting to give a guy he hadn't seen in years. He wasn't sure if he should hug him or just shake his hand. Matt seemed as equally confused as to what the correct etiquette was for such an occasion. They both made a couple of clumsy attempts at a handshake, until finally Matt just went in for the hug.

"Wow! You look totally different. I'm not sure if I would even have recognized you." Matt was hoping his comment sounded more like a compliment than an insult.

After each taking their seats, the waitress set their drinks in front of each of them while Matt ordered one for himself.

"Now you look exactly the same to me." Lucas smiled and leaned back in his chair. He grabbed Julie's hand and looked over at her. "Julie, this is Matt my old roommate from Virginia."

Julie smiled at Matt and said hello back. "So you're the dropout I've heard so much about."

"Yup that's me. I was quite the wonderer before I found my real passion."

Lucas was impressed. He didn't know that Matt was so fervent about his career choice. "So you really love advertising that much?"

"Not really." Matt snorted. "But it's a great paycheck and I'm pretty decent at it so what the hell, right?"

Lucas let out a small laugh. He saw Matt's point, but couldn't really imagine devoting his life to something he didn't completely love. He had almost forgotten that Jessica was even at the table, and tried to include her in the conversation. "So Jess –I'm sorry do you mind if I call you that?"

"Not at all, pretty much everyone does."

"So what do you do?" Lucas again tried to sound interested. He just didn't find Matt's girlfriend all that intriguing.

"I do hair and stuff."

Julie tried to stifle a laugh. "What kind of 'stuff' do you mean?"

Jessie didn't even notice Julie's teasing tone. "Well, like, I do waxing and all kinds of things. Not just hair. I actually have some pretty famous clients."

Julie was intrigued. "Really? That's pretty cool. Anyone I would know?"

"Um, do you remember that guy who played the delivery boy in that movie that came out about two or three years ago?"

Julie cleared her throat and brought her napkin to her mouth. "As good as that description is, no I don't think I know who you're talking about." She could tell that Jessie was probably a little immature for her age, and that her contribution to the conversation would be enlightening to say the least.

"Oh, well I gave him a haircut a couple of weeks ago. I got his autograph and everything!"

"Nice." Julie cleared her throat and turned her attention back to the guys. "You know Lucas, Jessie was telling me earlier that she went to college in South Carolina. Maybe you guys know some of the same people."

Lucas appreciated the fact that Julie was trying so hard to include Jessie in the conversation. It hadn't taken very long for him to realize that Matt probably wasn't with her for her intelligence. "Well I don't know. It's a pretty big state." He turned back to Jessie. "What college did you graduate from?"

"Oh I didn't graduate. I was only there through my sophomore year. It was in Fremont. Do you know where that is?"

Lucas felt a lump form in his throat. There was only one university in Fremont and it was the one that Sam had gone to when she left home, and him, behind. "Really? And you're probably what, thirty-one or thirty-two, right?"

"I just turned thirty a few months ago. Why?"

Lucas could feel everyone's eyes on him. He was sure they were all wondering why he wanted to know how old she was. "It's probably nothing. It's just that I used to date someone who went to college in Fremont. I'm sure you'd have no idea who she was. It's a big school, and we lost touch shortly after she started there."

Jessie gave Lucas a sympathetic look. "That's sad. But you know I was a pretty social person. Maybe I ran into her one or two times. What was her name?"

"Samantha." He stopped for a minute. It had been a long time since he had said her name out loud. "Samantha Weiler."

A look of total shock came over Jessie's face. Matt gave her a funny look. "What's up, Jess? Did you know her?"

"You have got to be shitting me!" Jessie couldn't take her eyes off of Lucas and she completely forgot to lower her voice for the sake of being in such a nice restaurant. "You're *The* Lucas?"

Lucas looked from Matt, to Julie, and then to Jessie. "What do you mean by that? Did you know her?" He tried to sound casual, but could tell he should brace himself for something he probably wasn't ready to hear.

"Of course I knew her." She still couldn't take the shocked looked off of her face. "She was my roommate."

Lucas felt his face pale at the word. It took a few moments to register, but if he looked closely enough he could somewhat remember Jessie – or Jessica if he remembered accurately - and the fact that they had briefly met a long time ago. If it hadn't been for this conversation he never would have remembered her. He took a long drink from his glass, downing it all in one gulp. Everyone at the table was watching him as he looked for the waitress and asked for another. A double this time.

Chapter 13

Lucas was back at his hotel room sitting on the edge of his bed. He had done his best to make it through the rest of dinner without seeming like he had just been hit by an emotional semi-truck. Jessie's admission had caught him so off guard that it almost knocked the wind out of him when she said Sam had been her roommate. He had tried to recover as fast as he could from the look of astonishment he was sure had registered on his face. By just mumbling an abrupt "that's nice", the conversation had quickly turned back to everyone's lives as they are now. Lucas had tried to contribute to the conversation but only seemed to be able to answer a question when someone asked it more than once. He knew that Julie could tell that his thoughts were preoccupied by something other than the group, but he had tried to brush it off as if he were just tired. He wasn't a betting man, but he ran his hands through his hair as he tried to determine what the odds of something like this truly were. He hadn't wanted to sound too interested in an old girlfriend while he was on a date with Julie so he didn't ask Jessie any questions even though he had been dying to find out if she knew what had happened to Sam all those years ago. There was no way he could have been prepared for something like this. Even though he sometimes found himself thinking about her, it was unintentional and more sporadic as the years progressed. But now, he wanted nothing more than to go over to Matt's apartment to talk to Jessie. It was nearly midnight, and if it wasn't for the sheer fact that he had somewhere important to be so early the next morning, he would have seriously considered it. He got up and started pacing the room. He couldn't believe that number one, Sam had somehow crept back into his life, but that number two, it was at the same time as him finally finding another woman he was interested in. He really wanted to get to know Julie more, but his interest in her had waned somewhat in the past few hours. He couldn't seem to take his thoughts off of Sam and the relationship they used to have with each other. It may have been when they were young but it was the only time that Lucas could remember ever truly being happy. It was true that he didn't know where a relationship with Julie could go. She was from Washington D.C. and he lived in South Carolina. However, a relationship with her seemed a hell of a lot more plausible than a relationship with a ghost from his past. He stayed up for hours replaying different memories of the five years he had dated Sam. He tossed and turned wondering what she was doing at that exact moment and what she might look like now. When they were dating, her hair had been a long chestnut brown and she had blue eyes that rivaled any ocean in color. She was tall, slender, and tan and had had a zest for life despite the obstacles it had thrown her. Lucas was sure that Sam would be married by now. She had always wanted a house full of children, a great marriage, and a successful career. And although none of those things included him as he always thought they would, he found himself hoping she was well and happy.

 He looked over at the clock and saw that it was a few minutes after three A.M. He knew he had to be up in just over three hours but sleep would not readily come. His head whirled with confusion, hope, and a little sadness. He was confused over whether or not he should pursue Jessie with questions about Sam. He was hopeful that if he did, it would bring him some sort of reconciliation. And finally, he was sad that no matter what he did, he might regret whichever action he took. Lucas finally fell asleep just before dawn. He got a rough two hours of slumber before waking for his first workshop of the day. Still perplexed by the events of the previous night, Lucas found himself yearning for home and wanting nothing more than to leave this big city that had brought his past clear into his present.

It was the end of the day and Lucas decided he just wanted to get a quick bite to eat and spend the rest of the night alone. He had spent his entire day trying to avoid Julie at the conference. It was a big building and there were a lot of classes and lectures going on, but it seemed that no matter what, he always turned the corner only to see her. He had just flagged down a taxi outside of the convention center when he felt a tap on his shoulder.

"Hey stranger."

Lucas turned to see Julie standing behind him, her arms folded across her chest. It was cold and he could see that she had left the building without her jacket. "What are you doing out here?" He asked. "It's freezing and you don't have a coat on. You should get back inside."

"Why so you can keep avoiding me?" Her eyes showed a hint of sadness, and he could see that she was visibly upset by his evasiveness.

"I'm sorry Julie. I haven't really been *avoiding* you. I've just been busy today."

She looked away from him.

"Did I do something wrong? I mean, I thought our dinner went well. You seemed a little distracted but other than that it was a nice night out. I just don't get it."

The cab driver shouted out the window that he couldn't wait all day. Lucas contemplated on whether he should just get in the taxi and avoid Julie for the next two days, forgetting she ever existed, or if he should stay and face her. He muttered an apology to the driver and shut the door just in time before the car sped away. "It's not you."

She interrupted him before he could go on.

"Wait. If you're going to give me the whole 'It's not you, it's me' bit, you might as well save it. I've heard that one before."

Lucas sighed.

"It's not that. I wish I could explain more." He didn't want to hurt her. In fact, standing this close to her he found that he actually wanted to spend time with her again. "Why don't we have dinner later? You can pick somewhere since you know the city a little bit better than I do. I'll go back to my hotel to shower and shave." He kissed her lightly on the cheek and saw her face brighten at the suggestion. "I'll call you in an hour ok? It'll just be you and me this time."

She didn't say anything right away and he could tell she was considering his offer carefully.

"Ok." She bit her bottom lip as if she still wasn't sure if she should have accepted. "But you better show up. If you end up leaving me sitting alone in some restaurant I'll have the bureau hunt you down."

"Fair enough." He kissed her again and turned to hail another cab. Before one came to a stop, he thought he should apologize once more for his behavior that day. "I'm sorry again for avoiding you."

"Ah, so you admit it." She grinned.

"Yeah, yeah. I've just had a lot on my mind since last night."

"I could tell. I wish you would tell me what was bothering you, maybe I could help." She noticed the taxi's turn signal and could tell one had finally noticed him standing on the curb waiting.

"Maybe we can talk at dinner." Lucas opened the door to the waiting cab and got in. "Let's keep it causal though. I only brought one suit with me. Actually, I only *own* one suit…pretty pathetic, huh?"

"Nah…I'm not much of a fancy dresser either so ditto on the casual thing. I don't get dressed up that often and you don't need to see me in the same clothes two days in a row." She leaned in and kissed him softly on the lips.

He was surprised by the forward action, but before he could say anything Julie was waving and heading back toward the building.

Lucas didn't think about anything other than Julie for the entire cab ride back to his hotel.

Just when Lucas was about ready to leave his room, the phone on the nightstand started ringing.

"Hello?" He wasn't sure who even knew where he was staying. He had already called Julie and made arrangements to meet at a diner around the corner from his hotel.

"Lucas?"

It was Jessie.

"Hey… Jessie. What's going on? Is everything ok?"

There was a brief pause.

"Everything is fine. I've just been thinking about you since last night and I thought maybe we could get together and talk."

This was something he had been dreading. He wasn't even sure if he wanted to know anything more about what had happened to Sam, but now that the offer was right in front of him he wasn't sure that he could turn it down. "What do you want to talk about?"

"I think you should know what happened."

"Are you talking about what I think you are?" He didn't want to assume anything. Jessie wasn't the smartest person he had ever met so just in case she was talking about anything other than Sam, he didn't want to presume what she had in mind.

"I could tell how stunned you were by what I said last night and I think you should know more."

Lucas looked at his watch. He knew Julie would be waiting but he wasn't sure if he could pass up this conversation. "Look Jess, I'm just about ready to meet someone for dinner. Can we…"

"Are you meeting Julie again?" She interrupted.

"Yes. Why?"

"I was just curious how serious the two of you were. I know you said you only met recently but if talking about Sam is too painful, I don't want to disrupt whatever it is you've got going on."

There it was again. Her name. "No, no. I really think we should talk. I was just going to say that if it was ok with you, I'd like to meet after dinner. Will that work for you?"

"That's perfect actually. I have to work until about nine o' clock. If you give me your cell number, I'll call you when I get out."

He agreed and gave Jessie his number. After hanging up, he was back to deciding if he even wanted to go tonight. It always seemed as if right when he was about to get close to Julie, something came up to ruin it. He determined that even if he didn't end up pursuing a relationship with Julie, he couldn't just ditch her at the last minute. He resolved to go to dinner and have a good time no matter what. Pushing thoughts of Sam away, Lucas pulled on his coat and left his room.

Julie was waiting for him when he got there.

Her face broke into a huge smile when she saw him. "I almost thought you weren't going to make it."

He leaned in to kiss her cheek. "I wouldn't leave you sitting here all alone." He took a seat across from her and smiled back. "What looks good to eat here?" He picked up a menu and browsed the selections.

"I'm actually not too hungry. I really wanted to talk more than anything." Her expression was serious.

Lucas set down his menu. "What's wrong?"

"I like you, and I think this could work." She paused. "I think you felt the same attraction as me when we met and we seem to have a good time together. I just..."

"What?"

"You just seem a little distant since Jessie mentioned your old girlfriend. And then today you *totally* avoided me. Is there something I should know?"

Lucas contemplated whether or not he should talk about Sam with Julie.

It was just kind of a shock to hear Sam's name is all."

Julie gestured with her hands.

"Ok, and?"

Lucas sighed and decided to tell her. He would just give her the condensed version.

"Sam was a girl I dated for over five years. We were young and completely crazy about each other. I mean, *in love*. When she was nineteen and I was twenty, she went away to college and everything was great for a while. But then..." He looked away from Julie and gazed out the window. It had started to snow.

"Then what?"

"But then... I don't know." Lucas sank back into his seat. "She just disconnected herself from me completely. She wouldn't answer her phone or any of my letters. After a few months I even called the police to see if she went missing."

"Why didn't you just ask her family?"

"She didn't have any. She only had me. That was the strangest part." Lucas rubbed his hands together. "Her mom died right before she left for school and her dad had taken off when she was really young."

"Any brothers or sisters?"

"Nope, she was an only child. I was literally the only family she had." Julie tried not to sound crass.

"Forgive me, but don't most teenage relationships end?"

Lucas shook his head.

"This was more than that. We were like one person." He looked down at the table and picked at the edge of his menu. "I know how it sounds, believe me. It's hard to understand how anyone could stay committed at that age, but you would have had to have known us back then. We were inseparable and crazy about one another." He had already told Julie more than he planned. "I just never was able to shake the feeling that something bad happened to her."

"It sounds to me like you're still in love with her." Julie said quietly.

"No." He didn't know how to explain what it was he felt. "I'm not in love with her anymore, but I'll never forget what we had." Those particular words made him stop talking for a moment. *Never forget.* He looked across the table at Julie and could see doubt in her eyes. She was quiet for a while and he didn't know what to say. "Look. That was all in the past. It was just strange and a little upsetting hearing her name is all." He tried to smile and reached for her hand.

"Are you sure you're over her? I don't need a dramatic relationship right now." She let him hold her hand. "I just thought we hit it off and could get to know each other."

"I totally agree." He stopped her before she said something he didn't want to hear. "Let's forget all about this and have a nice dinner, ok?"

She looked at him cautiously, but finally nodded and smiled.

"Ok. But you owe me big for having to sit through that dinner last night talking to Miss Intelligence of the year."

Lucas winced, remembering some of what he overheard Jessie talking to Julie about the night before. He hadn't been much of a talker and unfortunately Jessie had done most of the chatting.

"You're right. I totally owe you for that."

They spent the rest of the dinner talking, laughing and getting to know one another. By the time Lucas put Julie in a taxi and said goodnight to her, he was thoroughly smitten. She was smart, funny, and had a solid personality. They enjoyed similar things, had similar work interests and shared a lot of the same hobbies. He walked the two blocks back to his hotel whistling. Even though it was snowing hard and he wasn't used to the cold, Lucas was feeling like he was on fire. It had been a great date, and he was hoping there would be more in the future. The thought of the distance between where they each lived entered his mind, but he quickly vanquished those thoughts. He knew that if it was meant to be it would work out for them. After all this time he figured he deserved a little happiness and if he even dared, maybe a little love.

Chapter 14

Lucas could hear something ringing in the distance. He wasn't sure what it was but he did know that it was annoying him to no end. Without opening his eyes he reached for what he realized was the culprit of the noise. It was the voicemail signal on his cell phone. He couldn't imagine who would be leaving him a message so early in the morning until he realized it was nearly ten o'clock. He sat up and rubbed his eyes to rid them of any sleep that lingered before looking at the face of his phone. The call he missed was from a number he didn't recognize. When he dialed the number to retrieve his messages his thoughts went immediately to Julie. Maybe she was the one calling him. They had had a pretty nice dinner the evening before. But the voice he heard was not Julie's. It was Matt's girlfriend Jessie wondering what had happened the night before. Lucas realized he had forgotten all about meeting her after his dinner with Julie. She was calling to say that she had free time this morning if he was still interested. Lucas shut his phone and mulled over what he should do. After laying back down and weighing his options, he decided that he needed to know what had happened all those years before, even if it changed the rest of his life. Before he could change his mind, he called Jessie back and agreed to meet her in the restaurant of his hotel in half an hour.

That gave him just enough time to shower, dress, and have a cup of coffee.

It was just before eleven o'clock when he stepped off the elevator and headed toward the restaurant. He was following the signs that led the way and was about to turn the corner when he nearly bumped right into Julie.

"Hi!" She had a bright smile on her face and was obviously pleased to see him.

Lucas couldn't believe that he was facing yet another obstacle to finding out about the past that he so desperately needed resolution to. And it seemed as if every obstacle included this woman who had abruptly come into his life.

"Julie, hey…how are you?" He tried not to sound as if he were in a hurry and for some reason he found himself desperately hoping that Jessie wouldn't see the two of them together.

"I'm good, I'm good." She brushed her hair behind her ear and folded her arms across her chest. "You weren't at the workshop this morning, and I tried calling but there was no answer in your room. I stopped by hoping I would catch you." She let out a nervous laugh. "I guess I did." She watched him look around and then past her into the restaurant as if he had somewhere to be. "Are you…are you meeting someone or something?"

"Um, no…well yes. Sort of, I mean."

She let out a breath. "Oh, someone like another woman, someone?"

"Not technically." He didn't want Julie to think that he was on a date but he also thought that maybe if she knew who he was meeting that she would invite herself to come along. If she did that, he was afraid he wouldn't get all of the details out of Jessie that he needed.

"It's probably none of my business, but what does 'not technically' mean?" She unconsciously bit her lower lip while trying not to seem too eager for an answer.

"I'm not on a date if that's what you're thinking." A quick lie came to him. "I'm actually supposed to be meeting Matt in a few minutes in the lobby."

"But the lobby is the other way." She pointed toward the sign that was on the wall right next to them.

He wasn't sure if he should keep lying, but he thought he'd take a chance. Plastering a surprised look on his face he did his best to act innocent. "I get so turned around in this place." He put his hand on the small of her back and ushered her toward the lobby.

"Oh, ok…but I still don't get what you meant by 'not technically', is Matt actually a female or something? I mean, it wouldn't be the strangest thing I've ever heard." She let out a nervous laugh still unsure of what Lucas was up to.

"No, no it's nothing like that." Lucas searched for another lie, but he wasn't that good at it. Although he realized that since meeting Julie he had been doing quite a bit of it; starting with the whole pregnant wife story. "It's just that Matt talked about meeting up with another woman and he doesn't want Jessie to find out. He'd probably feel weird if you saw him with someone else after meeting Jessie the other night." Lucas bit his lip, waiting to see if Julie would believe such a bogus excuse. He also realized that if she did, she probably wasn't that great at her job.

She didn't say anything right away, but then she playfully tapped him on his stomach with the back of her hand.

"Alright Benson, I believe you."

Lucas sighed in relief.

"But I'd really like to see you later today. My flight leaves in the morning and I think we should talk about some stuff."

Lucas almost forgot that it was the last day of the conference and that they might not see each other after today. He needed some time to think about their situation before they make any kind of decisions, so he agreed to call her later to have dinner again. He gave her a kiss on the cheek and stood in the main doorway of the hotel. He watched her hail a cab and get in. She turned and gave him a quick wave before the driver sped away. He wanted to make sure that she was gone before he made his way back to meet Jessie. He had to stop himself from running, but only moments later he was back in front of the restaurant asking the hostess if anyone was there to meet him. It took her a moment, but she found that someone was indeed there to meet a Lucas. She motioned for him to follow her and it took only a second before he was seated at a booth across from Jessie. She was drinking a soda and reading a book. She looked up and smiled when he sat down and they both thanked the hostess.

"Hi." He wasn't sure how to start the conversation, but he thought "hi" was a safe bet.

Jessie leaned forward a little.

"You know, I feel kind of weird meeting like this. It's like we're trying to get away with something, you know?"

"I know. I just bumped into Julie outside. I kind of lied to her a little about who I was meeting."

"Why? She could have had lunch with us."

Lucas looked up as the waiter came over to their table and asked him if he wanted something to drink. He asked for a water and waited until he walked away to turn back to Jessie.

"I know. I just wasn't sure that either of us would feel comfortable talking about one of my ex-girlfriends in front of her."

Jessie nodded. "That's true. I didn't really think of it that way."

Lucas waited for her to initiate the conversation. She knew what he was there for so he didn't really feel like he needed to say anything.

Jessie realized he was waiting for her to start, and now that they were face to face she wasn't sure that she had the information he had waited too long for.

"I hope the information I have for you is worth all the trouble you went through. I mean, I don't even *exactly* know everything that happened but I think I have a good idea."

Lucas stayed silent. He wanted to just let her talk.

Jessie took a deep breath and tried to recall the events that took place eleven years ago. "I remember meeting you one or two times in the first couple weeks of school. You guys stayed in a lot and never came with me to any of the parties."

Lucas nodded, so far these were details he was already aware of.

"It was like, the middle of October and we had just gotten done with mid-terms. Sam had told me that you guys were planning on being together that weekend but at the last minute you cancelled saying something about going camping."

Lucas tried to recall going camping that year. It was a long time ago, but he didn't remember ever being much of an outdoorsman. He couldn't even remember ever having slept in a tent his whole life. He had dropped out of boy scouts before he was ever forced to sleep outside for the sake of some stupid badge.

Jessie started to talk again but he interrupted her.

"I wasn't camping…I just remembered what I was doing."

"What you were doing? Or do you mean, who?" She said it before she realized it.

"What is that supposed to mean?" Lucas took immediate offense to her accusation. Why would she for any reason assume that he had been with someone else?

"I'm sorry for blurting that out…but after you said that, I remembered that that is exactly what Sam assumed. She knew you hated camping so she didn't believe that that's what you were doing. She thought you were cheating on her."

"No, no! It was nothing like that!" Lucas couldn't believe what he just became aware of. The realization hit him like a ton of bricks - it was his own fault that things had turned out this way. He remembered why he had lied to her. "I told her I was going camping because I had just found out that I had been accepted into the program required to start at the police academy." Lucas looked down at his hands and ran his fingers through his hair.

"So why did you lie to her then? Why not just tell her that?"

"Because," He sighed, "she didn't want me to go." He tried to keep his hands from trembling. He wasn't sure what the rest of Jessie's story would entail but he hoped that Sam's decision to cut ties with him hadn't hinged solely on the assumption that he was cheating on her. If so, then it *was* his own fault. "I didn't tell her because she never wanted me to be a police officer. She was terrified of me going into that line of work because of the risks involved."

"Oh…Lucas, I am so sorry for assuming that you were cheating on her. Then and now."

Lucas sat back in his chair. For only being a few short sentences into the story his whole world had been turned upside down.

"I was afraid if I told her the truth, that she would talk me out of it. Back then, I would have done pretty much anything that she asked me to. I had been so supportive of her decision to go away to college that I was afraid of not getting the same in return from her." He paused and looked up at Jessie. "Does any of this make sense?"

She could tell that he was already deeply hurt by what she had told him. She was also afraid that if she told him the rest of what she suspected of happening, it would throw him right over the edge that he was already teetering on.

"I completely understand."

"I mean, I wasn't even sure if that was one hundred percent what I wanted to do with my life. I thought I should find out for sure before I upset her. If I had decided it wasn't what I wanted, she would have never had to know that I even applied to get in." He stopped talking when the waiter came over to ask them for their order.

"I'm sorry to interrupt I was just wondering if I could get you something besides drinks? I've been waiting for a good time to come over, but I didn't want to intrude on your conversation." The waiter looked at his watch. "Plus, my shift is over in like fifteen minutes, so…" He stopped talking before he made the pair feel like they weren't welcome to place an order. He did want to leave early though, if at all possible.

Lucas sized the waiter up, he was irritated at the interruption but figured the kid couldn't be much older than eighteen so he tried to cut him some slack. "I'm really not hungry…water is fine for me." Lucas returned the menu to the kid. Jessie said the same and gave the kid her menu as well.

They both heard him mutter something about not expecting a big tip, but they dismissed him and Lucas continued their conversation.

"OK, so I lied. It still doesn't explain why Sam would totally write me off. We had been together for a long time, even if she assumed that about me I think she would have tried to get an explanation."

"You're right… and I told her that she should talk to you first. I'm afraid, though, that what happened next might partially be my fault."

He couldn't decide if he actually wanted to hear the rest of the story, but Jessie persisted before he could say anything.

"She was so upset that I encouraged her to come to a party with me."

"Ok, so?"

"You don't understand. Sam *never* came out anywhere socially with me. She and I had gone a few places like out to eat together and stuff, but she never went to any parties. The fact that she even agreed to go blew me away. I was so excited that I lent her some of my party clothes and I even did her makeup."

"Sam never even wore makeup. She didn't need it." He wasn't sure if Jessie was painting in accurate picture of what happened.

"Exactly. The whole thing was totally out of her element. She looked like a completely different person when I was finished with her."

The waiter came back and hastily set a bill in front of Jessie for the soda that she had ordered. He didn't even wait for the money. Instead he moved on to his next table and ignored them for the rest of the time they were there.

"Ok, fine. So you guys went to a party. What's the big deal?"

Jessie continued. She told him how it was a fraternity party and that there was probably over two hundred people there. There was all kinds of drinking, smoking, and other things going on.

"Sounds like a blast." Lucas said flatly.

"Back then it was." She shook her head. "Anyway, we got separated a few minutes after arriving. There was some guy I was really into and we wandered away from Sam. I feel awful, but I actually think that I completely forgot that she was with me. I was a little self-absorbed back then."

"That's a shocker." It wasn't that hard for Lucas to picture.

The comment must have gone over her head, because she didn't even flinch at his words.

"I remember a few hours later seeing Sam upstairs sitting on a sofa talking to some guy."

"A guy? Who was it? What were they doing?" He tried to picture Sam in the way that Jessie was describing her but he was having a hard time doing so.

"Hey calm down… they were just talking. Besides, this was a long time ago, remember?"

"Sorry…go ahead." It was as if he was twenty years old again and listening to someone tell him that he was being cheated on.

"Anyway, they looked like they were having fun and it seemed innocent enough so I just left her alone."

Lucas interrupted her.

"Don't you know the kinds of awful things that happen to girls at those kind of parties? How could you just leave her alone like that?"

"Calm down *officer*, I realize that now but at the time I was just some dumb kid. I wasn't thinking. *Anyway*, before I knew it the night was over, it was morning and she hadn't come home."

A look of sheer terror took over his face.

"Did s-something happen to her?" He had almost forgotten that the police told him that they saw her alive and that she was ok. Now that he thought back though, he wondered if maybe that had the wrong person back then. It was possible that they met the wrong girl. His mind was whirling with terrible thoughts.

"Calm down, it's not like she died or anything." Jessie didn't realize how insensitive she sounded. She still couldn't grasp why Lucas was getting so upset. She understood that he had been in love with Sam, but it had been a long time ago. She couldn't believe he wasn't over her yet. Jessie couldn't even remember anything that special about Sam.

"Just keep going please."

"So anyway, she finally did come home sometime that morning. I had already left but she was there when I got back from having lunch with friends."

"So do you know what happened the night before?" Lucas had to know what Jessie knew. All sorts of bad things happen to young girls at parties. He had seen it more than once on the job.

Jessie seemed uncertain of what to say. "Please promise me that you won't get so upset that I regret telling you."

"Ok, ok I promise." Lucas would have promised his right arm to her if she had asked. He just needed to find out what had happened.

She let out a deep breath.

"I heard from a friend of a friend that Sam hooked up with someone that night." She waited before saying anything else. She knew this was probably hard for Lucas to hear.

He swallowed hard.

"Do you know who he was?"

"Not really. I heard that it was someone from the fraternity but Sam never talked to me about what happened and I didn't ask. To me it seemed like she was upset that she betrayed you and then who knows, maybe she never heard from the guy again. A one night stand kind of thing, you know?"

"I just have a hard time believing all of this. Was she drinking? Sam never really drank but I really can't see her doing this at all, let alone sober."

"I couldn't tell you. I didn't really see her much that night, like I said." Jessie reached over and squeezed Lucas's hand.

He pulled away and rubbed his face trying to put the pieces together.

"So basically what happened is that Sam thought I was cheating on her so she went to a party, got drunk, met some guy and ended up cheating on me?"

"That's about it. I think she was so ashamed of what happened that she was afraid to face you. She probably didn't think that you would ever forgive her."

"But I would have! I would have forgiven her for anything if she would have just talked to me." He wasn't sure how to process all that he had just heard. "Did she ever tell you why she wouldn't talk to me about it? I get that she was upset and embarrassed and even probably afraid I'd break up with her but I swear to you I wouldn't have. Did she tell you why?"

"Honestly, after that night we never really talked much about anything. She had me lie to you on the phone once or twice but after the whole incident she became even more reclusive than she had been before it happened. After the semester was over she asked for a room re-assignment and I hardly ever saw her after that. I bumped into her once at the beginning of our sophomore year but she wouldn't even say hi to me. I dropped out soon after that so I never really knew what else happened to her."

"I can't believe it. All this happened just because of some guy." Lucas felt miserable. He wasn't sure if he was glad he knew or if he just wished he had never come to New York and had never met Jessie.

"There is one more thing I didn't mention." Jessie bit her bottom lip in hesitation.

"Do I want to know?"

"This is really hard for me to say, but I do remember hearing something about Sam from some of my friends who had met her." She took a deep breath. "Um, someone ran into her a few months later and…" Jessie looked down and started picking at her manicured fingernail. "Lucas… Sam was pregnant."

Lucas stared at Jessie for almost a full minute not saying a word. She started to say something else but before she could Lucas got up and walked out of the restaurant.

Back in his hotel room Lucas sat down on his bed and stared at the wall. He couldn't believe what he had just heard. After he left the restaurant he came straight upstairs and locked himself in his room. He spent the first half hour pacing back and forth and fighting back tears, and the next half hour trying to hold himself back from hitting something. He knew if he let his emotions get out of control that he would probably end up putting his fist through the wall. Pregnant! How could Sam have been pregnant? For the last eleven years he had thought of her as the innocent girl that he had always known. Now he could only think of her as this cheating party girl who got knocked-up by the first guy she met in college. Lucas wasn't sure what he was supposed to do now. Should he try to find her? Should he forget all about her? On top of everything he remembered that he had promised Julie that he would meet her for dinner. How could he possibly go on a date now? The biggest mystery of his past had just hit him square in the face with answers he couldn't have imagined. There was only one thing he could think of doing. He took a deep breath and picked up the phone.

It was nearly four o'clock and Della was in the kitchen trying to make dinner without much success. It seemed like every time she turned around Oscar was getting in her way. When he was laying down he took up most of the floor space, when he was standing he wanted to do nothing but follow her every move. She was about ready to let him outside and intentionally forget to let him back in, when the phone rang.

"Get! Get out of my way you stupid mutt! I swear when my son gets home I'm going to give him an earful about your behavior!" She couldn't believe that she was talking to Oscar as if he was a human, but for now he was the closest thing she had to grandchildren, so what difference did it make? She reached for the phone on the wall, trying not to disturb the dog who had finally settled down into one spot. "Hello?" She could hear breathing on the other end but now words. "Hello? Who is this?"

"Mom?" Came the strained reply.

"Lucas? Is that you? What's wrong honey?" Della could feel a lump form in her throat. There was only one other time that she had heard this tone in Lucas's voice and it was the day that her husband had been shot on duty. Whatever he was about to say, couldn't be good news. She heard him clear his throat.

"Um, I'm not even sure why I'm calling…I just felt like I needed to talk to you."

"Ok sweetie, I'm listening." She untied her apron at the waist and sat in one of the kitchen chairs, bracing herself for whatever was about to come. Had he been in an accident? Had something happened to one of her other children that she didn't know about? Her mind raced with possibilities without letting her mouth jump to conclusions. Lucas lived a few short miles away, but her other three children were spread all over the country. Her son Jason, who is a free-lance writer for a sports magazine, lives in Denver and her two daughters, Christy and Chelsea, moved out to San Francisco last year. Christy is a chef at a four star restaurant; Chelsea a flight attendant.

Hearing his mom's voice helped calm Lucas enough to be able to talk to her. "Nothing is wrong, I'm fine. I just got some pretty upsetting news today about a…a friend I used to know."

Della breathed out a sigh of relief. She didn't want to Lucas to know about the awful things she had been thinking. "What friend? Is it someone that I would know?"

"Yes…you'd know her."

"It's a *her*? You don't mean…" Della knew that there was only one significant "her" in Lucas's past. Especially one significant enough to upset him to this degree.

"Exactly. Coincidentally I ran into her old college roommate. She's actually dating the guy I met up with while I was here. Do you remember Matt Creighton? He was my roommate for a while in Virginia."

"Samantha is dating Matt?" Della exclaimed in disbelief.

"*No-o.*" Lucas groaned. "Her roommate is dating Matt. So when we went to dinner the other night we were each talking about where we grew up, went to school, all that sort of stuff. When Julie asked Jessie where she went to school one thing led to another and Sam's name was all of a sudden front and center of the conversation."

"Wait a minute…who's Julie?"

Lucas knew he should leave it to his mother to completely miss the point. "Julie is this woman that I met at the conference on Monday. We've gone out a couple of times this week…it's nothing serious. Can I get back to my story now?"

"Yes, but only if you finish telling me about Julie when you're done."

He sighed, almost wishing he had never called his mother at all. "Anyway, Matt's girlfriend Jessie called me the next day and asked if we could meet up to talk. I knew what she wanted to talk about, I just wasn't sure if I was ready to hear it, you know?"

"I know." Della knew how difficult it had been on Lucas when Sam suddenly stopped seeing him. She was there through each stage of his grief. He had relied on her support when he was first confused by what was happening, and then after when he was angry with Sam, and then finally when he came to terms with everything and decided that he needed to move on. Even after all of those stages, though, there was still a constant sadness. She understood that her son had lost his girlfriend, his best friend, and his planned life partner all at once. It wasn't an easy thing for him to deal with and it was something that she never expected him to fully recover from. "So what did you find out?"

"It was awful. At first I started blaming myself because apparently Sam thought that I was being unfaithful to her and it was all because of some stupid harmless little lie that I told her. Do you remember when I started police academy training? I was supposed to go to Fremont the weekend of my first orientation but I didn't want her to know about me getting accepted because I knew she would worry about me. I told her I was going camping or something stupid like that and she assumed I was cheating on her."

"So because of that she never spoke to you again? That seems a little harsh. I can't really imagine Sam doing something like that. Can you?"

"There's more. I guess her roommate took her to some party where she met a guy and supposedly hooked up with him. After that night is when she started avoiding me. She would have Jessie lie to me on the phone and when I would go to visit she would purposely ignore me."

"Oh, honey I'm sorry you had to find out like this. And so many years later…but why do you think that she assumed that the two of you wouldn't be able to work it out?"

"That's not all. You see, Sam was…" Lucas's voice broke. He hadn't said the words out loud since he found out. "Sam was pregnant, mom."

Della froze. She knew her son was in a fragile state so she wanted to choose her words carefully so that she didn't upset him further. She hadn't heard her son cry since he was a little boy, and now this man on the other end of the line was weeping like a child. "Lucas, you need to be positive and continue to move on with your life. This doesn't change anything." She sat in her chair wringing her hands as she tried to sound strong and show belief in her own words.

Lucas thought about what his mom was saying to him. It sounded so simple, yet the advice carried the makings of an incredibly important decision. He took a moment to compose himself while his mom waited patiently on the other end. "I know you're right, but I just can't *help* but go back. I still miss her and I still love her…isn't that crazy? I don't even know who she is anymore but I *still* love her. Can you understand that? If she showed up on my doorstep right now and begged for me to take her back, I would. And I would do it without asking for any explanation. Do you know what it feels like to love someone that much?" He started to say more but there was a knock on his door. Lucas's heart pounded. There was no way it could be, yet…could it? He was so caught up in the conversation that he wasn't sure what was real and what was imagination. "Mom, someone's knocking, hang on for a second." He walked slowly to the door and took a deep breath.

"Who is it?"

When the response came he knew he had to end his phone call. Lucas opened the door.

"Mom, um… I'm going to have to call you back."

Chapter 15

Jessie stuck her key in the door to their apartment, unlocked it and walked in. She set her purse on the table in the entryway and noticed Matt sitting on the sofa in the living room.

"What are you doing home already? It's only four o'clock." She walked over to the sofa and sat down next to him.

"Where were you today?" He didn't even look up at her. He kept his gaze fixed on the beer he had in his hand.

"I was all over the place, why? What's wrong?"

He finally looked up at her. "Does all over the place include having lunch and holding hands with Lucas Benson?"

Jessie looked at him incredulously. "What are you accusing me of?"

"It's a simple question Jess."

"No, it's a stupid question is what it is." She stood to face him with her hands on her hips. "Yes I was with him, but I told you that I wanted to talk to him about Sam." She narrowed her gaze at him. "Were you following me or something? I mean, I just met this guy a few days ago and all of a sudden you think we're doing something together behind your back?"

Matt stood and walked toward the kitchenette.

"I went to his hotel today to see if he wanted to go to a game with me tonight." He dumped the remainder of his beer in the sink. "I ran into Julie in the lobby. She was obviously upset, telling me that she just saw the two of you at a table in the back of the restaurant and that you were holding hands. Geez Jessie, what am supposed to think?"

"Did you bother to come in and see for yourself?" She couldn't believe how out of context the two of them had taken the situation. "It was an innocent meeting, Matt. I told you I wanted to tell him what I knew about his old girlfriend. You saw how upset he was after he found out that I had known her. Should I just have ignored it and not said anything more to him?"

"You've just never given me a lot of reasons to trust you in the past, Jessie." He leaned back against the counter. "You know exactly what I'm talking about." He looked at her darkly.

Jessie threw her hands up in the air.

"I cannot believe that I am hearing this." She walked quickly toward him. "That was one time! And you and I weren't even that serious. I've apologized to you a thousand times. Do I have to keep being reminded of one mistake that I made?"

Matt was quiet. He knew that he was probably wrongly accusing her of something, but it was a touchy subject for the two of them.

When they first started dating, Matt was new at his firm and trying to get in good with his bosses. After he and Jessie had been dating for a few weeks, he invited her to a charity benefit that his company was throwing. A couple of hours into the night, Jessie was nowhere to be found. He had looked everywhere for her, he even had asked a couple of his female co-workers to look in the women's restroom for her. After about a half hour he wound up finding her in the coatroom making out with some random guy. He had been humiliated and devastated. Jessie was the first girl that he ever really had strong feelings for and this was clearly how she felt about him. The only reason he actually decided to give her another chance is because he figured it was just fate playing a little revenge game on him. He had never been a faithful person, so he thought he should give Jessie the benefit of the doubt. Over a year later, he's glad that he did but hearing gossip about her with another guy, especially a friend of his, just re-opens old wounds.

Matt sighed and hung his head. He rubbed his eyes to clear his head a little and finally looked up at her. He did have to admit that she genuinely seemed to be telling the truth. And he had no reason to think that either she or Lucas had any interest in one another. There certainly were no sparks flying between the two of them at dinner the other night. He supposed that it was possible he could be overreacting.

"Ok, I'm sorry." He walked over to her and grabbed both of her hands. "Why don't you tell me what actually happened?"

She wasn't sure that she should let him off the hook so easily. He had hurt her feelings and she didn't want him to think that she was a total pushover or someone that he could just beat down with his words and then decide to apologize when he felt like it. She tried to look mad until an unintentional smile crept up the corners of her mouth. She knew she couldn't stay mad at him forever. She just wasn't that kind of person. She gave him a small shove but that just made him pull her into a giant bear hug.

"I'm sorry honey. I didn't mean to jump to conclusions."

"I forgive you."

He could barely hear her because her face was mashed into his shirt, but he knew that he heard the word "forgive" so everything must be ok. He knew he had some making up to do, so he quickly swept her off of her feet and into his arms.

"Is this how it's always going to be?" He asked her.

"What do you mean?" She had no idea what he was talking about.

"I feel like I'm always screwing up and then I end up spending a whole weekend trying to apologize."

She gave him a devilish look as they made their way into the bedroom.

"Why do you think I always pick fights with you at the end of the week?" When he pretended to run towards her, she let out a half scream –half squeal that was loud enough for the neighbors to hear. He took care of that by shutting the door behind them with his foot.

Lucas wasn't sure what to say. He stood in the doorframe staring at Julie who was clearly upset.

"What's wrong?" He remembered his manners. "I'm sorry – I meant to ask you if you wanted to come in." When she didn't move he wasn't sure what to say next. "Ok, um…I'll just leave the door open and you can decide what you want to do." He opened the door all the way and walked to the other side of the room to put his cell phone on its charger. He could hear her walk into the room behind him and close the door. He didn't know what was wrong, but he didn't have much energy to do too much investigating into it. He turned around to find her staring at him with her arms crossed over her chest.

"Why did you keep asking me out?" Her face offered no smile.

He sighed and sat down on the bed.

"What do you mean? I thought we had a good time together. Isn't that why people go out more than once? To get to know one another?" He had obviously done something to upset her that much was clear. He just wasn't sure what it was.

"I just mean that, you and I are in a situation where we never have to see each other again if we really don't want to. So why would you pursue me if you were actually interested in that other girl?" She was biting the inside of her cheek to keep from crying. This was unusual territory for her. She wasn't used to getting emotionally involved with a guy. She had dated a lot in the past but never really connected with anyone. Lucas seemed different to her. She really thought that they shared something that was special enough for them to find out more about.

Lucas was taken aback.

"What other girl are you talking about?"

She briskly walked over to a chair that was positioned across from where he was sitting on the bed. "I saw you with her in the restaurant."

He was completely unprepared for this accusation. Why in the world would Julie think that he had any interest in Jessie? She was his friend's girlfriend.

"What do you think you saw?" He leaned closer to her. "And wait, I watched you get in a cab and pull away. What did you do, come back and spy on me?" Lucas clasped his hands together. "Oh wait, I forgot that's what you do. I should have known better than to get involved with a private investigator. You probably have my social security number and home address already too, right?" He knew he sounded cruel but he was floored by what she was accusing him of.

"That was low. Besides, I may have told you which firm I work for but if you would have ever bothered to ask more about me, you would know that I only work in administration. I'm not any kind of investigator like you assumed. My boss only sent me here for report writing and documentation reasons."

Lucas did feel kind of bad. He thought back over a lot of their conversation at their first dinner and then again the next night. They had talked about where they grew up and why they each went into this line of work, but now that he thought about it, he mostly talked about himself. And if he were completely truthful, he would admit that the topic of Sam had dominated the majority of their conversations. He was shocked at how so many years later; Sam could be such a huge part of his life. He decided that he needed to be honest with Julie.

"You are so right." He shook his head. "I have been completely wrapped up in my own life that I've probably ruined any chance I had with you." He looked up at her. "Julie, I'm really sorry. Especially for this whole Jessie thing, but it's not what you think."

She shrugged her shoulders.

"Then what is it? You can tell me. You don't have anything to lose. I'll just be another person you met in some city you went to." Her expression remained stoic.

Lucas sighed; he knew that it was either now or never. He could either completely unload his entire problematic past on Julie now and take a chance on her reaction, or he could blindly maneuver his way through the rest of whatever relationship they had together not knowing when his past would throw him the next curveball. He looked in Julie's big, green, earnest eyes and made a decision. He patted the bed next to him and invited her to sit down. He resolved to let go of Sam and the past that has haunted him for over a decade. Julie took a seat next to him and he told her everything about Sam, some he had already told her, but this time he went into detail. He finished his story with the information that Jessie had passed on to him just a few hours earlier. After the last word was spoken, Lucas and Julie spent a beautiful night together. It had been almost twelve years, but for the very first time, Lucas felt like he could finally move on.

Friday morning came, and with it came a sense of new beginnings. Lucas awoke without the heavy feeling on his shoulders and in his heart that he had grown accustomed to over the years. He looked over and watched Julie's chest rise and fall with each systematic breath she took. He couldn't believe how much his life had changed in just the past few days. A trip that he had been dreading for weeks had managed to reunite him with an old friend, bring him an amazing woman that he felt closer to every minute, and it had helped him let go of the past that had consumed most of his life up until the night before. He felt incredibly lucky to just be alive and to have had the chance to find love again. He couldn't believe he was even thinking in those terms. Love! Who could have imagined that he would ever be this happy again? Lucas wasn't sure what universal forces had brought him to Julie, but he was grateful for them. He figured he must have been gazing too intently as he watched Julie open her eyes and look over at him.

"Hi." She said the words lazily. Sleep was still clearly evident in her voice. "I could feel you staring at me." She closed her eyes and smiled.

"I wasn't staring. I was just…looking." He traced his fingers from her face, to her neck, to her shoulders and then down her arm. Their hands touched and he folded hers in his own.

She kept her eyes closed and just enjoyed the feel of his skin on hers. She was happier than she had been in a long time, but she felt torn between her newfound happiness and the sadness she felt from knowing that she would be leaving soon.

Lucas watched her face transform into a slight frown.

"What's wrong?"

She opened her eyes and turned on her side so that she was facing him.

"I don't want to leave you yet." Her eyes were downcast as she smoothed her hands over the softness of the hotel sheets.

"So don't." He said it simply and he meant it.

She looked up at him and brought her head back a bit.

"What do you mean? I have to. My flight leaves in like…" She looked past Lucas to the alarm clock on the nightstand. "Jesus, my flight leaves in like three hours! I haven't even packed yet!" She groaned miserably and covered her face with her hands. "What am I going to do? I cannot possibly get from here to my hotel to pack, shower and be at the airport in time. Weekend traffic is going to be hell with people coming into and leaving the city for the holidays."

Lucas was cautious before he spoke. He didn't want to rush anything but he also knew that he wasn't ready to say goodbye to her. "Change your flight and stay with me in the city for a few extra days. I'm not leaving until Sunday and you could just move your stuff in here with me so that you don't have to try and make a last minute hotel reservation."

She thought carefully for a minute about what he was saying, hoping to God that he realized the enormousness of what he was proposing. They barely knew each other and now he wanted them to share a hotel room for the weekend. If she agreed, it would be the most impulsive decision she had ever made in her whole life. She wasn't the type of person who jumped into things without contemplating all possible consequences. She bit her lip and before she knew it she had agreed.

"Ok I'll do it!" She covered her face with the sheet and let out an excited shriek. She was fortunate enough to have a lot of flexibility at work and she really had no major prior commitments to return home for. And although she was supposed to return to work on Saturday with a full report on the conference for her boss, she was certain she would be able to make up some sort of delay that would require her to stay for a few extra days. Maybe she would claim to be job shadowing at the New York office. Right now it didn't matter though, she was staying and that was all she was concerned with. She lifted the sheets up enough to be able to roll over on top of Lucas. He wrapped his arms around her and nuzzled his face in her chest.

"Hey, do you know what time it is?" She tried to pull away from him enough to look at his face but he only squeezed her tighter.

He didn't even bother to move his face to answer. The only thing Julie could hear was a muffled reply that only slightly resembled words.

"What? I can't understand a word you are saying."

Lucas conceded and raised his face enough for his mouth to be free. "I said, it doesn't matter what time it is, does it?"

"Well if I'm going to get any money back on my ticket I have to call within a certain timeframe to cancel or change my reservation. So yes, it does matter." She tried to pull away from him again but this only caused him to roll on top of her and pin her down.

She didn't realize how strong he was until he was above her, holding her down by her upper arms. She was exposed from the waist up and she could tell that he was enjoying what he was looking down at.

"You have to let go sometime." She grinned and took pleasure in watching him enjoy the sight of her naked body.

"Maybe I don't. What if I decide to hold on to you forever?"

"Then you'd have to marry me." She said jokingly.

"Ok."

Julie was sure she heard him wrong. He couldn't possibly have agreed to what was clearly a joke on her part.

"I'm sorry…what?" He had released his grip on her and was slouched back a little, yet still sitting on her.

"I said 'Ok.'"

He was grinning from ear to ear and Julie could plainly see that he was being very serious. She managed to pull herself into a sitting position. She took a deep breath and brought one of the pillows up to her chest.

"Are you serious?" Before she could say anything else, she had to be sure he wasn't joking.

"I'm dead serious. In fact, I've never been more serious about anything in my life." He sat up straighter and brought himself closer to her. "I'm crazy about you. And even though we don't know each other that well I feel like I want to spend the rest of my life getting to know you." He brought one hand up and brushed it through his hair. "Man Julie, I don't ever make rash decisions like this. I come from a small southern town and we usually think slower than we talk, so don't think this is normal for me." He took a deep breath and held it in, waiting for her to say something.

"I-I was totally kidding." She let out a nervous laugh. "It normally takes me an hour just to decide what I want to watch on television and usually by the time I do decide, whatever it is that I decided to watch is over."

He was about to apologize for making such a huge mistake, when she grabbed his hand and brought it to her chest. He could feel her heart pounding.

She let out a breath.

"Ok."

He thought he might faint.

"Seriously?"

"Seriously." She wrapped her arms around his neck. "I'm kinda crazy about you too, Benson."

"Holy crap."

This was not the response she was expecting.

"What's wrong?" She dropped her arms and pushed back on his chest. "If you tell me you were joking this whole time, I'm never speaking to you again."

Lucas started laughing. Something had just popped into his head and he couldn't believe he hadn't already thought of it. By now, he was laughing so hard he almost fell backwards off the bed. He took a minute to regain his composure and was finally able to look back up at her.

"Do you know that I don't even know your last name?" He watched her face change from a look of distress, to disbelief, and then finally to pure shock.

She covered her mouth with her hands.

"Oh my God, you are totally right!" They both sat there for a minute trying to go over each of their previous conversations with one another in their heads, all while attempting to grasp the fact that they had just gotten engaged.

He grabbed her hands and pulled them away from her face. He kissed the tops of each of them and looked her straight in the eyes.

"It doesn't matter to me. I mean, I do want to know what your last name is but I also want you to know that I don't regret what just happened. Not even a little bit." He intertwined his fingers with hers. "And if you'll still have me, I would be thrilled to move forward with our engagement."

She looked down at their interlocked hands and closed her eyes. She never imagined meeting someone as wonderful as Lucas and she certainly never envisioned her engagement to happen like this. Nonetheless, though, she was happy and certain that she was making the right choice. She breathed in his scent. Their scent, and nodded her head.

"I'll still have you." She pulled him close and hugged him tight. She brought her face close to his ear and whispered, "It's Sellick. My full name is Julie Andrea Sellick; and yes I'll marry you." She grinned and rested her forehead against his.

He thought for a minute about what had just happened and how he was ever going to explain this to his mother. This caused him to ask her a question.

"How do you think your parents are going to take it?"

"My parents are dead; but thanks for asking." She nudged him with her shoulder.

He groaned and leaned further into her.

"I really do have a lot to learn about you."

"It's fine…really. It was a long time ago. What about your parents though? Will they be upset?"

He contemplated his response, but decided to be honest.

"You have no idea."

She smiled.

"Well, I guess I'll just have to make them love me, won't I?"

Lucas was reassured by her smile. He nodded and pulled her on top of him. Looking up at her, he thought about the word "fiancé" and how he was going to have to get used to saying it. And he wasn't sure why, but in the midst of his thoughts, Samantha's face came to his mind. He could see her clear as day.

Try as he might, Lucas wondered if this ghost of his past would ever stop haunting him.

Chapter 16

Matt checked his appearance in the mirror before walking out of the apartment. He had agreed to meet Lucas and Julie for lunch downtown before they left for the airport. As he made his way down the stairwell, he thought about everything that Lucas had told him the night before when they had met for a late drink. He was still floored at the fact that Lucas had asked Julie to marry him. What was he thinking? Was he crazy? They had only known each other for a week! Matt shook his head at the thought. He couldn't imagine getting married yet and he and Jess had been together for over a year. Matt had noticed the look of sheer disappointment that had registered on Jessie's face when Lucas and Julie shared their news with them. She had tried to mask it, but had done a poor job of it. Matt knew that Jess wanted to get engaged more than anything. He was just afraid that she only wanted to get married for the idea of having all of the attention focused on her for the entire length of time that an engagement entailed. Plus, if he were truthful, he wasn't entirely sure that Jessie was the one he wanted to spend the rest of his life with. Dismissing all thoughts of weddings, Matt finally hailed a cab. It took about thirty minutes to get to the place they had agreed to meet from his apartment, with traffic at a standstill in some spots. Matt held on to the small gift wrapped package he had on his lap. It wasn't much, but he felt it necessary to get his old friend an engagement present. Luckily for him there was a small unique gifts store near his apartment building. He ducked his head in there before leaving for lunch to see if there was something appropriate for this type of an event. Luckily, he came across something that struck him as perfect for the couple. It was a book that looked like it had enough dust on it to account for its age; but what intrigued him the most was the title. It was titled *"Letters to someone I've never met"*, and it was a book written by William Remington, a man who had been married to his wife for nearly 60 years when she was overcome by Alzheimer's disease. The book was a collection of letters William had written to his wife about all the special moments of their life together. From births to deaths, marriages to divorces, and arguments to times of forgiveness, William had managed to re-introduce his entire married life to a woman he had known for so long but to a part of her he was only meeting for the first time. Matt didn't have time to scan through it all, but something about the title and the seemingly genuine heartfelt tone of the book appeared to be a perfect present to a couple just starting their lives together. The shopkeeper wrapped the book in a simple brown paper wrapping – after dusting it off – and tied a tan rattan bow around its middle. After stepping out of the cab, Matt stood in front of the restaurant staring at the package in his hands. He suddenly felt self-conscious about the gift and worried that Lucas and Julie wouldn't see the reason behind the gesture. Figuring it was too late to get something else Matt took a deep breath and pulled open the door to the restaurant. At the very least, he decided if they didn't like the book, he could just say Jessie picked it out. The thought made him smile.

Matt found Julie and Lucas sitting next to each other in a booth on the far side of the restaurant. They were holding hands and smiling at each other, looking every bit like a newly engaged couple.

Matt smiled at them when he approached their table.

"Well don't you two look cozy?"

Julie was beaming. She looked at Lucas quick and appeared to be asking for permission for something. He nodded his head at her as if to say "ok". Without waiting for Matt to ask, Julie thrust her left hand in Matt's direct line of vision. Sitting on her finger was an enormous, brand new, round cut diamond. It sparkled even under the dim lights hanging above their table. Matt had to take a step back.

"Wow." He couldn't even say anything else.

Julie giggled.

"I know! Can you believe how *huge* it is!" She wrapped her arms around Lucas's. "He got it for me this morning on the way here. I'm still in shock."

Lucas felt embarrassed by the spectacle that Matt and Julie were making of the situation. He had spent a good chunk of his savings on that ring, but he felt it was important for people to know that they were serious about one another.

Matt took a seat across from them and did his best to stop staring at the ring.

"So you never told me that small town policemen make that kind of money, dude." Matt whistled as he exhaled. "I'm impressed." He looked at the package he still had in his hands and suddenly wished he hadn't bothered with such a trivial gesture. To his dismay, Julie saw the gift before he could hide it under the table.

"Is that for us?" She looked at Matt with an expression of surprise. "Can I have it?"

Matt fumbled his words.

"Well, it's not really anything big. I mean, I just wanted to say, you know 'Congratulations' and to let you know that I'm like, happy for you guys…and stuff. That's all." He could feel his face redden by the second.

Lucas smiled at him.

"Thanks man. That's pretty awesome of you."

"Well, actually Jess picked it out so if you don't like it, I could totally return it." In his mind the "No Refunds" sign at the little shop was flashing at him in the back of his head.

Julie gingerly took the package from Matt as if she knew the contents were delicate. She untied the bow and carefully removed the wrapping. When she got to the inside she turned the book over to read the title. She stuck out her bottom lip a little as she read the dedication page of the book.

"This is beautiful. Thank you." She handed the book to Lucas. "Isn't this great?"

Lucas knew there was something appropriate to say for receiving this kind of gift but he didn't know what. He was pretty sure he understood the sentiment of the book – and even more sure that Jessie hadn't been the one to pick it out – but he didn't know how to respond.

"Thanks, man. It's great, I mean…I can't wait to read it."

Julie could feel Lucas's discomfort. She could understand that it was probably a little strange for two guys to give and receive such an intimate present. She felt like she needed to bust up the tension they were all feeling. She nudged Lucas in the side and reached over to squeeze Matt's hand, trying to look as sincere as possible. "

"Matt, even though I don't know everything about Lucas, I can guarantee that this will most likely be the most intellectual bathroom reading material he has ever had." She smiled at Matt and gave him a wink. They all kind of laughed and relaxed into their seats.

Lucas glanced at his watch and reminded them all to order so that they could reach the airport in time. They spent the next hour talking about their plans and telling Matt how they had spent all weekend playing trivia about each other's lives. Every so often, Julie would reach into her bag to touch the book that Matt had given them. She couldn't help but feel that his gift would be a significant part of her marriage to Lucas.

When they were finally seated on the plane, Julie couldn't stop staring at the ring on her finger. She chewed on her bottom lip with worry, wondering how Lucas's family would receiver her.

"Stop fidgeting. You'll be fine." Lucas put his hand over Julies. He had been watching Julie for a few minutes, and he could tell that she was anxious about the meeting that was drawing near. He could understand why she was so nervous but was certain that his family would put her at ease. Christmas was the following weekend, so Lucas and Julie made plans to stay in Bradyville through the New Year, and then figure everything else out after the commotion of the holidays and meeting the family was over. They had done some shopping over the weekend since Julie didn't have nearly enough clothes for the length of stay they had worked out. It was difficult finding appropriate clothes though; winter in South Carolina is dramatically different than winter in New York so the selection was limited.

"So should I say 'ya'll' at the ends of all of my sentences? I mean, I don't talk like you do. Do you think that is going to be a problem with your family?" Julie was trying to go over all of their differences in her head to find solutions to them now. Their accents were night and day opposites.

"Do I say 'ya'll' after everything I say?" Lucas thought it was cute that she was trying to be so perfect and likable for his parents. "Besides, my siblings live in Denver and San Francisco. God only knows what they talk like after living out west for so long."

"So everyone will be home then?" She tried not to feel even more overwhelmed. It was bad enough meeting parents, but she wasn't used to a big family. She had no brothers and sisters and her parents were killed in a car accident years ago. This was going to be a big change for her. She was hoping she would like it.

"Yup. Jason flew home yesterday I guess with his wife Becky. She's expecting a baby girl in May, so that should take some focus off of you. My parents don't get to see them much so I'm sure that will be a big cause for excitement."

"What about your sisters? Will they be there?"

The flight attendant was on the overhead speaker telling everyone to prepare for takeoff, Julie and Lucas simultaneously re-checked that their seatbelts were fastened.

"Christy is coming in on Wednesday and is staying until Monday but Chelsea isn't coming until Friday. She had an overseas flight come up last minute and I guess you get paid more for that so she took it."

"Will I like them? Or better yet, will they like me?"

Lucas thought about how to answer the question. He knew his sisters were good people but he also knew how nosy Chelsea could be and how skeptical Christy was about everybody. The combination might not be good.

"Well, with Chelsea just be honest –"

"As opposed to being dishonest?"

"No, as opposed to being impressive. She reads people really well and knows how to get information out of them. If you act like you're just trying to impress someone, she'll feed off of that and then that will just get Christy going about how our relationship will never work."

Julie looked at him with a horrified expression.

"Are you joking with me?" She threw her hands up. "I was really expecting you to say 'You'll love them and they'll love you. Everything will be perfect.' So much for that! Now you've got me all freaked out."

"I just didn't want you to be mad at me for not being honest with you. My sisters can be brutal but it's only because Christy never has and never will be in a successful relationship and Chelsea spends all of her time on airplanes with people who are probably flying places with their mistresses instead of their wives." He smiled at her. "Besides, the key person is my mom. My sisters are secondary characters when it comes to my family. If you get my mom to love you, then you're golden." He brought Julie's hand to his lips and kissed it gently. "I promise."

Julie relaxed in her seat and let all the information sink in. At least, she figured, she had a few days alone with Lucas's mom before his sisters arrived. That meant she had to work fast to get into her good graces.

Julie rested her head against Lucas's shoulder and listened to the hum of the jet engines outside of their window. She prayed silently that everything would work out. She wished there was someone she could go to for guidance, but other than her friends back home she had no family to turn to. This could be the family she's always longed for, so she knew in her heart that she needed to give this meeting her all. Before drifting into sleep, she swore to herself that she would not let this relationship fail despite all of the odds stacked against them. She would do whatever she needed to in order to keep Lucas happy. She didn't even seem to notice that when she squeezed Lucas's hand that there was no response. If she had been awake she probably would have questioned what he was staring at. To Lucas, the only thought in his mind was the long haired brunette sitting three rows in front of him. He spent the majority of the flight with Julie snoozing on his arm, and he praying that the mystery woman would turn around so that he could see her face.

He awoke when the fasten seatbelt sign above his head dinged and slowly dimmed away. They were on the ground and the passengers around them were all on their feet reaching for their carry-on luggage overhead. His last thought became his first as he stood and desperately tried to see beyond the crowd to look for the brunette woman. It was an impossible sea of impatient faces and arms reaching for luggage. The mystery woman was nowhere to be found. Lucas turned to face Julie staring up at him from her seat.

"What are you looking at?" She asked with a concerned look on her face.

He was embarrassed that yet again, his thoughts and actions had been hijacked by the face of his past.

"Sorry, it was nothing. I thought I saw someone I knew that's all." He smiled at her and sat back down. "We might as well wait until the aisle clears out to get off, huh?"

"Sure." She opened her purse and pulled out some lip gloss. "Do I look ok?"

"You look fine." He smiled, but his smile quickly faded when he saw her eyes narrow at him.

"Just 'fine'?"

He wasn't prepared for the reaction, but drawing on his years of growing up with sisters he knew he should correct his answer.

"I'm sorry, I meant you look great. Really."

She seemed pleased with the answer and put her lip gloss away, reaching for her cell phone. She turned it back on, knowing that it was safe since they were on the ground. She waited for the screen to light up and pressed a few buttons when it finally did. "Geez, I have ten missed calls and six new messages."

"Wow, someone must be wondering where you are." Lucas couldn't help but wonder who could be so desperately trying to reach Julie when she had no family to speak of. The pessimistic part of his brain made him wonder if there was another significant person in her life that he didn't know about. He watched her dial into her voicemail and listen to each message, seeming to delete some and save others. When she finally finished the plane was nearly empty of its passengers.

"Is something wrong?" He asked when she appeared to have listened to the last of the messages.

"No, no. It's nothing." She sighed. "Two messages were from friends wondering why I didn't come home last Thursday like I had told them I was going to. The rest were from my boss."

"What did he want?"

"He's not really grasping the whole point of the leave I requested. He said if there's no family emergency and I'm not sick, then he's not sure he can approve my request." Julie sighed. "I have to call him back when we get into the airport. I don't know what I'm going to do. I don't have enough vacation time to last me through the next two weeks and you and I promised each other we wouldn't talk about out plans until after the holidays."

"So quit." Lucas said it so simply he surprised himself.

"I can't just quit. What if we decide to move to my home?"

Lucas thought about her dilemma. Their dilemma. Although he knew he couldn't imagine living anywhere other than his hometown, they had promised each other that they would weigh all of their options and choose what was all around best for the both of them.

"Look Julie, there's lots of jobs out there. Your boss sounds like an asshole anyway from what you've told me, and you're definitely smart enough to get a job somewhere else. Why not just call him back and take care of this problem in the easiest way. We'll figure everything else out later." He kissed her cheek and tugged at the side of her mouth to make her smile.

She exhaled deeply. "I can't just live off of you though. I don't want you to think I can't hold up my half of a relationship. Are you absolutely sure about this?"

"It's only for a couple of weeks. I promise not to think that you're a freeloader." He smiled to make her feel better.

The flight attendant came over and asked them, politely, to exit the aircraft. Before he could answer the woman, he could hear Julie dialing the phone. He nodded to the attendant and turned in enough time to hear Julie utter two words into the phone.

"I quit." She looked up at Lucas and smiled, clicking her phone closed. "Hmm," she tapped her chin, "I wonder if he'll want to be reimbursed for this trip?" They both chuckled and exited the plane leaving their worries behind them.

Chapter 17

Della chewed her fingernails as she leaned against the window sill and watched Lucas pull into the driveway. She had been up half the night fretting about the information that was dumped on her over the weekend, while trying to make sure her house was spotless for their new guest. She was still coming to grips with her son's news. Engaged! What in the world was he thinking? Three days ago she was consoling his broken heart over a girl from his past after being told that this Julie was "nothing serious." And now they were engaged? After ending the phone call with Lucas on Saturday, Della spent an hour trying to muster up the courage to tell her husband. Although in most capacities he was a fairly understanding man, Paul always tended to be a little more demanding of Lucas. Whether it was choosing the right vehicle to drive or what line of work to go in, Paul wanted Lucas to always make the right decision. Truth be told, Lucas was just as eager to please Paul. All in all, the conversation had gone alright. He was understandably upset, confused and most of all curious. Della figured Paul must have known deep inside that with Lucas, the subject of serious relationships was somewhat off-limits. Although they all had doubted his relationship with Sam at some point, the scars from his link to her were clearly evident. Not even his cynical younger sisters would dare to poke at those old wounds. So with what appeared to be total acceptance, after only a few minutes Paul had shook his head and just said "ok". He then went back to reading his newspaper and lounging in his recliner. Pleased with the direction the conversation had gone, Della figured that she may as well fulfill Lucas's request of her and call each of his siblings to tell them the news. Each subsequent call went better and better. He started first with her youngest Christy, since Della knew she would give Lucas the hardest time. After reassuring her doubts and putting an immediate halt to Christy's banter, Della made her promise to be nice even if she literally bit her tongue off over the holiday break. Chelsea was next. Della had to leave a voicemail message on her cell phone since she was sure Chelsea was somewhere flying over an ocean. She calmly gave her the news and relayed the strict instructions she had given to Christy only minutes before. She reminded her of what good southern girls acted like and left another stern warning to be nice no matter what it took. Jason was the easiest of the three. Since he and Becky were coming in that night, Della waited to tell them in person. After Becky went to lie down, Della broke the news. He was so hyped up about the baby that was due in the spring that he barely gave more than a shrug and a smile. Della suspected that he didn't want to make too big of a deal about it since it had the potential of taking the focus off of his own happy situation. Everyone in the Benson family knew that Jason was more than just a bit vane, sharing the spotlight was never his strong suit. Above anything, Jason was looking forward to the girls fawning over his wife and him smoking cigars out on the porch with his dad and brother. It was after all, the first time since he found he was having this baby that his whole family would be together. Nothing was going to take away from that, especially some fluke engagement. Della didn't push the conversation. She was glad it was out of the way and that she'd have a day to forget about the shock and spend some time with her oldest son and his expanding family. Now, though, as she watched this strange woman exit her son's truck she did her best to force a smile and make good on her promise to make Julie feel welcome. She had to admit that she was pleased at the sight of Julie. She had striking green eyes and beautiful dark hair. She could clearly see why her son was so taken with her. Opening the front door she approached the porch steps and reached out her arms for an embrace. Lucas set his bag on the step and reached in to hug his mom.

"Not you, ya fool." She looked past Lucas and playfully shoved him out of the way. "This hug is reserved for that beautiful woman standing behind you."

Julie smiled and hoped her nervousness wasn't showing. She was glad for the immediate welcome and willingly stepped toward Della to receive the embrace.

"It's so great to meet ya, honey!" She gave Julie a quick squeeze and let her go to take a step back and get a better look. "My, my, you're as breathtaking as my son said you would be."

Julies face flared up with embarrassment. She wasn't used to receiving such a hearty compliment. Her looks had got her attention in the past, but it had never mattered as much as it mattered now. "*Well,*" she thought to herself, "*one down, four more to go.*" Although she was sure this one would be the easiest of the bunch.

"Thank you. That's so nice." She looked back at Lucas. "You're also as wonderful as Lucas bragged you'd be." She brushed her hair behind her ear. "He's said many wonderful things about you."

"Honey, if you keep saying the word 'wonderful' I'm gonna stop believing you." She laughed as she watched Julie realize her faux pas.

Julie realized Della was only kidding, but she still felt the need to defend herself.

"I swear I have a much greater vocabulary than what you've witnessed so far." She grinned, but looked to Lucas for additional help.

Lucas had been enjoying the exchange between his mother and Julie. He knew instantly that she'd fit in with the family. Recognizing that his help was needed, he came to his fiancé's rescue.

"That's true mom, in the few days that I've known her, Julie has probably used almost a hundred words." He knew the smack was coming so he just winced and waited for it. Sure enough, he caught a swift back hand directly to his gut. He feigned injury but received no sympathy.

"Hey, where's Oscar?"

Julie was confused. She thought she had memorized all of his sibling's names and Oscar was not ringing a bell.

"Who's Oscar?" She asked before Lucas's question was answered.

Della released what seemed to be an embellished sigh.

"That dog has been nothing but a pain in my rear end since you left. He literally paced this house from top to bottom the entire time you were gone. I very nearly called the police almost a dozen times thinking we were getting broke into." She gestured a thumb back towards the door. "Turns out teach time it was just that big ball of fur climbing on the furniture to look out the window." She shook her head and tried to appear annoyed. "He's probably upstairs on my bed."

Julie smiled at Della's obvious hidden adoration for this animal.

"So is Oscar a cute little dog that I'll want to cuddle up to at night?" She grinned.

Della's smile fell from her face as she shot a look at her son.

"You haven't told her?"

"Told me what?" Julie was confused.

Lucas was about to tell Julie just what kind of "lap dog" Oscar was when the need for explanation was yanked away in a flash of fur and panting. Apparently Oscar wanted to show Julie what kind of dog he was all by himself. And since he weighed more than her, it was pretty easy to take her down and show her.

Within an hour the whole family – minus two – was sitting in the family room enjoying warm beverages and each other's company. Oscar was content lying by the fireplace, making them all fear that he would burst into flames by how close he sat to it. This completed the cozy scene, Julie was relieved at the easy going nature of the Benson's and thoroughly enjoyed her conversations with Becky and Della. She could tell there was a competitive edge to Lucas's relationship with Jason but Julie assumed that was normal for brothers so close in age. Their need for approval was evident in the questions they threw at each other left and right regarding work, promotions, home renovations and even annual salaries. Della had tried to cut the conversation short many times, but to no avail. She would look to Paul for help but he actually appeared to be enjoying listening to the success stories of his two boys. He was pleased with Jason's career choice and gave him adequate accolades when it was necessary, but even Jason knew that it would take a whole lot of success to make up for the fact that Lucas was the one who had followed in their father's footsteps. No matter how many published articles there were, or even how many times his name was mentioned on one of the many cable sports channels, he could never quite measure up to his little brother. Lucas knew this. He also knew that it drove Jason crazy, and although he knew he shouldn't take pleasure in his brother's obvious envy, Lucas couldn't help but feel that it was a deserved emotion. After all, Jason was the one with the great job, beautiful wife, nice home and baby on the way. Lucas, up until now, mostly only had his career as his one shining accomplishment. However, he figured now that the playing field was closer to being even; he should probably ease up on Jason. After all, soon Lucas would also be married and who knows, maybe within a year or so he would also have a little one on the way. The thought made him ponder his recent engagement even more. He and Julie hadn't even begun to discuss children or whether they both even wanted them. It scared him a little to think that maybe Julie would turn out to be the type of person who has never wanted kids. Lucas knew that at some point he wanted to be a dad. He wasn't sure when but he did know that it was something that he had always pictured for himself. If he and Julie decided to stay in South Carolina and live in his home, he would be able to do all of those things that you do with your children when you live in a small town. He saw himself taking his children fishing down at the creek and playing at the beautiful park at the center of town. Although they had promised to be open to all decisions about where they would live, Lucas secretly hoped and prayed that Julie would agree to settle down here with him. As he sat in his parent's cozy family room he scanned the faces of the people surrounding him. He watched Julie's expressions change with earnest sincerity as she, Becky and Della got to know one another. They were undoubtedly talking about weddings, pregnancy, and babies and Lucas hoped that the conversation was helping to build roots between his family and his future bride. He felt that he had made the right choice in so hastily proposing to Julie, but he couldn't help but feel like this day and this excitement was meant for him and someone else. He didn't dare say, or even really think the name, but he knew she was someone who would unexpectedly haunt the big moments of the rest of his life. It should have been her. It shouldn't be this other beautiful dark haired woman who so quickly adhered to his family. Julie shouldn't be the one sitting here laughing with his mother and subconsciously twirling the new, sparkling ring on her left hand and peering down to make sure that it was really there. *It should be*...nope, he wouldn't think her name. If he said or thought her name it would create a hole of doubt in his mind and heart that he wasn't ready to deal with. The fact was that it is Julie that is sitting here in his family home. It is Julie that is proudly wearing the ring that he bought. It is Julie that he had asked to spend the rest of his life with him. He was happy with it, he was just surprised and a little perturbed that these other unwanted thoughts continually pierced his thoughts and held hostage his joy. He so badly wanted to keep control over his thoughts and to be able to put up some kind of mental barrier that would block them from entering. Each year it got a little easier, but in over a decade he still couldn't say that he didn't still love this ghost from his past. Hopefully by moving on with his life to this big of a degree, it would help stave off those unwanted reflections. He wasn't sure if it would help, but Lucas knew that he had to do something to ward off these old feelings. His gaze met Julie's and she gave him a smile that proved she was having a wonderful time. He failed to notice that he didn't smile back at her. It was as if he was looking at her without seeing; unable to respond to what should be a normal gesture between a blissfully happy couple. Although he didn't notice his lack of response, it read loud and clear to Julie.

Julie looked away from her conversation with the other two women for just a moment and happened to connect eyes with Lucas. She was having such a good time with his family and she wanted him to know it. She shot him her biggest grin, hoping that it proved to be sincere. She even blew him a quick kiss, but her smile quickly faltered when she received no response. His blank stare made it seem as if he was looking right through her. His eyebrows bore a furrow and his parted lips a near frown. This was not the look that a happily betrothed man gave his fiancé. This was the look of a sad, confused soul. Lucas's face showed feelings that Julie feared were true. She looked away from him and tried to return to the conversation that she was now lost among. A moment ago she was feeling Becky's belly for the tiny thump of the baby's kicks, wondering if she herself would ever become a mother. She even let herself venture into thoughts of her and Lucas and their two, maybe even three, children playing in the yard on a warm southern evening. Now, though, she wasn't sure that she should be thinking that far ahead. By the look on Lucas's face, Julie would be surprised to see a wedding; let alone a family.

They followed their afternoon of discussions by the fire with a pleasant home-cooked dinner. Della had made a hearty stew and some homemade biscuits that hit the spot for all of them. Julie had managed to forget about the doubt that had stricken Lucas's face earlier in the day. She forced herself to move on with the process of winning over her future in-laws and put the bad thoughts behind her. She was determined to do her best to make this engagement and eventual marriage work and she told herself that she wasn't going to keep reading into expressions and gestures. She would rely solely on open conversation and the trust that she knew they had in one another. She reminded herself of this again and she gave Lucas's foot a playful tap under the table. This action quickly prompted a playful smile from him and she felt relief wash through her body. Everything was going to be ok. She just knew it. She smiled back with a wink and went on finishing her dinner. Becky had complained of the smell of the beef cooking some time ago and had excused herself to go lie down. As the men finished their second or third bowls of stew, Paul invited his sons to step out to the porch to enjoy a cigar with him. They both eagerly accepted the invitation, knowing that this would be the best way to be excused from dishes duty. As the three exited the room, Julie stood to offer her assistance with cleaning up.

"Della, why don't you let me do the dishes? You made such a lovely meal it would be my pleasure to clean up." Although it was one of her least favorite household chores, Julie was not going to miss such an opportunity to impress Lucas's family.

"Oh honey, that is so sweet of you. However, you are my guest and I have a strict rule that I do not let my guests clean up my kitchen." Della gave Julie's chin a light squeeze as she walked past her to clear the other end of the table.

"Well if you won't let me do it myself, then I insist you let me help." Picking up her own dishes, Julie was determined to leave Della with no choice.

Della smiled at the gesture.

"Well alright then."

They talked as they washed, dried, and put away the dishes from that evening's meal. Della happily shared stories of Lucas's childhood including all of the embarrassing ones she could think of. In some way she was hoping this would help Lucas and Julie get to know one another better since they obviously couldn't have had much time to talk about their pasts. She liked Julie more and more with each passing hour and prayed that it would work out between the two of them despite the odds they faced. It was nearing ten when Lucas, Jason, and Paul made their way inside, bringing with them the chilly night air. It was Lucas's intention to spend the night in his own home since he lived just a few short miles away, but Della insisted it wouldn't be the same if they didn't all spend the holiday weeks under the same roof. She was endlessly traditional when it came to holidays and they all knew how much it would mean to her if everyone stayed together. Although Lucas was sure this would hinder the alone time he and Julie could have shared if they had stayed at his own house, he was hoping it wouldn't completely be a dead issue. He was sure they could *quietly* have just as good of a time as if his parents weren't just a few rooms away. They told each other goodnight and all made Jason promise to tell Becky to feel better soon and to let them know if she needed anything. He agreed and they all went their separate ways into their respective rooms to retire for the evening.

Within a few days the whole family was together again. It was Della's long time vision to have her entire family under one roof to share the holidays. With the exception of Lucas, the rest of her children were spread all over the country. Sometimes it just wasn't possible for them all to be together during important occasions. The girls made it home much less often than the boys. But with the baby coming in a few months, Della was sure Jason and Becky would be less able to travel. This made Della realize how much she needed to cherish this time they had together.

With the exception of the occasional sibling squabble, Christmas had gone smoothly. The girls had kept their promise to Della of being nice to Julie and not overbearing her with questions or making her feel uncomfortable.

Della knew it was most difficult for Christie, the youngest but nosiest of the group. Both Christie and Chelsea had already flown back home to get back to the personal and work lives they both seemed to love so much. Although she would miss all of her children Della was looking forward to getting to know her future daughter in law a bit more one-on-one. She and Paul were still recovering from the shock but were going to support the happy couple no matter what. Although everything seemed perfect now, Della was doing her best to suppress the nagging thoughts that this may not be the right thing for her son. She would be his cheerleader and support system throughout this part of his life and for once she would keep her true feelings to herself.

Chapter 18

The first several weeks of the New Year flew by for Samantha. The first issue of the magazine's re-vamp would be hitting shelves soon and she wanted it to be perfect. Nights were spent holed up at her computer at home and her days at the office allowed for little interruption. Personal calls and emails were ignored, meals were missed and doctor's appointments re-scheduled. Her job and the livelihoods of many people depended on the success of this one rash idea. Her life would have been much simpler if she had agreed with her boss and maintained things as they were. This was a huge leap of faith and she wanted it to be the shining marker of her career. Toni remained by her side through the process and continued to submit amazing articles filled with passion and warmth. Samantha was happy with her decision to promote Toni to the head of her writing staff and was pleased with the way she was helping supervise the project. It had taken months for the idea to appeal to all of the writers, editors, copy staff and other contributors but so far things were going smoothly. It was tough to tell how the new look and content would be received by their usual readers but all of the research Samantha had done was encouraging.

The last snowfall of the winter was beginning to melt away and New Yorkers all around her could sense that spring was fast approaching. The deadline of the first of April loomed over her head and she was determined to have a finished piece that she could be proud of.

The knock on her office door startled her and took Samantha from her intense focus on the final copy she was reviewing.

"Hey Sam, you want to grab some lunch?" Toni had poked her head in the door frame.

The mention of her not often used nickname caught her off guard for some reason.

"Wow, that's strange. Have you ever called me 'Sam' before?"

"Hmm, I guess not. Sorry!" Toni suddenly felt uncomfortable. "Does it bother you?"

Samantha sat back in her chair.

"No, no it's no big deal." She tried to find the right words. "It's just that I used to go by that nickname back in my hometown. It was used with great affection by a close friend. I guess I just haven't heard it in a while." She waved the awkwardness away. "Don't give it another thought." Samantha gave Toni a bright smile and shut her computer as she stood. "Let's go grab something…I'm starving."

They both buttoned up their coats as they exited the building into the chilly air outside and made their way to the small coffee shop on the corner. They walked in, saying hello to a few other regulars, and made their way to a table in the back.

"So how is the final copy looking?" Toni picked up her napkin to set across her lap, eagerly waiting to hear how her latest articles were looking. She desperately wanted to impress her boss and was hoping that her recent submissions were meshing well with the new look of the magazine. And besides looking for Samantha's approval she needed to hear that her job was secure. The latest medication she had been prescribed by her doctor was costing Toni a small fortune. Her co-pays had gone up and the cost of commuting to all of her appointments was killing her bank account. She was determined, though, to keep her illness from everyone around her and was beyond appreciative that Samantha had kept her promise to keep it a secret.

Samantha glanced at the items on the familiar menu as she responded.

"Good. Really good actually." She set the menu down and focused her attention on Toni. "Alexis is really pleased with the progress and seems to be on board – finally – with our decision to re-design." The waitress interrupted them to take their order.

"I'll have the soup and sandwich combo with a coffee." Toni gave her menu to the young girl scribbling away on her order pad.

Samantha waited for her to finish writing before agreeing to have the same. She waited for the waitress to leave and glanced around to make sure no one she knew was within earshot.

"So how are you feeling Toni?" She paused, wanting to choose her words carefully. "You seem really tired. I hope I'm not overworking you."

Toni's gaze fell toward her lap.

"I'm fine." She said delicately. "I just started a new medicine and it makes me a little sleepy and achy." Toni forced a smile. "Really, though, I'm fine. I like my new doctor and he seems to be really pleased with slow progression of the virus. He gave me a really positive prognosis for the next several years."

"That's great!" Samantha knew she sounded too cheery in her response but as much as she tried to seem natural with this topic it always made her feel uncomfortable. Being in journalism she rarely had to search for words but it seemed with Toni she felt like she never had the right things to say. It was really important to Samantha that Toni knew that she had the support system she needed in the workplace. Samantha was aware that she was the only person at the magazine who knew about Toni's health issues so she wanted to be sure that she remained a positive source of support in Toni's life.

"It is. I feel good overall and I've been reading and researching so many positive stories about people who have what I have and go on to live long happy lives with their loved ones." She instinctively lowered her voice at the mention of her illness.

The man sitting at the table behind Samantha scooted his chair back as he got up to leave. He bumped their table, accidentally spilling both coffees. He offered a quick apology saying he was in a hurry to leave and scurried away.

"Well that was strange! He could have at least offered to wipe up the spill. He must have been in a *big* hurry." Samantha brought her attention back to Toni. "I'm sorry…what were you saying?"

Toni collected her thoughts after the interruption and carried on. She wanted to be sure that Samantha was confidant in her abilities and not concerned with her health.

"I was just saying that everything is really good right now. I feel good and I've received nothing but positive news from my physician."

"Good…I'm really glad for you." Samantha paused as the waitress brought their food over and refilled their coffees.

"I mean, I may never have a close relationship with a guy or get married and have babies, but I'm healthy and that's what is important right now." Toni took a bit of her sandwich.

"You don't know that." Samantha said between bites. "I can tell you from experience that there are some amazing guys out there. You could find the perfect man to spend your life with regardless of your health concerns." She finished chewing before speaking again. "Don't completely write off the possibility of meeting the right person."

"It's pretty unlikely though." Toni contested. "How many guys want to deal with that?" She set her coffee down and clasped her hands together. "Are you telling me that you think there is a person out there willing to love someone that they can't be intimate with? That they can't have children with? A guy that has to constantly go to appointments and treatments and pharmacies and all of that other nonsense for me? Toni took another sip of her coffee. "I'm under no illusion that I'm not likely to live alone and die alone. And it will probably be at a younger age than I would have preferred but that's my life and I'm ok with it." Toni gave a genuine smile this time.

"Wow. You continue to amaze me." Samantha searched for the right words. "I admire your courage and determination. I hope you know what a remarkable young lady you are."

Toni knew that Samantha was sincere and only wanted the best for her. Tiring of the conversation being focused on her though, she tried to deflect with humor.

"Well I've got such a kick-ass job and boss…what do I need a man for?" Toni smiled to show her gratitude to the woman who over the last several months had become her mentor and close friend.

Samantha understood Toni's need to move on from the conversation and nodded. She raised her coffee mug and gave Toni's a light tap.

"Cheers to that." She smiled and changed the topic.

Back at the office it was chaos as usual. Articles were piling up on Samantha's desk and the phone was ringing nonstop from advertisers, contributors and critics. She spent the rest of the afternoon playing catch-up and trying to ignore the inkling that there was something bad about to happen. She thought that maybe it was something regarding Toni but all seemed well with her. Samantha was sure the magazine issue would be successful so she couldn't quite figure out what might be causing this feeling. She opened her desk drawer and rummaged around for some aspirin. She had a dull headache and her shoulders seemed to always been tense and sore lately. She found the bottle and thanked her lucky stars that there were still two small white tablets at the bottom of it. She popped the aspirin in her mouth and took a long drink from her diet soda to wash it down. The drink was flat and the pills were bitter but she plugged away at her work for the day waiting for the pills to kick in.

As the day wore into evening the offices around hers began to empty and she could hear the familiar voices wishing others a good night. When it became so quiet that she could no longer ignore the fact that she was probably the last one on her floor, Samantha decided to call it a night. She placed a few sticky notes on the article she was reviewing and shut down her laptop. When her day planner came into her line of sight she decided to jot down a reminder to herself about scheduling her annual physical. It had been awhile since she had seen her doctor and the headaches she was frequently experiencing were starting to become bothersome. Samantha threw on her coat, grabbed her purse and flicked her light switch as she left her office.

A few weeks later, Prestige finally released its first issue of the newly redesigned magazine and the launch party was scheduled for the upcoming Saturday evening. It was Tuesday, and Samantha found herself sitting in the exam room at her doctor's office waiting to be seen. She knew her doctor well and was looking forward to catching up with her at this appointment. She looked around at the brochure racks on the wall but nothing seemed especially exciting to read. Deciding to just wait patiently Samantha tried not to stare at the clock and count the minutes until Dr. Robinson came in. A few moments later there was a light knock as the exam door opened.

"Hi Dr. Robinson, how are you?" Samantha's natural smile started to fade when her doctor didn't seem her normal self. Samantha could see a manila envelope in Susan Robinson's hand and hoped the contents weren't the source of her doctor's gloom.

Susan shook Samantha's hand.

"It's good to see you again Samantha, sorry for the wait." She gave a tight smile and held Samantha's hand a bit longer than usual.

"Is something wrong?" Samantha tried to be sound casual but there was obvious tension in the room. What would she do if it were bad news? She didn't have anyone here with her to hold her hand or give words of encouragement. A million thoughts raced through Samantha's mind. She was at a good weight, she didn't smoke and she rarely drank alcohol. She thought back to the tests Dr. Robinson had ordered prior to this visit. There were some quick blood draws, a mammogram, a bone density scan but nothing out of the ordinary. Could something have shown up on her scan? Did she have a brain tumor and that's what was causing the headaches? She was terrified of what was coming.

Dr. Robinson could tell that Samantha's mind was racing so she tried to be gentle with her words.

"Samantha we found something on your mammogram. There appears to be a large mass on your left breast." She turned to the lighted fixture mounted on the wall and clipped the mammogram film to it so that Samantha could follow what she was saying. "If you notice in this gray area here where all the normal breast tissue is everything looks healthy… this is your right breast scan." Dr. Robinson pointed out all of the normal healthy tissue on the scan so that Samantha could see what it should look like. She then attached the second film to the screen and pointed to the large white area that was clearly noticeable even to someone without medical training. "This is your left breast scan." She paused to give Samantha a moment to digest the information. "As you can see there is large mass about the size of a golf ball. Due to its size and placement I'm concerned it could be an aggressive form of breast cancer. I want to run additional tests to determine if it has spread to your lymph nodes or any surrounding parts of your body."

"Wait, wait, wait a minute." Samantha tried to gather her thoughts. "How is this possible? I take very good care of myself. I eat right and get plenty of exercise. I mean I know I work a lot and don't get much sleep sometimes but I really am a healthy person. I scheduled this appointment because I was having headaches and shoulder pain. How can I have cancer?"

"Breast cancer cells can invade other cells and tissues throughout the body. In some cases, breast cancer spreads to tissues within and around the shoulder, leading to pain in that area. And there are many reasons beyond diet and exercise that can cause a person to be diagnosed with cancer. It can be genetics, environmental factors…plenty of reasons. Some studies suggest women who have never had children or breastfed can have a higher risk of having breast cancer later in life. There is research going on all over the country regarding cancer – especially breast cancer. The important thing to focus on is that it isn't the death sentence it used to be. The survival rate is the highest it's ever been."

Samantha couldn't find the words. Her mind was swirling with thoughts of treatment and surgeries and all of the other things that come along with this dreaded disease. She founded herself tunneling back twelve years.

"But I had a baby." It was almost a whisper.

Dr. Robinson was visibly stunned.

"What? How do I not know this I've been treating you for several years? I didn't know you had a child. How old?" She scanned Samantha's chart to see if she had missed something buried deep within the file. "And you've never talked about him or her…I'm confused." She pulled her stool over to the table where Samantha was sitting.

"I don't *have* a child. I *had* a child." The tears were streaming down Samantha's face. She didn't even know she was crying until the first drops fell into her lap. The thin paper gown she was wearing soaked up the droplets leaving her lap covered in water spots.

"Samantha, do you want to talk about this now? It's been an emotional visit with everything else. Maybe we can schedule a time to meet in my office. Or I can refer you to a friend of mine if you'd like." She clasped Samantha's hand in her own. "It's really important that we focus on the next steps in your treatment process first so we can find out exactly what we're dealing with. I'm concerned that this could be a fairly advanced stage of the disease and I want to be as aggressive as we can be right away to give you the best possible options."

Samantha knew Dr. Robinson was being kind and was probably spending a great deal more time with her now than she would most patients but she couldn't listen to it anymore. She couldn't deal with it right at that moment. All she could focus on was getting off of that exam table and out of that office. She needed to be around people and noises. She needed normal people and normal noises. She didn't want to hear the minutes ticking on the clock. She didn't want to feel the crinkling of the paper on the exam table a second longer. She wasn't even sure what she muttered as she jumped down from the table and began to hastily pull her clothes on. Samantha gathered her purse and coat and rushed past the doctor. She would deal with it tomorrow or the next day. Right now she just needed to go somewhere and breathe.

Samantha spent the month of May getting MRI's, having surgery and starting chemotherapy. She took a leave of absence from her job without much explanation and wasn't sure if she would ever go back. The magazine's first issue was received with praise by critics and the general public. She was confident that the team she had in place would continue to research, write and publish meaningful articles and stories and that Prestige would flourish even without her direct involvement. She had agreed to be available for consultations when needed by phone or email but other than that she had handed her main responsibilities over to Toni and it seemed to be going well for everyone. Today she was meeting with her therapist who was a friend of Dr. Robinson. Samantha had met with the psychologist twice already and was happy to have someone to talk to outside her normal circle of friends. Plus, the office was a short distance from Samantha's apartment so it was an easy commute even on days she wasn't feeling so great.

After making the short three block walk from her apartment to the therapist, Samantha was winded. The treatments took a toll on her body and she was finding even normal activities difficult. She was grateful to reach the second floor office and was greeted by the therapist.

"Hey Samantha it's good to see you again." Linda Samson was a tall, thin, dark haired woman in her forties. She dressed in comfortable clothes, wore very little make up and had a warm presence about her at all times. Samantha found it very easy to open up to her.

"Thanks…sorry I'm late. It took me a bit longer this time." Samantha took her usual seat on the sofa and mentally prepared herself for the session.

"No problem…we can take as much time as you need. How did you feel after our last session? We covered a lot last week."

"Pretty good. It's difficult to talk about what happened to me in college and giving the baby up and everything. I've never really talked about it with anyone. It felt nice to get it out…I felt relieved in some ways."

"I'm glad to hear that. You should feel a sense of relief when you leave here." She crossed her legs and leaned forward a bit toward Samantha. "So we talked last week about you possibly going back to your hometown. Have you given it any more thought?"

Samantha hadn't stopped thinking about this possibility since she spoke with Linda last week.

"Yes I've thought about it constantly. I think I need to go back." She paused. "I think I need to find her."

"That's a big step you know. You're dealing with a lot in your life right now. If you find this baby you gave up twelve years ago you will be forcing her to deal with all of it as well. That's a lot for a girl to handle. She may not even know she was adopted. When is the last time you spoke to her adoptive mother?"

"The day I handed the baby over." Samantha was crying now. "I haven't seen her since."

"Do you know if she has ever been told that she was adopted?"

Samantha was trying to remember every detail of that day. Had they discussed those things? Did she give the adoptive mother her opinion on any of those important details? It was such a blur and it happened so long ago. Samantha had spent so many years trying to forget about that day. It wasn't easy to bring it back to the surface of her mind.

"It wasn't handled through an agency or anything. It was sort of, um, an illegal adoption I guess." She could feel Linda's eyes on her even as she looked at the floor. Although a therapist should not pass judgment,

Samantha couldn't help but feel guilty and ashamed as she talked about it out loud.

"Could you even find the adoptive mother if you wanted to? Was she referred to you by someone you know?"

Linda had been able to get Samantha to talk about things that she never wanted to talk about with anyone. In the last two weeks they discussed her mother's alcoholism and sudden passing. They talked about Samantha's time in college, the pregnancy and subsequent adoption, and obviously they had discussed Lucas. *Lucas.* She hadn't spoken his name in so many years. To be thinking and talking about him so freely all of a sudden was still strange to Samantha. And now they were talking about her daughter. The daughter that was conceived as a result of a shameful act with someone she did not know. She was convinced, though, that she needed to go back and fix things. She needed to face the parts of her life that she had been too afraid to face all those years ago.

"Yes I can find her. I know exactly where Caroline has my daughter."

Chapter 19

Wedding preparations were in full swing. Julie and Della spent every other day on the phone with each other mulling over the finest details. They had grown close since Christmas and Julie was really starting to feel like this was the family she was always meant to be a part of. Since both of her parents were deceased, she treasured every moment she spent with Lucas's parents. Paul was like a father to her and Della was like a mother and close friend. They shopped together, went out to dinner together and spent nights in watching movies while the guys were out doing whatever it was they did in their spare time. The wedding was to take place in August and there was still so much to do. The family had just spent a relaxing Memorial Day weekend at their lake house celebrating over the news of Jason and Becky's new baby girl and now that they were back it was really time to tackle the last minute wedding duties.

"Lucas you *have* to get fitted on Thursday. The tailor needs time to get all of the measurements and then have the suits made. All of the other groomsmen have to go in on Friday. Please don't make me be mean to you about this." Julie was trying really hard not to turn into the proverbial bridezilla but when Lucas wasn't keeping in sync with her plans it was difficult to keep calm.

"I will do my best but I do have a job you know." Lucas understood the importance of the whole bride thing – well mostly understood – but he found himself getting increasingly frustrated with the process. He knew he loved Julie but sometimes he felt like the closer she got to his family, the further he felt from her. It was a strange dynamic they had created with this engagement. He had to introduce her to his whole life *after* making the decision to spend their future together. She quit her job, moved out of state to be with him, and essentially started her life over in his hometown. Some days he woke up feeling like the luckiest guy in the world and other days he felt like he barely knew her. They were too far into the planning now to talk about postponing the wedding but most of the time that was exactly what he wanted to do. He knew she could sense his distance when they went over any of the wedding details even though he tried his best to hide it. She never mentioned anything to him but sometimes he caught her twisting her ring around finger and staring off into the distance as if she had her own concerns about their future.

Julie plastered on a smile.

"I understand you have a job. I just need you to take twenty minutes on your lunch hour and go get measured."

"It's easy for you to just take twenty minutes whenever you need to because you don't work." He regretted it as soon as it came out of his mouth. The job topic was a sore spot for Julie and he knew it. He was the one who suggested she quit her job to move to South Carolina with him and although it seemed easy at the time Julie hadn't had much luck finding a decent job. He could see her eyes glisten with tears but she looked away before he saw too much emotion.

"It's fine, just go whenever you have time I guess." She set the planning book down that she was working from and left the room.

Lucas sighed and sank into the sofa in his living room. He rubbed his face with his hands and looked around what used to be his home. It was now *their* home. There were traces of Julie everywhere he looked. How had that even happened? He didn't remember her putting up framed photos of her parents. People he had never and would never meet. Her shoes were lined up by the front door and her magazines were spread on the coffee table. He looked around feeling like this was the first time he was realizing that she would be a permanent fixture in his home and in his life. Was this right? Did he make a mistake? Lucas tried to call on those feelings he had during his week in New York where they met and fell in love so quickly. It seems like years ago and yesterday all at the same time. He never remembered a time in his life when he felt so conflicted…especially about something so life changing. He sat there for nearly an hour mentally weighing his options and retracing the last few months of their time together. He loved her. He knew he loved her. She was beautiful and smart and talented. His family loved her and in that respect it was hard to imagine a time when she wasn't a part of their lives. He was going to marry her in nine weeks just like they had planned. He would go to her and apologize for behaving like a selfish asshole. Things would be great and they would be happy. It was just cold feet. *Wasn't it?*

The next weekend Julie was feeling much better about the progress of the wedding the planning. Lucas had apologized and had even managed to find time to get his measurements taken. Everything was happening right on schedule. The wedding was eight weeks away and Lucas seemed more on board with everything that was going on. Up until last week she had a growing concern that he would decide not to go through with the ceremony. She knew he felt strongly about her and he told her that he loved her but more often than not she sensed his mind was somewhere else or on someone else. She was too afraid to ask though. She was afraid if she did dig into that possibility that she would get an answer she wasn't prepared to deal with. Nope. Everything was fine…great even. She was crazy about his family and was finally beginning to adjust to the southern way of life. Her next challenge was to talk about starting a family but she wanted to get through the wedding first. As she sat on the couch going over her never-ending checklist the phone rang, startling her. It was Della.

"Hi Della…how are you?"

Della was happy to hear the cheery tone in Julie's voice. She was concerned there was trouble between her and Lucas lately.

"I'm great sweetie how are you doing? Are you starting to feel overwhelmed?" She chuckled.

"Oh my gosh *starting* to feel overwhelmed? This is craziness. I had no idea what went into planning a wedding."

"It's a lot of work for sure. Have all of your bridesmaids booked their plane tickets?" Della knew that Julie missed her friends from back home tremendously. It would be a good boost to her spirits to have some familiar people around her during such an important time.

"Just about everyone has. Emily is having a hard time finding a good flight back. Her daughter is starting kindergarten that following Monday and so she wants to be home right after the wedding. It will work out though." Julie was happy to be talking about her old friends. She missed home like crazy and couldn't wait to see all of her guests. It meant a lot to her that so many people were willing to fly down for her wedding. The last time she was home was in January to pack up her apartment and take care of all of the loose ends that moving entailed. She was really looking forward to seeing everyone.

"Well listen, the reason I called was to see what day the invitations needed to be picked up. They really need to go out this week don't you think?"

There was silence on the other end of the receiver.

"Julie, honey, are you still there? I can pick them up it's not a problem I was just thinking about it when I was at the post office today."

Julie cleared her throat.

"Um, well, Lucas said he picked them up already. They were done last Friday." She couldn't think of anything else to say and Della could sense that she had just stirred the pot.

"Oh, well, they're probably in his truck with him. I bet he picked them up and they're on his front seat right now. Listen, don't you worry about anything. How about we talk a little bit later?"

Before Della finished her sentence Julie hung up. She knew Della was going to call Lucas and try to fix the mess she just started. Julie was going to beat her to it though. She flipped through her notepad and found the name and number of the printer. She dialed as quickly as she could and asked for the person she had been dealing with when the invitations were ordered. Just as she suspected the invitations had never been picked up. In fact, the gal on the phone was happy to explain that she called Lucas and left several messages to let him know they were ready. Julie was both angry and hurt and tried to determine which emotion she should deal with first. She looked up in time to see Lucas pull into the driveway and sure enough he was on his phone. It was, no doubt, his mother calling to warn him of what she started. She saw him get out of his truck and walk to the side door. She could hear the familiar sounds of his keys dropping on the kitchen counter and of his boots being kicked into the mudroom. She could hear him coming up behind her but she didn't turn around. She wanted to be composed when she confronted him. He didn't give her the chance.

"Babe, I'm sorry I forgot."

"Do you want to get married? We don't have to but *please* tell me now. Don't let me get to that church in front of God and everyone else on that day just to hope that you will show up."

"Yes I want to get married. I'm just dealing with a lot of stress at work right now."

Julie finally turned to face him.

"I totally understand that you work and I don't. But when you forget something like picking up our *wedding* invitations it makes me think that subconsciously you don't want it to happen. It's like you think that if you don't send them out then the day will just never arrive." She was shaking now. "But it will arrive Lucas. We sent out the save-the-date cards. We have dresses on order. We paid for a cake and food for three hundred people. You need to decide now. Not in two months…now."

"I thought we went over this. I'm just dealing with a lot. I'm sorry. I do love you and I want to get married I'm just stressed." He unbuttoned his shirt and walked out of the room. "I'll pick up the Goddamn invitations tomorrow." It was the last thing she heard before he slammed their bedroom door behind him.

Chapter 20

It was muggier than she remembered. The drive down from New York to South Carolina was long and hot especially in July. Samantha watched her thermometer inch upwards with every state she drove through. She took her time getting down there. She didn't listen to music and didn't talk on her phone. It was twenty three hours of the quiet that she needed to figure out what she was going to say to Caroline and to Lucas and to her daughter. She had no idea what she was about to embark on. Would Caroline be willing to see her? She thought about calling ahead but was afraid that if she heard hesitation then she would decide not to go through with the trip. She would track Caroline down and be sure to catch her when she was alone. They would have to figure out together how to take the next steps. And Lucas. What was she going to say to him? He could be married with a family by now and what about his parents? They had been such an integral part of her life at one point in time. She had no idea what they even thought about her now. What had Lucas told them about her? There really wasn't much he could tell them she supposed. He didn't know the true story himself.

It was just about seven o'clock in the morning when she reached Richland County. Caroline had relocated after she came for the baby. They both decided that it was best that she not return home with a baby she couldn't explain. She didn't have any family in the area and since Samantha called her when she was only three months along, Caroline had plenty of time to come up with a reason for leaving. Plus she was a natural at making up stories and sticking to them so besides the fact that Samantha had no one else to turn to at the time, Caroline was the perfect woman for the job. Not that those were Samantha's only reasons for choosing Caroline to adopt her baby. Caroline didn't have any children, she was trustworthy and successful at building her own business so she could provide for the baby and she was one of the only people in Samantha's life that never judged her. She was a good person and Samantha knew back then that she was entrusting her baby to the right person.

Caroline had sent her address to Samantha shortly after moving to Richland. Samantha hoped that she was still there after twelve years. When Samantha found the house it was just as she pictured it would be. The house was pink – literally all pink – with blue shutters. This was definitely Caroline's house. There were sparkly wind chimes hanging from the porch right next to the sign for 'Carol's Hair'. Samantha grinned to herself. She supposed that Caroline had shortened her name to sound more like a mom. It was just the sort of thing Caroline would have done.

Now that Samantha was here, sitting in her car parked across the street from Caroline's house, she wasn't sure what to do next. She couldn't very well just walk up to the front door. What if the girl answered? What would she do or say? She chewed on her thumbnail as she stared at the house and contemplated her options. Lost in her thoughts Samantha was startled by a light screech and the sound of air brakes. A school bus had stopped in front of the little pink house. A school bus? It was the middle of the summer, why would there be a school bus? With her car window rolled down she heard a screen door slam shut. She hadn't quite realized how worried she was about seeing her daughter's face for the first time. What if she looked like her father? Her father. What will Samantha tell her about him? She knew nothing herself. How would she explain the situation in words that would be delicate enough for this child to understand? Samantha didn't even understand. Every time she thought about that night and about that guy she felt she would be sick. She wanted to scream out her hurt and her anger and her sadness toward this person she never knew but had lost so much to. She would have to figure it out. She had come too far not to come full circle with everything. This was just the beginning. Samantha let out a small choked sob. There she was. It was her daughter and unmistakably so. She looked exactly like Samantha. It was strange to be staring at a smaller version of herself yet seeing for the first time someone she didn't know. Samantha watched the young girl walk down the sidewalk carrying a purple sleeping bag with a yellow duffle bag slung over her shoulder. She was obviously going somewhere for longer than the day. This could be the perfect opportunity to spend some time with Caroline alone. Samantha had to sit on her hands to keep from bolting out of the car and running over to the girl and showering her with hugs and kisses. When the little girl was on the bus and out of her line of sight Samantha finally caught a glimpse of Caroline on the front porch. She was waving and blowing kisses in the direction of the bus as it began to pull away from the curb. Samantha felt her stomach settle a bit. As much as she wanted to hug her daughter and hold her and apologize to her, Samantha knew she would have to wait. She had to deal with one thing at a time. Samantha drew in her breath, pulled on the door handle and got out of the car.

Caroline was standing motionless on the porch as Samantha slowly approached her. Samantha couldn't believe how good Caroline looked. It was as if the last twelve years had never happened. The only difference in her appearance was the clothes she was wearing. Gone were the tight fitting pants and cheetah print tops. Her hair was a bit tamer also but still just as blonde. Samantha wasn't sure what to say first or how to say it.

"Well I was wondering when this day would come." Caroline's smile was genuine but she made no move toward Samantha.

"I'm sorry to just drop in without warning." Samantha felt awkward and out of place. "I was afraid to call. I didn't know what to say."

Caroline drew in her breath.

"Well come on in. Let's have some coffee and talk."

Samantha followed her into the house and shut the door behind her.

"Your home is lovely. Really sweet."

"Well listen to you. You went and got yourself one of those fancy New York accents. I can't even tell you were ever from the south."

Samantha wasn't sure at what point her accent had changed but right now she *felt* like she belonged here as much as she sounded like it. She took a seat at the small white kitchen table and watched Caroline busy herself with making a pot of coffee.

"She's beautiful." Neither of them had to say who Samantha was talking about.

"Yes she is. She looks just like you." Caroline took a seat across from Samantha and handed her a mug. It was a pink ceramic homemade mug with 'Happy Mother's Day' scribbled in a child's handwriting. Samantha wasn't sure if Caroline had given her that mug on purpose or if the home was just so filled with things that connected the two that it was impossible to avoid.

"What's her name?" Samantha was eager to put one to the girl's face.

"It's Emma." Caroline smiled as she blew the steam from her mug. "Doesn't she look just like an Emma?"

Samantha shook her head and bit her lip. The tears were unavoidable.

"I've made such a mess of my life and of your life and Emma's. I'm so sorry for everything."

"Oh honey. You have no idea. You gave me the best gift you could have. I have treasured every single second that I've spent with that little girl." Caroline reached across and took Samantha's hand in her own. "She's so sweet and kind and funny." She squeezed a bit harder. "She was my second chance."

Samantha wiped her tears with her free hand.

"What do you mean?"

"I mean that I was meant to be a mother a long time ago and I was too afraid to let it happen. Caroline drew in a ragged breath and looked down at the table. "I got pregnant when I was sixteen years old by my boyfriend at the time. He was so handsome and I thought I was so in love with him." She brought her eyes back up to meet Samantha's. "He told me that if I kept the baby he would leave me. I was so scared. I couldn't imagine my world without this *boy*." She paused. "So I did it. I had an abortion when I was about nine weeks pregnant. I didn't have the money or my parent's consent to go to a real clinic so I went to some guy my boyfriend found out about." Caroline's eyes went empty. "I couldn't have any more children after what he did to me."

"Oh God...Caroline I'm so sorry. I had no idea." Samantha could feel the pain radiate from across the table.

"Yup that's my story. My boyfriend left me shortly after the abortion. He was eighteen and out of school so he took off and moved out west somewhere. I finished high school and went to beauty school right after. Then I moved from New Jersey to South Carolina so that I could feel like that part of my life never happened. I've never told anyone."

"That's why you agreed to help me?" Samantha was reflecting back on her time working with Caroline. She couldn't remember hearing anything about Caroline's past or her family. It made sense that she did her best to keep the town gossip pointed in any direction but her own.

"Oh honey I would have helped you no matter what. I always knew how special you were and how much you wanted the chance to make yourself a success." She smiled. "But yes, in some way I felt like this was God's way of forgiving me and granting me the opportunity to do things right this time. I hope I have."

"I'm sure you've done an amazing job." Samantha meant every word of it but she was cautious how to approach the next step in this journey. "So what do we do? I mean I don't want to just barge in on your life and assume you owe me anything because you don't." How was she supposed to say what she wanted? How do you just ask for the child back that you gave up so many years earlier?

"You mean have I told Emma that she was adopted and am I going to tell her about you and let you meet her?" Caroline was never one to beat around the bush.

"Yes. Have you told her about me?" Samantha gripped the edge of the table.

"I've told her she was adopted. I mean, it was going to come up at some point wasn't it?" Caroline laughed a bit. "First of all we look *nothing* alike. And then there's that pesky issue of family history for medical reasons, school projects etc. I suppose I could have just made up stuff along the way but that wouldn't exactly win me Mother of the Year would it?"

"Does she know about me specifically? Does she know my name and where I live?" Samantha hoped she wasn't overstepping her boundaries but this was all new territory for her.

"No she doesn't know specifics. I've told her that her mother was very young and unable to care for her at the time but that you were a wonderful and beautiful person and that hopefully she would get to meet you someday. I told her the truth." Caroline stood to get more coffee."

"So can I meet her?" Samantha could see Caroline tense up a bit at the question even though she must have known it was coming.

"Of course you can meet her." She paused. "You can meet her when she gets back." She walked back to the table and refilled both coffee mugs and then sat back down. "Emma is at camp for the week. She'll be back Friday afternoon."

It was only Monday. Samantha wasn't sure she could wait that long.

"Wow…crazy timing huh?" Samantha sagged down in her chair. She felt sadness mixed with some relief. As excited as she was about meeting her daughter for the first time she was worried about how Emma would take the news. "Well I guess we can spend some time together before she gets back. Would you mind telling me more about her?"

Caroline knew that this was as difficult for Samantha as it was for her. They were going to have to figure it all out together.

"Of course I will." Caroline smiled. "Would you like to see her room?"

They spent the next several hours flipping through photo albums, watching home videos, and admiring school achievements. They cried together and they laughed together. As the afternoon wore into evening Samantha was afraid to say goodbye. She didn't want the day to end as much as she wanted the week to fly by. Caroline had offered for Samantha to stay in her home for the week but Samantha was afraid to impose too much, too quickly.

"Well I know one place you could go while you wait for Emma to get back."

Samantha knew what she was going to say before the words even came out.

"I know." Samantha took a deep breath. "I should go home."

Chapter 21

Lucas sat at his desk staring at the box of wedding invitations he had just picked up from the printer. He hadn't even opened them to see if they were correct. For all he knew he could have just picked up a stranger's package filled with graduation invitations. It was all a little overwhelming. The invitations were supposed to have gone out two weeks ago after the huge fight he had first with his mother, and then with Julie. They both thought he had cold feet and he spent the better part of that night convincing both of them that he was just stressed out at work. He was afraid they might be right though. He was starting to get the feeling that maybe he and Julie had rushed into all of this. Who in their right mind gets engaged after one week together? And then it's not like they planned for the wedding to happen a few years down the road. Nope. They set the date for eight months later. It would have been sooner except that the reception venue Julie wanted wasn't available until August. So here they were only weeks away from what was supposed to be the happiest day of their lives but the knot in his stomach just kept getting bigger and bigger. Maybe he could just throw the box away and blame the post office. It was possible that three hundred invitations could get lost right? This was crazy. If he was having this many doubts why didn't he just call it off? This kind of thing happened all of the time right? It was better to do it now than a month after the wedding or even worse, the day of. What would he do though? Julie had moved her entire life down here for him. He wasn't sure that he could be that cruel. Although getting married just to be nice wasn't exactly the right thing to do either. He wished he could fast forward the next few months and just find out what happened after the fact. If only it were that easy.

His radio started to beep with a call coming in when he heard a knock on the glass office door.

"Come in." He started to stand when he looked up and the air went out him. He sank back into his chair and tried to determine if he was dreaming or if this was the best possible version of reality that he could imagine. He was staring at Sam.

"Hi." Samantha wasn't sure what else to say.

She was beautiful. She looked exactly as she did the last time he saw her except her hair was longer and there was the unmistakable appearance that came from life experiences.

"What are you doing here?" He stood but wasn't sure he could move. "I haven't seen you since…" His voice trailed off. He wasn't sure how to word it. No matter what he said it would sound like an accusation. She was, undeniably, the reason that they never saw each other again but at that very moment it didn't matter. None of it mattered. It was like it never happened. It was like they were both teenagers again and they had their whole lives ahead of them.

"I know. I can't even begin to apologize for what I did to you and I don't deserve even a moment of your time. I had to come back though. I had to tell you the truth." Samantha shifted her weight and looked uncomfortable.

"Um, well come in I guess."

"Thank you." Samantha was relieved that he didn't tell her to go to hell and demand that she leave his office.

Lucas offered her a seat and went out to tell the clerk to block all of his calls. He was sure it looked suspicious meeting privately with a strange beautiful woman but he didn't care. He wanted to go back in his office, lock the door and never come back out.

"So how are you? How have you been?" He was cautious not to bombard her. He could plainly see that she had no wedding ring on her finger and she appeared to be alone as there was no one in the waiting area or in the one lone car he could see in the parking lot from his office window.

"I'm fine, thanks. It was a long drive so I'm tired but otherwise, really good. How are you?"

"Are we really going to do this Sam? We could go back in forth for an hour with the formalities of catching up but we both know that's not why you're here." He could feel some of the hurt creeping into his words. "Why did you come back?"

Samantha looked down at her hands.

"You're right. I'm sorry. I just don't know exactly what to say or how to start."

"Why don't you start by telling me why you shut me out? What happened that made you feel like you never wanted to see me again?" He was trying to keep calm. He didn't want her to leave but he wanted her to just be honest and put him out of the misery he had been in for the last decade.

"I missed you." She started. "I missed you so much that I thought about quitting school. It was so hard and so different from what I was used to. My roommate was awful to live with and I was homesick." She drew in a breath. "You were supposed to visit me for a weekend and you called at the last minute with some excuse that you were going camping or something like that. I was upset. I was certain you were cheating on me and barely could get out of bed that afternoon." Saying it out loud it sounded childish. Samantha knew she would have to explain herself in a way that proved how hurt she really had been at the time. She shook her head. "No. I wasn't upset, I was devastated. I had just lost my mom and had no other family. You were my whole world and not in a teenage fairytale kind of way. You were literally my entire life."

"So you didn't give me a chance to explain?" Lucas knew more to the story than Samantha realized due to his meeting Jessie back in December but he wanted to hear it all in Sam's words.

"There wasn't time. My roommate Jessica convinced me to go out with her that night to a party at one of the fraternities. She ditched me as soon as we got there and I found myself alone and trying to get out of the house. I ran into this guy who seemed really nice and offered me a chance to take a breather and just sit and talk. He said all of the right things and made all the right moves. I didn't even see it coming." Samantha kept her eyes fixed on the floor. She was too embarrassed to look at him. "When I woke up the next morning I was naked, sick and embarrassed. I didn't know where I was or what had happened. It turns out the guy didn't even go to school there and I never saw him again. At the hospital they said I was drugged." She finally looked Lucas in the eyes. "How could I face you after that? I made you wait all those years for me to be ready and then I threw it away because I was *mad at you*? You didn't deserve that. You didn't deserve the way I disregarded you. It wasn't my fault I was raped but it was my fault that I put myself in the position to get raped. I couldn't bring myself to admit what I had done." She stopped talking. She had to catch her breath and regroup her thoughts.

Lucas could tell she needed him to say something. The story she was telling him was a familiar one to him. He had dealt with rape victims more than once in his years of being a police officer but it never got easier especially when it was someone close to him. He could picture this faceless, heartless asshole and wanted nothing more than to find him and kill him. This guy who probably went on to live a perfectly normal and happy life not giving a thought to the events of that night had no idea of the lives he ruined.

"So that was it? You had sex with some guy and you felt you couldn't tell me or give me the chance to help you deal with it? You should have known me better than that. I could have forgiven you for anything. You didn't give me the opportunity."

Samantha couldn't listen to him any longer.

"I was pregnant!" The tears were falling fast. "What was I supposed to do? Come to you and ask you to raise this illegitimate child with me when we were just teenagers? I had betrayed you in the worst way and I was terrified of what you would think of me. How could you trust me? And what would your parents think? That was not an option for us at the time. I couldn't do that to them, to you or to us."

He knew that she had been pregnant but she never mentioned whether or not she actually had the baby. Lucas assumed she would have had an abortion but maybe he was wrong. Had she actually raised this baby on her own? He knew she was fragile so he tried to sound as gentle as possible.

"What happened to the baby? I mean, was everything ok or did you…" He couldn't say the word for some reason. He wanted to let her say whatever she needed to say.

"I had the baby on August second of the next year. She weighed seven pounds and she was beautiful. I only saw her for a brief moment. I never even held her." Samantha covered her face with her hands. "She'll be eleven in a few weeks." Her shoulders heaved with each sob.

Lucas couldn't keep distance between them any longer. He pulled a chair close to hers and gathered her in his arms. He still couldn't believe this was happening. He couldn't believe that Sam was actually here in his office and that he was touching her. At some point over the years he had made himself believe that this moment would never come. She smelled the same and felt the same. He wanted that moment to last the rest of his life. He truly felt that if he died tomorrow he would be satisfied. How was it possible that a person could have that much of an effect on him?

"So you gave her up for adoption?" It was of course what she would have done. He should have known she could never have ended a life.

"Yes. I signed the papers immediately after she was born so that I didn't have the opportunity to change my mind." Samantha debated whether or not to tell him who the adoptive mother was.

"Have you ever seen her? I mean, since the adoption, did you ever meet her?"

"I've seen her yes, but just briefly." Samantha pressed her lips together and clasped her hands in her lap. "Caroline Connelly adopted the baby. I met with her before I came here and I saw Emma – that's what Caroline named the baby – for a moment, but I didn't meet her yet. We're still figuring all of that out."

Lucas wasn't sure what clicked in his mind. He stood up so quickly he even caught himself off guard. He walked behind his desk and grabbed his keys and shut down his laptop.

"Come on, let's go." He was in such a hurry he knocked a large box off of his desk and onto the floor.

Samantha wasn't sure what was happening but she was willing to follow him wherever he needed her to. The ball was in his court for now.

"Oh hey, let me help you with that." She bent down and picked up the package nearly knocking the lid off. "Is this anything you need to take with you?" She was staring at him with those big blue eyes of hers and holding the box of invitations in her hands.

It was the first time Julie entered his mind since Sam walked through his door. He contemplated telling Sam what was in the box and then shook his head. He walked toward her and took the box from her hands and tossed it on the table next to his desk.

"Nope…it's nothing I need now." He grabbed her hand and walked out of his office and through the back door of the police station into the parking lot where he faced his first dilemma. "Can we take your car?"

Samantha wasn't sure where they were going.

"Sure…you'll have to drive though since I don't know where we're headed."

"Not a problem." He took the keys from her hand and walked to the driver's side of the only car in the back parking lot. His heart was racing and his palms were sweating. He felt like he was a teenager again and he was sneaking out of the house to be with Sam.

He drove a few miles out of town and turned down a dirt road in an area she could barely remember. He drove down the long lane into a wooded area. She saw a tiny rustic cabin come into view with a small lake just beyond the yard.

"Where are we?" She felt nervous and excited. She hadn't expected to be alone with him any longer than it would take to tell her story to him and apologize for what she had done. Now they were alone together and the sense of anticipation and anxiousness was almost too much to take.

"My dad and I come here to fish sometimes. It was my grandpa's place before he died. I never brought you here?"

"I don't think so. We went to your family lake house once or twice but I don't remember this." She looked out her window as he parked her car next to the cabin.

"Don't get too excited…it's definitely a guy shack." He grinned and opened his door to get out of the car and come around to her side. He opened her door for her and reached for her hand.

It was still so surreal. He couldn't believe that this was actually happening.

They walked up the few steps to the porch and opened the door with a key that had been hidden behind the light fixture.

They weren't two steps into the house when he grabbed her hands and pulled her close to him. Her breath was soft on his mouth and it took every ounce of his strength to not be too forceful with her. He teetered between wanted to take everything from her that he never had the chance to before and wanting the moment to go slow and last forever.

She let him lead her into the back of the cabin where there was a double bed covered only by a single sheet.

They stood facing each other, neither one knowing exactly what to do next.

Samantha decided to help him out. Without breaking his gaze she slowly unbuttoned his uniform shirt. They took their time undressing. When he tried to lift up her shirt she hesitated. He didn't want to press the issue or make her feel uncomfortable so instead he lifted her up to him. She wrapped her legs around his waist and buried her face in his neck. He smelled of aftershave and tears. It was almost too much.

He brought her down to the bed and kissed her softly. She let out small cry and put her arms around him. The moment was everything they both had waited almost fifteen years for. Neither of them said a word as they expressed their love for one another in that small bed in his cabin in the woods.

It had started to sprinkle outside and the sound of the rain on the tin roof was a perfect backdrop to their first night together.

When it was over they laid next to each other face to face. Lucas traced each of her features with his fingers. He felt like he needed to keep touching her or she would vanish again.

The feeling of his fingers on her face and arms made Samantha drift into sleep. She felt herself being pulled closer to his body and she could have sworn he whispered the words 'Thank you' although she was not sure who he was talking to. He fell asleep next to her not caring about anything but that very moment and whatever force it was that brought her back to him.

Chapter 22

No one had heard from Lucas since that morning. Julie was pacing their living room at eight o'clock contemplating what she should do next. He should have been home two hours ago. She already called Della and neither she nor Paul had seen him. His patrol car was still in the lot and the clerk said she hadn't heard from him all afternoon. Could something terrible have happened? Julie was trying her hardest not to give in to the feeling that it wasn't a tragic accident that kept him from coming home. There was a tiny voice in her head telling her that he couldn't go through with the wedding and this was his way of breaking it to her. Paul had told her to remain calm and give it a few hours. He assured her there were plenty of legitimate reasons that would keep Lucas from coming home on time, although he didn't elaborate on any of them. She agreed to wait no later than ten o'clock and then she was going to look for him. As the minutes ticked by she grew more and more fearful. She couldn't shake the sense that something bad was about to happen very soon.

It was the slamming of a car door that startled Lucas awake. He tried to focus his eyes on his surroundings but the room had grown dark and he assumed it was well into the evening. He looked down hoping to see Sam still next to him and he let out a relieved sigh when he made out her outline in the dark. He heard footsteps on the porch and bolted out of bed. He threw his pants on as quickly as possibly not even bothering to zip them up. He grabbed his t shirt and headed for the kitchen. With his back to the wall he peeked through the window of the corner of his eye. He recognized the truck that was outside and saw his father's silhouette out on the porch. Before Paul could knock, Lucas opened the door and met him outside so as not to wake Sam.

Paul did not appear to be pleased with his son's appearance.

"What are you doing and whose car is that?" He poked his thumb over his shoulder toward Samantha's vehicle.

"Dad, I know this looks bad but let me explain." He tried to keep his voice down. Everything seemed louder in the darkness.

"You better explain quick. Your mother is worried sick and Julie is ready to send out a search party. Are you sneaking around with another woman?"

Lucas couldn't stand to see the disappointment on his dad's face.

"Yes I'm here with another woman but it's not what you think."

Paul's eyes narrowed at his son.

"Are you joking? What else could it be?"

Lucas hesitated.

"I'm here with Sam, dad. She came back today and one thing led to another. I don't know exactly what is happening but I have to find out where this is going."

Paul took a step back. He hadn't heard that name in so long it took a moment to realize who Lucas was talking about.

"*Sam?*" He didn't know what else to say. "Do you mean…"

"Yes dad…it's Sam. I can't explain it all right now and I don't expect you to understand but please, just cover for me. I don't know what you can say and I didn't mean to get you involved but I can't deal with mom and Julie right now. I need to get this settled first."

Paul looked Lucas up and down.

"It looks like you settled things just fine."

Lucas leaned back against the door.

"Come on, dad don't do that to me. That's not just what this is about. I promise I will explain everything to you as soon as I can. Just help me. Please?"

Paul looked away and rolled his shoulders.

"Fine. Just for tonight. I have no idea what I'm going to say but you better get this mess figured out and cleaned up quick. You have a fiancé sitting at home terrified that something has happened to you. She doesn't deserve this." He shook his head and looked down. "I raised you better than that."

As much as it killed Lucas to see his dad disappointed in him he needed Paul to leave quickly and quietly.

When Paul was finally in his truck and backing out of the driveway, Lucas went back in the house and softly closed the door. He turned to see Samantha sitting up in bed with tears in her eyes.

"Who is Julie?" She whispered.

They sat next to each other on the bed in silence. Lucas had spent the last hour explaining to Samantha who Julie was and about the wedding. He told her all about his trip to New York, how he met Sam's old roommate, and everything that had been happening since then. Samantha didn't say a word, she just let him talk. She was having a difficult time coping with the fact that she just slept with a man who had a fiancé at home. This trip to her hometown was supposed to be about repairing relationships not tearing them apart. If she had known about Julie before coming here she never would have ended up in bed with Lucas. Or would she have? Did she secretly hope all along that this is exactly where they would be? She tried to convince herself that this was all about forgiveness but deep down maybe she had hoped that she and Lucas could pick right back up where they left off. With the recent revelation about his current relationship Samantha silently vowed that she would not continue to see Lucas unless he was no longer engaged.

"You have to tell her about me." Samantha turned to face Lucas, resting her hand on his leg. "I won't see you again until you've talked with her. I think we both just got caught up in the emotions of the moment. You might feel differently about me when you see Julie. You may realize that you made a mistake in bringing me here and decide you never want to see me again." She took his face in her hands. "Whoever you choose is up to you. I will support whatever decision you make…I'm sure this can't be easy."

Lucas knew in his heart what he wanted and who he wanted. It would be difficult to break the news to Julie but it had to be done. He had waited almost twelve years to see Sam again and he was not going to lose her this time regardless of the consequences.

"Sam I love you." He pulled back from her and clasped her hands between his own. "I've always loved you and I have been waiting so long to have you back. I've been waiting to kiss you, to touch you and to hold you again. I'm not giving that up." He kissed the tops of her hands gently. "I'll never give you up again."

Samantha went weak with his words and felt a sensation of relief wash over her. Maybe it would be fine. Maybe they would get to end up together after all. They had overcome so many obstacles already that surely they could forge ahead. She would support him by giving him as much time as he needed to work the details out with Julie.

"When do you have to leave?" Samantha knew he would have to go home eventually but she was desperate to make the most of whatever time they did have for the night.

"My dad is going to cover for me for now. I promised to be back by morning." Lucas ran his fingers through his hair. "I have no idea what he is going to say or how I'm going to explain where I've been." He brushed off the thoughts of home. "For now, though, I just want to be with you. Whatever that means and however you need me. I'm here." He leaned forward and gently kissed her forehead, her nose and her lips.

"I've missed you." She whispered into his ear.

Samantha held onto Lucas as tightly as she could. She could see the calmness of the lake out the window behind him and longed for life to become as peaceful and still as that water. She knew, though, that more rough times were ahead. Especially since there was one more secret she had yet to divulge.

Chapter 23

Julie stared out the window watching Lucas pull his car into the driveway. She had spent most of the night before packing up her things and mentally preparing herself for what she knew was coming. When she heard the back door open and close, she sensed his deceit coming at her with each footstep.

She didn't even bother to turn around when he entered the room behind her.

"Don't even try to say it." She finally turned to face him. "Your dad is a worse liar than you and I knew the moment he called that you were up to something else." Julie hastily wiped a tear from the corner of her eye.

For the first time Lucas could really see what he had been doing to her. She didn't look like the same vibrant, tenacious woman he met several months earlier. Now that he could really *see* her he noticed the circles under her eyes and the paleness to her skin. She didn't look like the glowing bride-to-be she was supposed to. She looked tired and miserable and he knew it was all his fault.

"Julie I'm so sorry. I don't even know what to say." He lifted his hands slightly at his sides and then dropped them in defeat. "She came back. I wasn't expecting it and I wasn't looking for it but there she was. I'm so sorry."

"I figured it was her." Julie and Lucas talked about Sam back in New York and his mother had filled Julie in on the extent of the damage she had done to him. Until now, though, she didn't truly understand. There was something different about Lucas. He looked…complete. It was as if a small part of him had been missing and all of a sudden someone had finally pieced the puzzle together. There was light in his eyes. "Please don't blame this all on her though." Julie leaned back against the wall. "You jumped ship a long time ago. This wedding was never going to happen and you know it." She crossed her arms and hugged her middle. "I sure knew it. I just tried my best to ignore the fact that you had no interest in actually marrying me. I was just the temp."

"So what are we going to do now?" Lucas didn't want to put it all on her. He wanted to help her transition to the next phase.

"Um, well I talked to my girlfriend and she's going to meet me at the airport back home. My flight leaves in a few hours."

"Is there anything I need to do or anyone I can call?" He was starting to realize the gravity of the situation. There were deposits on flowers, food, cake and a band. There were decorations and dresses already purchased. People had brought gifts to the shower and likely had already shopped for the wedding. This decision he was making would affect a lot of people. He knew Julie had family and friends flying in from all over the country to attend this wedding. She was being incredibly relaxed about the whole ordeal. Either that or she was too hurt and embarrassed to let her true feelings show.

"No I think we can take care of it all. Your mom starting making some phone calls this morning." She looked down at the floor. "My dress is being shipped home. I guess I'm going to donate it or something."

An awkward silence fell between the two of them. Lucas wasn't sure if he should give her a hug or offer to take her bags out to her car. They each stood at their respective corners of the room for a few minutes. He looked around and noticed that the pictures had all been taken down. Her running shoes weren't lying in the corner of the living room and her jacket wasn't hanging on the coat rack. It was if she had never been there at all. She shrugged her shoulders and looked around the room one last time.

"I guess this is it."

He watched her sling her purse over her shoulder and reach into her pocket. In her hand was a small white box.

"I can't keep this." She handed the engagement ring back to Lucas.

"Yes you can…it's the least I can do. Sell it and do something with the money. I bought it for you."

She wasn't sure if she should feel grateful or indignant.

"Ok then. I guess I should go." She started to walk past him.

"Can I help you with your bags?" He instinctively grabbed her hand as she walked by. They both seemed startled by the touch of each other's skin.

"No I've got them all but thank you."

They both turned when they heard the sound of the taxi pulling up the driveway. He watched her pause briefly in the breezeway as she walked through the house. And then she was gone.

When the cab pulled away he walked to the door to make sure it had closed. On the table next to the door was the little white box.

Lucas spent the next two days dealing with his mother and phone calls from his sisters. They didn't understand what he was doing or how he could let someone like Julie walk away. They had never understood his relationship with Sam and it didn't matter to any of them how he felt and how amazing it was to be with her again.

Lucas and Sam met up each night at the cabin and spent their time talking, laughing and loving each other. Neither of them was quite ready to spend a night together in Lucas's home. It seemed almost disrespectful to Julie. They didn't want to flaunt their relationship to anyone or give people the satisfaction of validating the gossip that was flying around town. They were careful to take things slow and not ask for too much from one another.

It was Wednesday and Samantha was planning on driving back to Caroline's Friday morning. They needed to have a plan in place for when Emma got home from camp. Samantha wasn't sure how she wanted to introduce herself yet. It was a difficult thing to know how to navigate.

That night Lucas and Samantha were sitting in front of the fireplace. She had her head rested on his lap as he traced her cheek bones with his finger. She knew it was time to tell him the rest of her story and why she had come back after being away for so long.

"Lucas?" She said it so quietly she barely heard her own voice.

"What's up babe?" He leaned closer to listen.

"I have something I need to tell you." She swallowed hard as she felt his body tense up beneath her.

"There's more? I thought we got everything out of the way." He tried to sound casual but there was obvious concern in his voice.

Samantha licked her lips nervously.

"A few months before I came back I, um, I had some health issues."

Lucas wasn't sure what she was about to say.

"Ok…well is everything good now?" He braced himself.

Samantha felt the tears sting her eyes.

"Not really." She took a deep breath. "I had a large tumor removed from my breast."

Lucas flashed back to each of their nights together. This explained why Sam always kept her shirt on. She didn't want him to see the evidence.

"So they removed it all right? You're ok now?" It was more of a demand than a question.

Samantha sighed and sat up to face him.

"No Lucas, I'm not ok now. I did a few rounds of radiation after the surgery and even kept a few of my chemotherapy appointments. The treatments were awful. I have so much empathy now for people who go through them for long periods of time. There truly is nothing like it." She bit the inside of her cheek to keep from crying again. "At my last appointment my doctor had some disappointing news. It appeared as if the treatments weren't doing much and when they did another scan it showed that the cancer had spread to my lungs and my lymph nodes. Theoretically I could finish my treatments and see if it slows the progression of the cancer. Unfortunately due to the number of tumors that were found and how hard the treatments are on my body, my doctor and I decided I should focus on quality of life at this point…not quantity."

Lucas felt like the wind had been knocked out of him. How much was he supposed to be able to take? How was it that this woman that he loved so fiercely had drifted out of his life without explanation? How could she return and allow him this happiness to then be taken away by such tragic circumstances?

"So what happens now? Can't we get another opinion?" Lucas searched his brain for options. Surely there was another doctor she could see. He would find her the best oncologist in the world if he had to.

"My doctor is a close friend of mine and she referred me to the top oncologist in the New York area and maybe even in the country. I was given every opportunity to continue treatment and to try experimental drugs. I did weeks of my own research. It's not good no matter which avenue I choose. I have to deal with this diagnosis realistically."

"I mean, did they give you a timeline or anything? I don't really know what to think."

"Six months…maybe." Samantha knew this was difficult for him to hear. No matter how many times she had rehearsed how she would break this news she couldn't fully be prepared for the pain that was showing on his face.

"I just got you back." Hot tears rolled down his cheeks. "I can't lose you now. I just can't. I won't." He pulled her into his lap and hugged her so tightly she thought she'd taken her last breath.

Samantha had never seen Lucas cry this way. There was nothing she could say to make him feel better. She just let him hold her as they sat together in the dark.

On Friday morning they were getting ready to leave for the two hour drive to Caroline's. Lucas had taken the week off of work and Samantha was grateful that he was willing to go with her yet she was still nervous about what was to come. The plan was that they would meet up and talk about how to approach Emma with the news and what their roles would be in each other's lives after the fact. Samantha knew this was her last chance to make amends with the daughter she had given up so long ago and she was determined to do everything in her power to make the right choices this time around. Lucas opened the car door for Samantha and flashed a reassuring smile at her as she got in. He made his way around to the driver's side and slammed the door shut behind him.

"Are you ready for this?"

Samantha bit her lower lip.

"Yes and no. I've waited so long to meet her I just hope everything goes ok."

"It will. I know it." Lucas gave her knee a light squeeze and turned his head to watch behind him as he backed out of the driveway.

They were both quiet during the ride. Lucas figured she needed more time to mull over what she was going to say so he just held her hand and let her stay lost in her thoughts.

It was just before noon when they reached Caroline's house. Lucas shifted the car into park and turned off the ignition.

"Well of course this is her house." He stared at the bright pink house in amusement. "I shouldn't have expected anything else."

Caroline was waiting for them on the front porch.

"Hey ya'll!" She called out. "How was the drive?"

Lucas and Samantha clutched hands and they made their way up the walk. Samantha shielded her eyes from the sun.

"It was fine. How are you?"

It was strange for Caroline to see Samantha and Lucas together. It was as if no time and million years had passed all at once.

"I'm good. Come on in." Caroline gave Lucas a squeeze on the shoulder as he walk by her. "It's good to see you." She winked at him as he nodded and smiled in response.

They all sat around the kitchen table exchanging pleasantries and giving compliments. Samantha briefly filled Caroline in on the past few days and how she and Lucas were somewhat together again. It was strange to say it out loud but it felt good.

"So let's get down to brass tacks. What are you going to want from Emma once you tell her?"

Caroline's worry was evident all over her face. Samantha understood why she was nervous. She was obviously thinking now that Lucas and Samantha were together they were planning to come in and scoop Emma up to be a part of their new happy family.

"Well…I was thinking that we would let her say whatever she needed to say and we would just go from there. I don't want to force anything on her. She knows you as her mother I just want to be as delicate as possible."

Lucas didn't chime in once. This wasn't a conversation he had any place in and he didn't want Caroline to feel as if they were ganging up on her in any way.

Caroline fidgeted with her napkin.

"I think that's good. You just have to know that Emma is an incredibly sweet child. She does get her feelings hurt easily but tries to hide her emotion. We just have to be extra cautious." She then asked what they were all thinking. "Are you going to take her with you?" Her voice was shaky.

"I-I don't know. It's not that easy." Samantha glanced over at Lucas. "I have some health issues that I've been dealing with. I'm not sure it's in Emma's best interest to move away from here and stay with me. I want her to know I'm her biological mother but to be honest I don't know how long I'll be around."

Samantha could feel Caroline's gaze on her as she stared at the table. "What are you saying?"

"I'm saying that I'm dying." She brought her head up and looked squarely at Caroline and then focused on Lucas. It was the first time she had said those exact words.

Caroline wasn't sure how to respond. Before she had the chance to speak they all heard the screen door open and slam shut.

"Hey mom!"

And there she was. Emma came bounding into the kitchen with her duffle and sleeping bag slung over her shoulder. She stopped when she saw Samantha and Lucas.

"Who are you guys?" Emma stared at them with obvious curiosity.

Caroline glanced at Samantha who looked over at Lucas. Samantha interrupted before Caroline could answer.

"We're old friends of your mom's." She smiled at Emma and for the first time really took in all of her features. Samantha couldn't believe she was standing this close to her daughter. She took a deep breath and suddenly had the clarity she was hoping for. Samantha knew what she was going to say to her daughter. "Your mom invited us over for dinner is that ok?"

Emma shrugged her shoulders.

"Sure, whatever. It's nice to meet you guys. I'm Emma." She didn't wait for a response from either Lucas or Samantha. She threw her arms around Caroline's neck and gave her a quick hug. "I missed you."

"Oh baby I missed you to." Caroline gave Emma a big bear hug back and looked at Samantha over her shoulder. "Hey Emma why don't you go throw your stuff in your room and take a quick shower. I'm sure you want to get all that wilderness off of you huh?" She let Emma go and gave her a smile and a pat on the butt.

"Ok. Have fun with this laundry mom 'cuz it is *stinky!*" Emma grinned at Caroline as she ran from the room.

No one said anything until they heard the bathroom door shut and the water turn on.

"Wow she's beautiful. She looks just like you Sam." Lucas couldn't believe how much Emma looked like her mother. He had secretly been afraid that he would meet Emma and see the face of some strange guy who was Sam's attacker. Instead, he saw a younger version of the woman he loved.

"Don't tell her." Samantha's words startled both Caroline and Lucas.

"What do you mean?" Caroline wasn't sure what changed Samantha's mind.

"I'm saying don't tell her. She's *your* daughter, not mine." Samantha could see the obvious bond that Caroline and Emma had with one another. She looked around Caroline's house and saw traces of Emma everywhere. It was clear that this is where Emma was meant to be. She couldn't take that away from either of them. "Let me just be around her for a little while. We'll have dinner and I can talk with her about normal stuff but I can't tell her the truth about me now. She's obviously an amazing young girl and I don't want to change any bit of who she is. It wouldn't be fair." It was one of the hardest decisions Samantha had ever made second only to giving Emma up the first time. It felt like she was giving her baby away all over again but she knew in her heart it was the right thing to do.

"Are you sure?" Caroline was overwhelmed. She felt relief and sadness all at once.

Lucas took Samantha's hand.

"You're positive this is what you want to do?" He squeezed her hand under the table.

"Yes. I'm completely sure. I don't know how long I'll be around and I don't want to put that on Emma."

They could hear rustling in the bathroom down the hall and moments later the door opened and Emma appeared.

They all spent the afternoon sitting on the porch and talking. Samantha was impressed with how smart and polite Emma was. She was able to ask Emma everything she wanted to, from Emma's favorite color to which boy she had a crush on. She truly felt like she got what she was looking for out of the trip. Emma was a perfectly lovely young lady and she had a great mom to look after her.

They had a wonderful dinner together and Samantha was thankful for the time she was able to spend with Emma and Caroline.

When it was getting obvious that Emma was tired and ready for bed Samantha suggested it was time she and Lucas get going. She hugged both Caroline and Emma and they all said their goodnights and walked together to the car. Samantha gave Emma one last hug without explanation, knowing that it probably caught Emma off guard. She smiled at Caroline and got in the car.

She and Lucas waved as they watched Caroline and Emma fade in the distance behind them. Emma was gone for good.

Epilogue

The months that Samantha and Lucas had together were wonderful. They spent their time taking short road trips and getting reacquainted with his family. Her cancer had spread more rapidly than doctors predicted it would and by Christmas she was gone. Lucas didn't regret any decisions he had made that year. He wasn't sure if he would ever find love again or if he even wanted to. He had peace in his heart knowing that Samantha was truly his forever and that she died knowing how much he loved her. He understood how lucky he was to know what true love and happiness felt like. He only hoped that he had done everything he could to make her feel the same way he did in the final moments of her life. She left this world giving those around her everything she had and leaving behind the greatest gift of all in Emma.

Sitting in the small cabin on the lake where he and Samantha had spent their first and last night together, Lucas vowed to remember each and every day. It was up to him to never forget. Despite his heartache, the experience was definitely worth the fall.